"Gloria Lamerino is a kick to travel with—witty, charming, and wise. *The Beryllium Murder* is the best of a solid, grown-up series, well-plotted and well-peopled, with dialogue that keeps you smiling."

—Shelley Singer, author of *Royal Flush*

"*The Beryllium Murder* has got it all. It's the periodic table of reading pleasure, including each of the elements that make a mystery sizzle. A good-hearted protagonist, a twisted and intriguing puzzle, sparkling humor, believable characters, and even some physics that a nonscientist can enjoy. What a gas!"

—Jaqueline Girdner, author of *Murder on the Astral Plane*

"Gloria Lamerino, retired physicist extraordinaire, is sexy and spunky and can mix it up with the best of them.... Camille Minichino has a way of bringing science to life for us nonscientists!"

—Rhys Bowen, author of *Evanly Chairs*

"Lamerino's blend of courage, reasoning and perseverance, and a well-constructed plot, make for another attractive mystery in an impressive series."

—*Publishers Weekly*

"...an engaging yarn...keep(s) readers' interest to the end."

—*Booklist*

Previously published Worldwide Mystery title by
CAMILLE MINICHINO

THE LITHIUM MURDER

The Beryllium Murder

Camille Minichino

WORLDWIDE®

TORONTO • NEW YORK • LONDON
AMSTERDAM • PARIS • SYDNEY • HAMBURG
STOCKHOLM • ATHENS • TOKYO • MILAN
MADRID • WARSAW • BUDAPEST • AUCKLAND

For
RICHARD RUFER,
my husband and greatest supporter;
ROBERT DURKIN,
my cousin and expert consultant;
and
PENNY WARNER,
my mentor and friend

THE BERYLLIUM MURDER

A Worldwide Mystery/October 2001

First published by HarperCollins Publishers Inc.

ISBN 0-373-26400-3

Printed in U.S.A.

Acknowledgments

My thanks to all who helped in the preparation of this novel. I'd like to acknowledge the technical assistance of Rion Causey, Pete Davis and Ken Wilson. Any misinterpretations of their advice are entirely my responsibility. I'd also like to acknowledge the special guidance from my agent, Elaine Koster; my editor, Betty Kelly; and her assistant, Alice Lee.

ONE

"YOU *ARE* COMING back, Gloria?" Matt asked me in as soft a voice as he could manage under the circumstances. He had a hard time leaning his boxy frame across the fake end table that separated our plastic seats in the waiting area of Boston's Logan Airport.

I held up my red, white, and blue ticket envelope.

"You've seen my itinerary. Round-trip. In fact, I gave you a copy, didn't I?"

"Just checking."

He patted my ticketed hand, and I thought how wonderful it was to feel connected to Sergeant Matt Gennaro of the Revere Police Department. I'd been living in my hometown a few miles north of Boston for one year, after three decades in California, and this was going to be my first trip back to the West Coast. Matt was on the short list of reasons why I'd decided to make Revere, Massachusetts, home once again.

For a few minutes, we sat in comfortable silence except for an occasional laugh at the unintelligible announcements emanating from the loudspeaker at the podium. One message sounded like DUTCH...DISEMBARK...FOUR SEVEN FOUR SIX...THANK...HAVE...DAY. Matt and I agreed that if civil defense depended on airport PA systems, we were all in trouble.

We pieced together information from other waiting passengers, and finally understood the reason for the delay of Flight 67 to San Francisco. My plane shared a boarding ramp with a jumbo jet from Amsterdam that had just landed, and regulation four million something or other prohibited international passengers from mixing with any other group before passing through customs.

I looked at the long line of weary travelers, separated from us by a clear Plexiglas window, trudging down the ramp toward customs clearance.

"It might be a while before we board," I told Matt. "You don't have to wait."

"I know I don't. I like being here." This time he gave my hand a pat that was close to a caress. I looked around the room as if I expected to see a private investigator hired by Matt's wife or my husband snapping a photo from behind the flower cart. But, in fact, neither of us had any other attachments. Matt was in his eleventh year as a widower, and my brief engagement more than thirty years before had ended with my fiancé's death. We were free, consenting adults of a certain age.

Then why was I blushing at such a simple gesture? I wondered. For once I was happy to have dark Neapolitan skin that didn't reveal shades of red to any great extent.

"I'm glad to have you here," I said, proud that I hadn't whimpered.

Matt smiled and crossed one leg over the other, his body shifting to settle in for a while. It was Thursday, and he was in his gray suit, keeping to his office wardrobe schedule, airport trip or not. I wore loose-fitting dark green knit pants, even more comfortable since I'd lost a few pounds during my year back in Revere. Only fifteen more and I'd be down to the upper limit for "medium-frame males" on the insurance charts. Never mind that at five three, I was actually a small-frame female.

"About the purpose for this trip..." Matt said.

I ran my fingers around the edges of my lapel pin, tracing the silver image of Boston's USS *Constitution*—a pitiful attempt to avert Matt's eyes as I gave him a partial answer. "To see Elaine and some other friends."

"And it's pure coincidence that there's this mysterious death in her backyard, more or less?"

"Of course," I said, stiffening in my chair, as if I'd just been accused of first-degree murder myself. "I didn't plan Gary Larkin's death to coincide with my visit."

"Did you know him well?"

"I wouldn't say we were close. I knew him casually. We both worked at BUL—the Lab—as we called it, but in different research divisions. Do you have to know your homicide victims well to want to find their killers?" I tried to keep my tone light and playful, hoping not to alert Matt to the difference between his career as a police investigator and mine as a snoopy retired physicist. "As long as I'm out there, I might as well look into Gary's death."

"Didn't I hear Elaine say the Berkeley police had ruled it an accident?"

"It probably was," I said, waving my hand as if to dismiss any other possibility.

Either my comment or my gesture evoked a loud laugh from Matt, who thought I saw foul play in every death since my first contract as his technical consultant.

He reached inside his jacket pocket.

"In case you're right, and it wasn't an accident, I have something for you," he said, handing me a long white envelope.

As soon as I saw the official blue seal of the RPD in the upper-left-hand corner, I knew he'd done the favor I'd asked and written to an acquaintance in the Berkeley Police Department. I also knew it hadn't been easy for him.

"I'm really grateful for this, Matt."

"It might not work. I only met this guy a few times, at conferences. And you know what I'm going to say next."

I nodded. "I'll be careful," I said in the same bland tone that came from my computer, telling me I had E-mail. I'd already started reading the letter.

May 31
To Inspector Dennis Russell, Berkeley Police Department
Dear Dennis,

I skipped past the opening paragraph, with polite questions about Dennis's family, and moved to the section I was hoping for.

This letter is also to introduce Dr. Gloria Lamerino, a retired physicist who we've used as a consultant for the past year on our science-related cases. She's been invaluable solving no fewer than six homicides for us in the past year.

I resisted the urge to correct the grammar and punctuation, but couldn't let the error in arithmetic slide. I pointed to the phrase "six homicides."

"Seven, if you count Al," I said, referring to my fiancé, whose death more than thirty years ago no longer remained a mystery.

"Don't push it."

I smiled and kept reading, only slightly distracted by the entourage of uniformed attendants boarding my plane.

Dr. Lamerino has a personal interest in the Larkin case now on your desk. I think you'd find her very helpful, unless you know a lot more about beryllium than I do! I'm recommending a PSA for her, for the week or so that she'll be out there. She comes in handy when your usual technical experts are also suspects.

A PSA, a Personal Services Agreement—a contract. Matt's words meant as much to me as the college recommendation Miss Alma Wiley wrote for me when I was seventeen years old and graduating from Revere High School. I pushed aside the voice of my dead mother, Josephine. *Ask him if all you are to him is "handy,"* she whispered. I could always count on Josephine to supply the negative to balance any positive. I was getting better at ignoring her, though.

"This is perfect," I said.

I folded the letter and gave Matt a wide grin.

AN HOUR LATER I was in the air, my graying hair propped against a tiny, cold window, reading a biography of Gertrude Goldhaber, a key researcher in nuclear fission. In an interview, Goldhaber, whose husband and two sons were also physicists, told a reporter she'd fallen in love with numbers at the age of four and decided on a career in physics and mathematics when she was in her teens. I wondered how I could work Goldhaber into the series of science talks I gave in my on-again, off-again friend Peter Mastrone's Revere High School Italian class. Maybe it was time to move away from the contributions of Italians and become more inclusive.

I passed up the in-flight movie since all the actors were under thirty. Thanks to a care package from Rose Galigani, I could also skip the hot entree. Leftovers from a Galigani meal—an eggplant sandwich in this case—were many orders of magnitude better than first-run food from the airline's lunch wagon.

Putting aside the Goldhaber book, I pulled out my notes on the Larkin case. My West Coast best friend, Elaine Cody, had visited me in Revere two weeks before and told me of Gary's death at fifty-two. I hadn't known him well—Gary was one of more than a thousand engineers and scientists at the lab where I'd worked—but he'd had a high-profile job in the fusion energy program, so I knew his work with beryllium. I'd also been on a task force with him, and was impressed by his dedication to new forms of commercial energy.

This news had come at the anniversary party Rose had thrown for me. I'd been back in Revere for a year. Like a sailor with a girl in every port, I had a best friend on each coast, and Rose Galigani was it on the East Coast. I lived in an apartment above the funeral home she and her husband, Frank, operated. Wakes in Galigani's Mortuary on Tuttle Street had been the scene of more than one suspect interview as I took advantage of what were supposed to be my temporary living quarters.

"He had an accident with some beryllium powder," Elaine had reported, halfway through her party cake and ice cream. "They say he died almost immediately."

True to my growing reputation for finding the science in every murder and the murder in science "accidents," I'd decided on the spot that Gary knew too much about beryllium to have mishandled the deadly powder. And I'd said as much that evening, bringing the party atmosphere to a halt.

"Are you going to try to solve this case from three thousand miles away?" Elaine had asked. "Maybe you'd better come home with me."

"Maybe I'd better."

"What case?" Matt had asked almost simultaneously with the Galiganis.

"Think of it as good timing," I'd said. "My year here is up and it's time to watch the sun set in the west again."

TWO

ELAINE CODY MET ME at San Francisco International Airport with a two-pound box of See's chocolates and a single perfect sunflower. An onlooker would hardly guess from our elaborate greeting that we'd left each other less than a week before on the other coast. A glance at Elaine's beige knit pants and silk sweater set, with a matching leather purse, might lead the same stranger to believe that she'd just come from a photo shoot for an upscale San Francisco boutique. But I knew this was a standard going-to-town outfit for my classy friend.

"No balloons, as requested," she said, pinning me with a two-inch-diameter gold button that read "California Semi-Native." For all her elegance, Elaine wasn't above a bit of pop culture. The sunflower tickled my nose and I greeted my erstwhile state with a loud sneeze, as if I were allergic to it.

At one o'clock on a Thursday afternoon we had a rare traffic-free trip across the Bay Bridge and into Berkeley. Although it wasn't on the way to her house, Elaine drove to the Elmwood district, south of campus, an area busy with shops, ethnic restaurants, and an old-style drugstore with a soda fountain. She pulled up in front of a white stucco fourplex on Ashby, a main thoroughfare in the neighborhood.

"This is where Gary Larkin moved after his divorce," Elaine told me. "His was the apartment on the bottom right. Even though he died in the lab, I thought you might want to see his place." She shrugged her shoulders. "Not that we can get in. But maybe you can pick up some vibes or something."

"Thanks, Elaine. I really appreciate this," I said, putting my hand on her arm.

"I kept a stack of newspaper clippings for you, too. Just, you know..."

I gave her a reassuring smile. "I'll be careful. Don't worry."

Police work wasn't exactly my friends' idea of a best-bet new career for a fifty-six-year-old woman, so when Elaine came through with support like this, it meant a lot to me. I knew Elaine, like Rose Galigani, Matt Gennaro, and who knew who else, worried about my safety as I went around trying to solve murder cases. So far, I'd gotten away with only one serious injury—a gunshot wound in my shoulder. I figured a few scratches, a broken wrist, and the sore muscles I got from a romp with a pile of Galigani's caskets didn't count as damage worth talking about.

"By the way, I didn't know the Larkins were divorced," I said. "I sent a sympathy card to his wife at an address I had on Hilgard Street and it didn't come back."

"I heard she moved in with her boyfriend off Claremont. But when did you have time to send a card, anyway? It was only four days ago I told you Gary died."

"I mailed it right away on Sunday night. So it probably will come back to me eventually. Darn."

"Anyway, I didn't think you knew them that well."

I hoped Elaine wouldn't notice my flush of embarrassment. "Well enough for a card," I said in a weak voice. "Her name is Marlene."

Elaine squinted at me with a look that said she saw through my ploy. "You're something else, Gloria. You just want an excuse to talk to her."

"I might give her a call."

"I guess she doesn't have to know you're aware they were divorced."

"Now you're talking."

Elaine hit her forehead with the palm of her hand in mock alarm. "What's happening to me?" she asked. "I'm starting to think like you. Might as well go all the way. Do you want to walk around here?" She swept her arm in an arc that encompassed Gary's house and yard.

"I'm not in that much of a hurry. Let's go home first."

Elaine put her army green Saab in drive and headed for the University of California campus, pointing out the sights on the way, as if I were a tourist.

"Remember Lamonte?" she asked me, waving toward the

heavy, white-bearded black man who sold pretzels from a wagon outside the Sather Gate entrance to the campus. "He's still here."

"I've only been gone a year, Elaine."

"I'm just trying to orient you again. Revisit some of your old haunts."

We cruised around streets with the world-class bookstores and coffee shops Berkeley was famous for—Peet's, Black Oak, Saul's—all within walking distance of the two-bedroom condo I'd owned for more than twenty years. Elaine had been with me when I'd bought the house near Walnut Square a few years into my postdoctoral life, and she'd been with me when I retired, packed up, and moved east.

Elaine slowed down as we approached my old condo. She turned her head to me, her shoulder-length gray-blond hair falling in soft straight lines around her face. She used a lift of her eyebrows to ask the question.

"Yes, I miss all this," I said. "But this part of my life is over. And I love my new one."

"I could tell. Matt's really nice. No more nagging you about coming back to California. I'm resigned." Elaine glanced at me and gave me another lift of her neat, brown-crayon eyebrows. "Maybe I'll move east."

Before I could suppress it, my sharp intake of breath gave me away.

"Oh no," I said as if I'd come upon a toxic waste spill. "I don't mean to sound like a soap opera episode, but..."

Elaine laughed, apparently pleased that I'd fallen for her tease.

"I'm kidding, Gloria. Peter and I were a one-night-only couple. We had a great time at your party—and afterward, I must admit. But that's all. Besides, I'm now committed to José."

"Have I ever heard about José?"

"Not yet, but you will."

I sat back in my seat, relieved that Elaine was not involved with my onetime boyfriend Peter Mastrone, whom she'd met at my party in Revere. Nothing romantic had ever transpired between Peter and me as adults, but during the year I'd been back in Revere, he behaved as though we'd always been meant for each other. I'd hoped he would concentrate his attentions on someone else, but I didn't relish a complication like Elaine and Peter as an item.

Nor could I believe Elaine would tolerate Peter's sexism and arrogance for long.

"Peter's a very difficult personality," I said.

"I know. But I've tried all the easy ones."

We laughed and traded memories of Elaine's two husbands and more than her share of beaux. It amazed me that she was still friendly with most of them.

"What were those mathematical expressions you always used for our social lives?" Elaine asked.

"'A countable infinity' for you," I said. "And mine 'asymptotically approached zero.'"

"It just takes one," we said together as we'd done so often in the past.

ELAINE'S HOUSE WAS a two-tone brown wooden Tudor in an old neighborhood on the north side of campus. With its lush shrubbery and lack of Spanish tile roofs, the area looked more like an established East Coast community, except that the trees were cedars and eucalyptus instead of elms and maples. I remembered when Elaine bought the house in the late seventies, three months after I'd moved into my condo, a few blocks away.

"I may be a California native," she'd said, "but I'm not pink stucco."

The first thing I saw when I stepped into the familiar living room was a silver Mylar balloon tied to my favorite chair, a high-backed rocker with a green corduroy chair pad and pillow.

"You said no balloons at the airport. You didn't mention my house."

I felt another surge of gratitude that Elaine was my friend and gave her a better hug than we'd managed in the crowded airport with my carry-on luggage between us.

I sat on the rocker and took in the simple decor. Elaine's collection of Hummel figurines, lining the mantel, were the only knickknacks other than tastefully framed photographs. Built-in dark oak bookshelves on either side of the brick fireplace revealed her predilection for a wide assortment of contemporary fiction by women writers—Joyce Carol Oates, J. California Cooper, Margaret Drabble—and other authors I'd never heard of.

"You're so literate. It's a wonder we can be friends," I told her, thinking of the narrow spectrum of volumes I owned, covering only scientific biography and current nonfiction from the science and technology section of bookstores on the Internet.

Elaine laughed. "I keep hoping you'll branch out. I put a Marguerite Duras novel by your bed upstairs."

At the foot of the rocker was a basket full of special items for me—my favorite pear-scented soap, made only on Telegraph, Berkeley's avenue of street artists; a stiff yellow envelope with photographs from the party at the Galiganis' home back in Revere; an extra-large Cal T-shirt for my extra-large frame; a bag of dried California fruits and nuts.

At the bottom of the basket I saw a lab-green folder with news clippings sticking out. For as long as I could, I resisted the urge to delve into the file before acknowledging Elaine's treats. I made a fuss over the sweet-smelling soap and the photographs, examining a group shot of the Galigani family and Matt.

Elaine's grin told me she knew where my real interest was.

"Would you mind reading me the Larkin folder, Gloria?"

"If you insist."

I picked up the oldest piece first, a clipping dated Wednesday, May 17, the day after the alleged accident, and read aloud to Elaine.

Berkeley lab beryllium engineer Gary Larkin, 52, died last night at Berkeley University Laboratory. Laboratory officials say Larkin was found near his workbench after returning from a business trip. "He probably should have gone home first to get some rest instead of pushing himself to finish this work," said Dr. Sidney Kellerman, a spokesperson for Larkin's group and his neighbor on Ashby. "You've got to be alert when you're handling a substance like beryllium."

Beryllium (pronounced ber-il-lee-um) is found in mineral rocks, coal, soil, and volcanic dust. It is mined from beryl, which in its very pure form is better known as the gem aquamarine. Destined for beautiful jewelry in one form, and lethal for humans in another, beryllium is a two-faced metal.

I screwed up my nose. "Who writes this stuff?" I asked.

"A rookie at *The Berkeley Spirit*, probably. And meanwhile, my extraordinary writing talents are wasted at the lab."

Immodest as it sounded, Elaine had a point.

I continued looking through the pile of clippings, most of them from the internal lab newsletter, which had little information. The Larkin story was covered in one major local newspaper, and was given only a few inches at the back.

"What I need is the police report," I told Elaine. "I have a letter from Matt introducing me to a Dennis Russell, a Berkeley homicide inspector. I'll give him a call later. Let's forget this for now and pick up where we left off last week."

Elaine took me up on my offer to chat and went to make coffee while I unpacked. From the second-floor guest room I could see parts of both the campus and the lab where Gary had worked and died. And my workplace for almost thirty years.

Also the source of my pension, I thought. I was still amazed every month when a check arrived, in spite of my not having been at work. Although I'd taken early retirement at fifty-five, I'd been at the lab long enough to take home a reasonable percentage of my full-time salary. It was hard to beat an apartment above your friends' business for a simple lifestyle, and as long as I could keep landlady Rose Galigani from revamping my wardrobe, I could be financially comfortable for a long time.

I looked in the direction of the towering campanile of the university's campus. In my mind, no city in the country could compete with Berkeley as a symbol of the sixties. People's Park. Mario Savio. The free speech movement. Fellini and Bergman films so full of meaning they kept us up all night discussing the symbolism. Or maybe we'd just wanted to stay up all night.

For the most part, I'd skipped the heavy-duty soul-searching and the hootenannies. "Have to go to the lab," I'd say. "Have to make my measurements."

I stared out Elaine's tastefully treated window and wondered if I'd missed anything by not learning to play the guitar. I pictured the thin, frail-looking flower children with long unmanicured hair who were part of the movement. Maybe that's why I didn't fit in, I thought. I had thick black hair and too much heft. Even then I couldn't wear hip-huggers with wide belts without looking like Santa Claus on his day off.

I'd convinced myself that I didn't need to protest or wave peace signs and that those who did were drugged-out dropouts. I was doing good for the world in my own way, uncovering the mysteries of a titanium dioxide crystal shaped like a tiny amber pyramid. Who knew what humanitarian purpose might be served by my data in the future? But once in a while I was tempted to relive the sixties and reevaluate my political apathy. Especially now as I faced the campanile, a somber gray needle shape against the afternoon sun. I was sure I'd be able to hear strains of "Blowin' in the Wind" if I tried hard enough.

Instead I heard Elaine. "Coffee's ready."

Her call knocked the imaginary aroma of marijuana-laced brownies from my nostrils and replaced it with the real bouquet of Peet's French roast coming from her living room. With a shake of my head, I abandoned my late-blooming consciousness-raising session.

Downstairs, I took my position on the rocker and Elaine curled up on her floral chintz sofa. Elaine briefed me on José Martinez, her newest Latin-American love interest.

"He has the most sexy facial hair, if you'll pardon me." I smiled at Elaine's usual apology for using libidinous references, a testimony to my lack of a love life for the whole time we were friends in California. "Just because I don't date, it doesn't mean I don't know the facts of life," I'd tell her, aware that she'd feel compelled to edit a sentence with three negatives.

As if she'd been tuned in on my memory, Elaine retracted her expression of regret. "Oh, I forgot, you're now an active member of the group of adults who..."

"Never mind me. Continue your description of José, please."

"It's the new look—an upside-down T, with the horizontal part across his chin." She ran a finger along her own hairless chin as she described the pattern. I assumed she was about to give me the dimensions of his biceps, when the phone rang.

"It's for you," Elaine said, swinging her white telephone receiver by its cord. She handed it to me with a smirk and a wiggle of her shoulders, in the manner of a twelve-year-old girl excited about her friend's getting a call from the cute boy across the street.

I grinned and took the telephone.

Matt's voice sounded too close to be coming from three time zones away. As we chatted about my flight and his dinner with the Galiganis, I had a sudden wish to be at his side. After a few minutes, he cleared his throat, as if to get ready for an unpleasant topic.

"It's pouring back here," he said. "My cellar's flooded. And that's the good news."

A large knot took over my stomach.

"What's wrong?"

"That letter I gave you—I faxed a copy to Dennis Russell. As a courtesy, to prepare him. I got an E-mail message back saying you won't be needed."

I let out a long sigh and adjusted my body to a more appropriate level of panic. Nothing disastrous. Nothing I had to fly home for. But disappointing nonetheless.

"What did he say, exactly?"

"I'll read it to you. Very short. More like a telegram. 'Larkin lab death accidental. Case has been closed. Thanks anyway. Regards, et cetera.'"

"Well, I guess that's that. I'll have more time to shop."

My voice came out high-pitched, a giveaway to anyone who knew me. And, if I'd thought first, I never would have mentioned shopping, which everyone knows I hate.

"Gloria..."

"I won't do anything dumb," I said.

THREE

AFTER MATT AND I hung up, I told Elaine the disappointing news. I'd already reconciled myself to doing without my usual home team advantage—attending the murder victim's wake on the ground floor of the building I lived in. And in the past I'd managed to continue my sleuthing after Matt took me off a case out of concern for my safety. Now it seemed I didn't have any official permission even to start investigating Gary Larkin's death.

"How am I going to get anywhere if I don't have cooperation from the police?" I asked Elaine, merely to give vent to my frustration. I never thought she'd provide an answer.

"I know some people," Elaine said in a flat voice, sounding like a well-connected wise guy instead of the mild-mannered technical writer she'd been for three decades.

"What kind of people?" I whispered as if the house might be bugged.

"Remember my old friend Hattie from Oakland? The one I used to have lunch with every week? Well, she died last year—"

"Hattie died?"

Elaine apparently misinterpreted the concern in my voice. "She was not murdered, Gloria. Hattie was ninety-four years old, in a nursing home. Her heart gave out."

"I wasn't going to investigate Hattie's death, Elaine."

"Right." Elaine rolled her eyes, implying she had no reason to believe me. "My point is, her granddaughter, Terry Spender, is a cop right here in Berkeley."

I set my china mug on Elaine's coffee table and leaned forward, nearly tipping the rocker by the sudden shift in the center of mass.

"So?"

"So, I could call her and see if she knows anything about the

case. Maybe she could get you a copy of some reports
or...something."

"You'd do that? Elaine, that would be wonderful." I put my
hands together, fingers pointing up, as if Elaine had answered
my prayers.

"Well, I know you're not going to shop anyway."

I picked up the telephone and handed it to Elaine.

"No rush," I said.

IT TOOK ELAINE about half an hour to reach Terry.

"Tonight's good for her. Otherwise it might be weeks," she
said, holding the phone receiver against her breast. "Are you
ready?"

"I'm ready."

Elaine set up the meeting, but declined my invitation to join
us in the interview.

"It might get gruesome," she said, wrinkling her nose and
wringing her hands like an actress in a B-grade horror movie.

"She's not the coroner," I said. "Cops don't always have to
get gruesome."

"You're right, I guess. After all she's not the official embalmer for the county, like someone else I know."

I laughed, knowing Elaine was referring to the Galigani family
back in Revere. Robert, the oldest of the three Galigani children,
had spent some time as a trade embalmer, carrying out undertak-
ing procedures for four other northeastern Massachusetts mor-
tuaries besides his parents'. He hardly ever had a day off, and
he was never allowed to tell work-related stories at social gath-
erings.

"Had to drain through a brachial artery this morning," he'd
say, and suddenly he'd be the only one eating dessert.

"I hate to leave you alone my first evening here," I told
Elaine.

"Well, I, uh, have a couple of backup ideas."

"Oh?"

"I might invite José for dinner."

"So, I might have been in the way if it weren't for my date
with Officer Terry Spender?"

Elaine threw a floral chintz pillow at me, reinforcing the image of the sorority house conversation we were having.

"No," she said. "I do want you to meet him."

"Maybe he'll still be here when I get back."

"Maybe he will. We have a couple of hours before you meet Terry," Elaine said. "Any requests?"

"We could go shopping," I said, taking Elaine's coffee mug and mine to the sink. "Or watch TV. Or drive up to the lab." I tried to sound neutral, as if all these options held equal interest for me, but Elaine wasn't fooled.

"Come on," she said. "If we're lucky we'll run into suspects in the Gary Larkin murder investigation."

"Now you're talking."

ON THE PLANE RIDE to California, I'd pictured myself driving up the steep, narrow road to the lab for the first time in a year. I'd wondered how I'd feel. Now, sitting in Elaine's Saab, my mind followed the path of a strange mathematical algorithm, compressing my thirty years as a physicist on this site into one twelve-month period, as if to match my one year back in Revere. To give them equal importance? A sign of old age? Maybe just jet lag.

I stopped playing amateur psychologist on myself and trained my eyes on the extraordinary view that had once been part of my daily commute. The road up to the lab had been carved into a dense, wooded area on a hillside east of the University of California Berkeley campus. The enormous expanse of trees, majestic and still on this windless day, was the ideal natural laboratory for Berkeley's biology and environmental science researchers.

Elaine was quiet on the drive, as if she understood my need to put my head in order. It felt like cleaning out an office file drawer, wondering how to sort the folders. Chronologically? Alphabetically? By order of importance? Only this time the files were the people and events and choices I'd made in my life.

By the time we parked, we were high up over the San Francisco Bay, with the buildings of three separate government-funded laboratories and a science museum all around us, the campus spread out at our feet. The official name for the lab Gary and I'd worked at, and where Elaine still worked, was Berkeley University Laboratory, BUL for short. It offered fraternity brothers limitless opportunity for jokes and puns.

I remembered taking visitors to this spot to see the imposing view—the buildings of Oakland, the San Francisco skyline, Alcatraz island, and, on a clear day, three magnificent bridges. There was hardly a breath of wind on this afternoon, however, causing a thick layer of fog to hover over the water, masking everything beyond the Berkeley marina. I was forced to use my memory to re-create the splendid vista.

On the way to the main BUL building, above the Lawrence Hall of Science, Elaine reminded me of my current status.

"You know, with only a retiree badge, you're pretty limited as to where you can go in there."

"I was thinking we could go to the library. Is that still an area where I just need to be in the company of an employee?"

"Right. I can be your escort," Elaine said, offering me her arm in an elaborate gesture, then withdrawing it. "But what good is the library going to do you?"

"You'll see."

"I'm sure I will."

We walked into one of the newer buildings on the lab site, one that didn't look like an ailing World War II barrack. The library and information services functions were operated out of a suite of small rooms at one end of the building.

The turnover among the nontechnical staff was higher than it was for the scientists and engineers, so I wasn't surprised that I didn't recognize the young woman with a ponytail the color of straw seated behind the library's reference counter. Technical people found BUL a wondrous playground of high-tech toys and stayed for decades. You could carry your administrative or clerical skills to any company in the Bay Area, but there weren't too many places that offered a closet full of atomic-force microscopes and super-strength magnets for research.

"Hi, Courtney," Elaine said, addressing the young woman, who didn't look old enough to be working anywhere but on Revere Beach, twirling cotton candy. "I want to introduce you to my friend, Dr. Gloria Lamerino. She was with the spectroscopy group in Building 3 until she retired about a year ago."

"Oh, how sweet. Well, welcome back," Courtney said in a bright, cheery voice, speaking very slowly. "My grandmother retired a few months ago. She and my granddad are traveling everywhere." Courtney swept her arms around in a circle, reminding me of a child's gesture to represent the whole world. "They're having a great time."

"So am I," I said with a sigh of resignation.

I realized that, at fifty-six, with Courtney probably in her early twenties, I wasn't that far from her grandmother's age range. Moreover, since I'd passed up every opportunity to look younger—coloring my hair, losing weight, covering my cheeks with age-defying makeup creams—I shouldn't have been surprised that I appeared two generations removed from a Generation Xer. I looked down at the lapel pin I was wearing—I'd changed into a linen jacket with a tiny copper enamel solar system—and regretted it did nothing to lighten my image as an old woman.

"We're going to browse around for a while," Elaine said to Courtney. She was still wearing her youthful-but-sophisticated beige outfit, and didn't look like anyone's grandmother, although she was only a couple of years younger than I was.

"Feel free," Courtney said, indicating the collection of books, reports, and periodicals she presided over.

Elaine looked at me as if to ask "now what?" and I led her to the bank of computer terminals along the side wall. At four-thirty in the afternoon, a half hour before quitting time, the library was nearly empty. One middle-aged man stood in front of a bookcase a few feet away, giving me a chance to review the standard lab engineer uniform—gray pants and striped shirt, with a clean white undershirt showing at the neck, plus the ever-present pocket protector with a row of pens, pencils, and small tools. The outfit was the same on the younger engineers except they wore jeans instead of polyester pants with no belt loops.

"Why don't you have a seat," I said to Elaine, nearly pushing her into a dark blue government-grade easy chair near the shelf of current journals. "I'll only be a minute here."

I stood in front of a computer monitor and punched in the

letters to start a search of the library's database. I clicked on
AUTHOR SEARCH and typed in LARKIN, GARY. I felt an
excitement that had been missing since I'd heard Matt read Inspector Russell's rejection of me as a helpmate to the Berkeley
PD.

The cursor blinked for a few seconds, an old-fashioned bright
orange on black, then the screen showed a list of reports authored
or coauthored by Gary Larkin. I scrolled through several pages
before I came to the end. Gary had been a prolific writer, it
seemed. His program covered all phases of beryllium production
and current applications to fusion energy. Even if I weren't curious about how the author died, I had some interesting reading
ahead of me, I thought.

Passing up the tiny pieces of paper and miniature pencils sup-
plied by the library, I pulled my own notebook and pen from my
purse and copied the call letters from the six publications with
the most recent dates.

"Okay," I said to Elaine, who'd found an old issue of *News-
week* on the rack. I waved my paper in front of her. "I need to
see if Courtney will get these for me. I'll be right back."

Before she could quiz me, I walked over to the reference desk
and handed Courtney my list of numbers.

"Do you have give-away copies of these reports?" I asked
her.

Courtney looked confused for a moment. She squinted at my
paper, one hand in the pocket of her tight-fitting white slacks, as
if she were trying to picture her grandmother reading technical
report TRB-1467-96.

"I'll see if we have extras back there," she said at last.
"They're pretty new—looks like nothing older than January of
this year, so it shouldn't be a problem."

It may have been my imagination, but I thought she gave me
a suspicious look. I thought of telling her I was really a young
male, a spy in disguise, left over from the Cold War, but I wasn't
sure she'd get the joke.

"Thanks, Courtney," I said as she disappeared into the stacks.

"What are you up to?" Elaine asked, coming next to me.

"I'm just putting together a little light reading on beryllium. Have to keep up with the field, you know."

"I don't think so, Gloria. What were those reports you asked for?"

"Here they come," I said.

Courtney returned with five of the six reports I'd asked for, spreading them on the counter in front of me.

"For some reason, this one has been pulled from the shelves," she said, pointing a long metallic blue fingernail at one of the call numbers on my wish list.

"No problem. These five will do. Thanks for your help, Courtney."

I picked up the stack of reports. Their shiny, clear plastic covers reflected the wide overhead lights, and I had to tilt them at an angle to read the titles and authors. Courtney left her post to take a telephone call, but Elaine didn't budge. She rested both her hands on my left shoulder, straining to see what I was holding.

"Five out of six is almost a record for me," I said.

"That's the truth. They never have any copies of what I want. Let me see what you have."

"These are the last few reports Gary Larkin wrote," I told her, to make it a little easier for her. "I wanted to see who his coauthors were, since they're likely to be his most recent colleagues."

"Why is that important?"

"Let's see," I said. Ignoring her question, I fingered each report in turn. "We have two with Kellerman and Johnson, two with Kellerman and Carver, and one with Kellerman, Carver, and Johnson. The one I don't have is with Kellerman only, but I have enough of his anyway."

"Oh, wait a minute," Elaine said in a high-pitched whisper, although no one was in earshot. "You think one of those men killed Gary?"

"Not necessarily one of the men," I said, pointing to Johnson's first name—Rita. "It could have been the woman."

FOUR

UPSTAIRS IN ELAINE'S guest room, I put the five beryllium reports variously by Larkin, Carver, Kellerman, and Johnson on the night table next to my bed, and changed for my dinner with Terry Spender.

With Elaine's cooperation and her network of friends, I'd obtained the phone number and new name of Marlene Larkin, now Marlene Korner. I made a call but left no message. I didn't think my tenuous connection to her ex-husband would hold up as a good reason for a chat unless I could talk to her directly.

As I dressed for dinner with a policewoman, I congratulated myself on bringing the right jewelry, an NYPD tie clip. I thought Terry might be amused by the piece, a present to Matt from a policeman friend who'd moved to Manhattan. Matt had passed it on to me for my collection of scatter pins.

"I can't see myself advertising the New York City Police Department," he'd said.

"I thought all detectives collected these things—tie clips, patches, caps, insignia from other departments?"

"Never got into it."

"So you don't want me to bring you one from a police department in California?"

"I'm hoping you won't go near a police station while you're out there."

Matt's wish, bordering on an admonition, went through my head while I prepared to worm my way into the Berkeley PD. As far as I remembered, I hadn't made Matt any promises. Besides, although it was useless at the moment, he'd reneged and given me a letter of introduction to Inspector Russell, in my mind signifying his approval of my snoopy ways.

Following my common practice, I arranged the rest of my outfit around my choice of pin. I dressed in my navy blue suit, clipped the blue-and-gold NYPD insignia to an off-white scarf draped casually over my blouse.

"I'm ready to go," I told Elaine.

OUR PLAN WAS THAT she would drive me to Angelo's Seafood Restaurant on the Berkeley marina, and Terry would drive me back at the end of the evening.

"What time shall I come back? I don't want to walk in on...anything," I said. We eased our way into stop-and-go traffic on University Avenue, a wide thoroughfare running east to west, beginning on campus and ending three miles later in the waters of the San Francisco Bay.

Elaine laughed at my suggestion of breaking up a romantic interlude, but turned serious in the next minute.

"I talked to José while you were dressing. From the sound of his voice, this is probably not going to be a fun night."

"You think he's going to break up with you?"

"No. Somehow this feels different. And I'm an expert at detecting the preamble to 'let's just be friends.' I don't think the problem has to do with us."

"Maybe it's work-related. He's a graphics artist, right?"

"Could be. He was at work and couldn't really talk. Or it could be his kid. He has a son in high school. Seventeen years old. José's had full custody since Manuel was eight. The boy is kind of a loner, which worries José. Well, enough of that."

"You'll know soon enough," I said.

At the next red light, Elaine leaned over her steering wheel and waved her hand toward the intersection of University and San Pablo.

"There's Siad's," she said. "A new Kenyan restaurant. I keep forgetting to tell you. I contacted some of the old dinner crowd and we're all going there on Saturday night. Delicious curry dishes. Ordinarily I wouldn't have to say this to a houseguest, but try to keep your calendar clear of forensic activities."

"I'm surprised there's anyone left in the group," I said, thinking of the one social club I'd belonged to while I lived in the Bay Area, a dozen or so lab people and their significant others. We'd met monthly at different ethnic restaurants in Berkeley and surrounding towns. Of the original members, two people had been murdered by a third, who was now serving time in a Massachusetts prison.

"We're still pretty active. José comes more regularly than he used to. And there are some other new people in the group. They're all dying to meet you. Well, I don't mean *dying*..."

"I get it," I said, suppressing a guilt-ridden laugh at the expense of murder victims I'd known. "Who are the new members?"

"Not Kellerman, Carver, or Johnson, if that's what you're hoping."

I gave her a weak smile, unable to deny her accusation.

"How about Marlene Korner and boyfriend?"

"Not them either."

"Then I guess I'll have to go to Siad's just for the food."

ELAINE DROPPED ME OFF at Angelo's a little before seven o'clock. I had the feeling she was going back home immediately to change out of her "sensible" clothes and into something more appropriate for her evening with José Martinez. I hoped the "little problem" he'd warned her about wouldn't spoil their time together.

I took a table by the window and sat facing the reception area. Elaine had given me a photograph of Hattie's young granddaughter, Terry, in full uniform—dark blue pants and short-sleeved shirt with SPENDER embroidered in gold over her right pocket. I studied the snapshot and could see no stray hair peeking from under her cap. She had patches on both sleeves and a wide black belt loaded with equipment. A gun that I recognized as a semiautomatic, a pager, and a baton were clearly visible.

Although I couldn't tell from the photograph, I guessed from my association with Revere PD beat cops the back of her belt was heavy with handcuffs, rubber gloves, a knife, pepper spray, and several sizes of flashlights. Terry looked like a child ready for a parade, dressed up in her father's clothes. I'd wanted to ask Elaine if she knew any real cops she could introduce me to. My feminist side was embarrassed that I meant tall men with large, bulging muscles.

In the picture, Terry was standing with her mother in front of the Berkeley police station. Her gun was holstered on her right hip, causing that arm to curve outward in an unflattering way. Or else she was getting ready to draw it and take her mother into custody, I thought.

The photograph did not prepare me for the stunning young woman who walked into the restaurant. She looked around as if she expected to meet someone, and I noticed at least two young men who seemed to wish they were the ones. She wore a pale green sleeveless dress and straw sandals, her blond hair cascading to her shoulders. A large beaded tote bag, which I hoped was filled with police reports, statements, and crime scene information, hung at her side. Only her wide, perfect smile as she talked to the maitre d' reminded me of the cop in the snapshot.

I took a chance and went over to her.

"Excuse me, are you Terry Spender?"

"Uh-huh. Dr. Lamerino?"

"Yes. And it's Gloria. I'm so glad you could come. I have a table by the window."

Moments later I sat across from Terry and took in her flawless complexion and her hair, thick and silky enough for a shampoo commercial.

"You look like a TV cop," I told her. "Too pretty to actually be on a real-life police force and wrestle with the bad guys."

"Thanks," she said, her voice low. She sat up straight and seemed comfortable with the compliment, though not in a conceited way.

A waitress approached us with "Hi, I'm Brianna" and wrote down Terry's request for a glass of white wine with ice. I asked for a refill of my iced tea, wondering who would name a child Brianna. After a father named Brian perhaps? I saw the name as a handicap to a serious career. If I'd had children, I thought, I'd have named them after the particles of physics. Positron Lamerino had a nice ring, for example.

The restaurant was more crowded than I'd have expected on a week night, but I could see why its location, with floor-to-ceiling windows facing the bay, made it very popular at sunset.

"Terry," I said, "I'm going to ask you something I've always hated being asked myself."

"How did a nice girl like me get into police work?"

I let out a no-going-back sigh, remembering all the times I'd been asked the same question about being a woman in physics. *How does anyone get into anything?* I'd wanted to reply, but I had to acknowledge that usually there was an interesting tale behind a woman in a male-dominated field, or vice versa. Fortunately, Terry didn't appear to be put off by my question, and shared her story.

"I went to junior college, and after two years I still didn't know what I wanted to do, so I took off for Hawaii to figure it out."

"That's a nice place to think. I was on Maui for a vacation once."

"I lived on Oahu, visited Maui a lot. I loved it there—all the islands are beautiful. But I had to earn money, so I took a job as a security guard at a mall."

"Was that exciting?" I asked, unable to imagine much mall crime in Hawaii.

"There were incidents all the time. We'd be chasing someone through the stores. Shoplifting, or personal robbery, or a fight. And we'd have these radios, talking back and forth, and we'd trap them just before the exit. It was more exciting than any other job I'd had going through school."

"Sounds like good training for your current profession."

"It was. I met some cops through the security company I worked for, and I decided to go for it. But I came back here first, to be near my family."

Our waitress returned with Terry's wine and took our dinner orders—cioppino all around.

"Elaine tells me you're a scientist and also a detective yourself," Terry said.

"Well, not quite a detective. I've had a few contracts with the police department back in my hometown in Massachusetts. I helped with a couple of homicides that were science-related."

"According to Elaine, you've put your life on the line, and nearly got yourself killed."

"Elaine and I are big fans of each other," I said with a laugh. "My involvement is nothing compared to yours, at risk everyday." And Matt's, I thought, thinking of a photo I'd seen of him in uniform when he was younger.

"Yeah, the scariest feeling in the world is, you're scrambling with some guys resisting arrest, and then you see your own gun on the ground across the yard." Terry shook her head and looked at a spot high in the air, as if she'd forgotten I was at the table with her. "Then I get home and talk to my girlfriends, and they're whining about how they got a paper cut at work."

"I'm impressed, and grateful to anyone who's willing to be in law enforcement." I hoped Terry couldn't tell my thoughts had strayed to include a police department three thousand miles away. "How does your family feel about your choosing this profession?" I asked, partly as a stall before broaching my main agenda for the evening, and partly because I was intrigued by my adventure-seeking companion. Until my new career as a paradetective, the only excitement I'd sought was mental—like the thrill of tuning a laser to the bright red line of a neon spectrum. When I was Terry's age, I would have run from the sight of a gun in an alley, even an unmanned one.

"My mom was a little nervous in the beginning," Terry said. "So I invited her on a ride-along."

"Did that help?"

Terry shook her head.

"A call comes over the radio, to go to this alley where a fight had broken out. We get there and see guys all bloody, fists flying. And my mom yells, 'Call the police!' 'I am the police,' I tell her."

Brianna arrived in time to hear Terry's rendition of her mother's cry and joined our laughter, though I couldn't imagine she knew the context. Brianna the waitress, Courtney the librarian, Terry the cop—was everyone in California blond and did they all look younger than drinking age? Was it this way while I lived here, or is it a new phenomenon? Maybe working on a half-dozen murder cases in a year had aged me, making everyone look like the grandchild I'd never have.

I scooped a small bay scallop from my bowl.

"This is delicious," I said, wondering how many more irrelevant comments I could make. At least we hadn't commented on the weather yet, I mused, wishing I'd asked Elaine exactly what she'd told Terry. I couldn't think of a pleasant, small-talk description of what I wanted from her: off-the-record help in an under-the-table investigation. A hyphenated project.

The word "entrapment" came to my mind. Maybe Terry and Inspector Russell were in collusion to trap me into asking for unauthorized material. I envisioned myself making my one phone call to Elaine from the local jail.

To my relief, Terry broached the subject. "Elaine said you're interested in the Larkin case at BUL. Are you going to be looking into it?"

Here's the tricky part, I thought. I cleared my throat and gave Terry an answer more fitting a politician than a scientist trained in logic and straight talk.

"I have some misgivings about the conclusion that Gary Larkin inhaled the beryllium accidentally."

"I guess that means you won't be working with Inspector Russell's approval?"

"No, I won't. And thanks for cutting to the chase."

"Well, I don't have to know all the details. I got you a copy of the file. What I did was black out all the names, so this becomes a generic document. Like the samples we give to rookies or to the press sometimes."

Terry reached into the large purse at her feet and pulled out a brown envelope. I looked at her, wondering whether to accept my good fortune without further questions. She seemed to sense my curiosity about her exceptional level of cooperation.

"Russell can be a pr—, uh, hard to get along with," she said, passing me the envelope. "Elaine's told me a lot about you and I figure we should use all the help we can get. I know you're not some loose cannon."

Don't tell that to Sergeant Matt Gennaro of the Revere Police Department, I thought. Or to Rose Galigani of the Galigani Mortuary.

I stirred the broth in my bowl, adding to the fishy odor of the air around us. "Thank you," I said. "I'm really grateful for the chance to read the file. I'll probably come to the same conclusion Inspector Russell did.''

From the look on Terry's face, I guessed she didn't believe that anymore than I did.

FIVE

TERRY DROPPED ME OFF at Elaine's a little after ten o'clock, handing me a card with at least four ways to reach her.

"By the way, nice tie clip," she'd said. "Would you like one from the Berkeley PD?"

"I certainly would." Even though I may have to hide it from Matt, I added silently.

I walked up the stairs to Elaine's porch, feeling the same giddy lightness that came over me when I embarked on a research project or, more often lately, when I started a new contract with Matt and the Revere PD.

I clutched the envelope Terry had given me to my breast, as if it were new data from the spectrograph I'd used daily in my old life as a physicist. I remembered cradling a newly exposed photographic plate as I walked to my dark room, eager to examine the marks that would reveal the structure of my experimental sample. This time I was hoping for similar revelations about the death of a human being I'd once known.

Elaine's street was crowded with cars and sport utility vehicles and vans that could belong only to soccer moms, unlike the colorful vans of the sixties, the ones you hoped your daughter wasn't in. I had no way to tell whether one of the cars belonged to José Martinez. I glanced up at Elaine's bedroom windows as I put my key in the lock, wondering how to interpret the lack of lights on the top floor. I coughed loudly to announce my presence.

When I stepped into the dimly lit living room, I could tell that, as Elaine had predicted, it hadn't been a fun evening. Elaine and José were side by side on the sofa, not touching, both with grim faces. Not the compromising position I'd prepared myself for. The fire had died, and the room had a chill that I remembered as appropriate for any late evening in Berkeley, even in early June.

"Manuel is missing," Elaine said. Her tone was matter-of-fact, as if I'd been there all evening and needed only a simple reminder of the problem.

"Manuel?"

"José's son, remember? He's seventeen. He'll be a senior next fall. José hasn't seen him since early yesterday morning."

"I'm so sorry," I said. I dropped my purse and Terry's envelope and sat on the rocker in front of them, hoping for some inspiration that might be comforting. None came, but José had enough composure to introduce himself and to welcome me back to California.

"I've been looking forward to meeting you, even before this happened," he said. "Now it seems you've come into my life just in time." José's dark eyes locked onto mine as he took both my hands in his. He'd stood up and assumed a posture that was half bow, half genuflection, accomplishing an elegant greeting even in his distraught state. His slight, charming accent and broad smile reminded me of Latin lovers in old movies—with the dashing good looks that Elaine seemed drawn to, the kind that accompany a sword and a bright red cloak. The patches of gray spotting his new-look facial hair seemed only to enhance the romantic image.

I was sure that my own "I'm glad to meet you, too" labeled me as boring and inarticulate. I struggled to redeem myself. "I'm sorry to interrupt you," I said, falling short of my expectations.

"We were just talking about you," Elaine said. "I told José what an outstanding detective you've become. Just what we need right now." In the silence of the room, I could have sworn I heard my brain clicking away, processing the meaning of their words. Hoping I was mistaken, I chose to ignore what was sounding like a request for my services as a faux policewoman to investigate the disappearance of a teenager. I cleared my throat.

"You've called the police, haven't you?"

"Yes, yes," José said. He paced in front of the fireplace, head down, hands waving. "They say they're looking."

"They entered him into their network—MUPS, Missing Unidentified Persons System. And they called the area hospitals,"

Elaine said, showing she'd done her best to become an expert in the missing persons procedure for the sake of her friend.

José shook his head and waved his hands in a wider arc. "But I don't think they're taking this very seriously. One of the cops told me teenagers leave home routinely, and then come back when they're ready. Less than two days, he said. That's not unusual. And he's almost eighteen, practically an adult. But, I know, that's not my Manuel."

"And you've called his friends, places where he might hang out?"

"Yes, and everyone of my neighbors. They're all worried. But no one knows anything."

"You have to help us, Gloria," Elaine said.

Was this the same Elaine who thought my living in a building where dead bodies came and went was too dangerous? I asked myself. Let alone her thoughts on my consulting work for the Revere Police Department.

I wasn't used to Elaine's lack of composure. Though her hair and makeup were still perfect, it seemed to me that new wrinkles had appeared around her eyes, making her seem closer than usual to her fifty-three years of age. Only three years my junior, Elaine was never asked if she'd like the senior discount. Thanks in part to my much grayer hair and wider girth, I'd been getting 10 percent off lunch specials for quite a while. Tonight, I was afraid we both looked eligible for the front seats on a bus.

"I don't know what I can do that the police aren't already doing," I said, my voice weak as I observed the neediness in my West Coast best friend.

"You're such a good thinker, Gloria," Elaine said. "I've watched you figure out problems. You find evidence. You put things together."

"You could look around his room for one thing," José said. "For a clue. The police didn't think that was necessary yet. Instead they asked me questions like, is he homosexual? Is he likely to be carrying a weapon? Does he do drugs? Does he have tattoos?" José spat out the last word as if the idea of a picture on his son's arm was even more offensive than the suggestion of a coke habit.

"But I have no training in how to find a missing person."

Elaine sat up straight, appearing to bristle at my whiny voice.

"And you have a degree in homicide?" she asked in a sarcastic tone that caused me pain.

"No, but…"

José stopped pacing and looked at me. His gray-and-black-striped sweater emphasized what I imagined to be a trapped, prisonlike feeling at best, and I wondered if he'd chosen it deliberately. The patches of gray hair around his temples seemed to spread as we talked.

"I can understand that you wouldn't want to be involved," he said.

"That's not it." I glanced back and forth between him and Elaine, trying to think of a way to explain my discomfort at taking on yet another task that properly belonged to the police. I was already treading on dangerous ground in the Larkin case. I looked at the Berkeley PD envelop leaning against my ankle as if it were warning me not to take on another case without official sanction.

But I glanced at Elaine, and in the next moment, I knew what I had to do. "Let's sit down and make some notes," I said.

Elaine sprang from the sofa, a smile brightening her face. "I'll make another pot of coffee."

To me, it sounded like "Gloria's on the job."

FOR THE NEXT HOUR or so, the three of us brainstormed while I learned the basic facts. No one had called with a ransom demand. Not surprising, since José was not wealthy. Also, he described Manuel as a well-built teenager, taller than his father at about five feet ten. Not the usual target for kidnappers.

I had a fleeting wish for a missing persons manual and had to mask a grin at the unexpressed pun. I was stuck with reciting the most obvious of questions.

Where was Manuel's mother? In Bakersfield, six and a half hours away in southern California. She had remarried and had no apparent motive to abduct her son, as sometimes happens with noncustodial parents. José had always had uncontested custody from an amicable divorce proceeding. He'd persuaded the police not to contact Liz, his ex-wife, yet, so as not to worry her.

When had José last seen his son? The day before, early Wednesday morning, when he left for school wearing a bright red hooded Stanford sweatshirt and carrying a plain blue backpack. Manuel didn't have a car, but he did own a state-of-the-art bicycle. The school and library were within walking or biking distance. He took a bus when the weather was bad.

Extracurricular activities? Manuel didn't have many interests except his computer, José admitted. But with prodding from his father, Manuel had just joined the band, which practiced on Wednesdays after school. The music teacher had told José Manuel was present for the whole rehearsal and left with the others at four-thirty. He'd noticed nothing unusual about Manuel that day.

Who were Manuel's close friends? Did he have any obvious enemies? In his absence, Manuel took on the proportions of the dream child—popular yet studious, into computers but a reader of poetry, a friend to all. José had provided the police with a list of his friends. There was no one who didn't like him.

I tapped my pencil on my notepad, ready to move to more personal questions.

"Does Manuel have a girlfriend?" I asked.

José shook his head. "He went to the dances, but there was no one special. He had a lot of different girls he studied with."

Right, I thought, but decided to drop that angle for the moment.

I left the hardest question for last, one I felt guilty asking, given José's distress.

"I have to ask you this, José. Was there any kind of disagreement or argument between you and Manuel during the last few days?"

"No. No. None whatsoever," José said. "Unless you count the usual, make sure you're home in time to do your math, and eat enough vegetables. I swear." José held up his right hand, ready to take an oath.

One glance at his dejected face and tired, earnest eyes, and I believed him. I felt a wave of sadness, and a new appreciation for the policewomen and policemen whose daily job was to ask tough, insinuating questions of distraught relatives.

In spite of the coffee refills coming from Elaine's kitchen, by midnight we caught ourselves yawning in unison and called an end to the session.

We made a date to meet José at his house the next morning—the same morning, to be accurate—to look around Manuel's room and check out his computer. For what, I didn't know, but my friends' faith in me would have to do for probable cause.

"I KNOW YOU'D LIKE to focus on Gary Larkin's death," Elaine said when we were alone. "But this is so important to José."

I'd taken José's spot on the couch, thinking I could settle there for the night in case I couldn't make it up the stairs. I was losing the battle with my body, which knew that it was after three in the morning, eastern Daylight Saving Time, the zone where I'd started the day.

"How well do you know José?" I asked Elaine. "It seems I was still hearing about Bruce only a couple of weeks ago." Bruce Derin was a plumber Elaine had met during a crisis at a rental property she owned in north Berkeley.

"Bruce is history. And it's true, I've only been dating José seriously for about a month. But I've known him a long time. You probably don't remember, but he came to our dinner group once in a while even before you left a year ago. He was a graphics artist at the lab, then left to work for a software company out in the tri-valley area. He's at a place called DrawWare, believe it or not, in Pleasanton."

"I can't say I remember him, but the group got pretty big for a while. Have you ever met Manuel?"

"A few times. He came to the group's Christmas dinner. And he was there when we celebrated José's birthday in February. Oh, I keep meaning to tell you; it's the same day as yours, February fifteenth." Elaine delivered this news with a disproportionate measure of excitement, as if to add one more reason for me to pursue the Martinez case. Obligation by reason of identical birthdays. "Manuel's a good kid, even if he doesn't have a lot of friends. Last week he came over and did some yard work for me. We talked about maybe setting up a regular schedule since my gardener retired. He'd never just run off like this." Elaine sounded convinced that Manuel's commitment to her bushes alone would be enough to keep him from running away.

"That's not a lot to go on," I said, though I hated to disillusion her.

"I know. And I know this is not your expertise. But just take a look around his room. There might be something that José hasn't seen. You could check his computer, see if he left a clue there."

"Was he in the habit of leaving notes to his father on his computer?"

"Probably not."

"And do you think he's just at a friend's house for two days and neglected to call home?"

"Probably not. What are you saying, Gloria?" Elaine stood up and wrapped her arms across her chest. Her green silk evening outfit was a few shades lighter than her living room carpet, giving my out-of-focus eyes the sense that, like Manuel Martinez, she'd also disappeared, perhaps into a nighttime forest. I knew I'd sounded harsh and decided to yield to my exhausted state and be quiet, before I upset her even more.

"I'm too tired to know what I'm saying right now. So don't pay any attention to me." I checked my watch, having to blink a few times before I could read it. One-fifteen. Or four-fifteen, if you'd flown across the country the day before. "Why don't we go to bed? Are you planning to come with me to José's?"

"I might as well. I'd arranged to take the day off anyway. To take you shopping."

Elaine grinned at her own joke, the first smile I'd seen in many hours. I was happy we could end the evening with a good laugh.

UPSTAIRS IN THE lovely guest room Elaine had prepared for me, I lay on the bed, unable to sleep. I stared across the room at her San Francisco Symphony poster from the late nineteen eighties. I remembered waiting while she shopped for it in the lobby of the concert hall—in a different lifetime, it seemed. Before I'd retired. Before Matt.

Tired as I was, it still took a long time to clear my mind. What had I gotten myself into? I wished for a quick, happy solution. Manuel on the doorstep, apologetic after the first drunken binge of his young life. Manuel in the emergency room, calling for José as he awakens from amnesia after a fall from his bicycle. Manuel phoning from his mother's kitchen in Bakersfield, suddenly finding in his pocket the note he'd meant to leave for José. A spontaneous trip to visit Mom, nothing more.

In the last moments before sleep, I realized I hadn't thought of the Gary Larkin case since I'd met José. I hadn't yet looked at the five beryllium articles I'd gotten from the library or the police reports Terry had given me, and I hadn't tried to reach Marlene Korner again. How did I end up so busy, with two cases to work on? A missing person and a murder, with nothing in common. Two cases to hide from Matt.

Through eyes that were mere slits, I glanced at a photo of Matt I'd brought with me and put on the dresser. It was a snapshot from our first trip together, to a bed-and-breakfast on the way to Cape Cod. From under a beige canvas hat, he smiled at me. Because he doesn't know how little I pay attention to his advice, I thought.

As I drifted off, images of José's teenage son mixed with a likeness of Gary Larkin. Gary's clothing alternated between a white plastic clean room suit, a Stanford sweatshirt, and a Revere Beach T-shirt.

SIX

IF ELAINE'S NEIGHBORS saw us leave her house at nine on Friday morning, they would have assumed she was entertaining her mother. The dark circles that lined my eyes even on a good day had expanded and taken on the color of material best left at the bottom of a petri dish. Elaine, on the other hand, looked ready for a day's work selling cosmetics. Her day-off attire consisted of a long, straight, denim jumper over a white turtleneck. A pale blue sweater slung over one shoulder gave her a casual, jaunty air.

"I feel so much better this morning," she said to me. "Probably because you're here," she added, patting my back as I maneuvered into the Saab.

While Elaine walked to the driver's side, I constructed a half-truth. "So do I. The guest bed is very comfortable."

"I know you're going to find something, Gloria."

I could tell by Elaine's response that she was in denial about how tired I was, and how pressured to do a job I was unprepared for. I mentally forgave her for the rare insensitivity. I breathed in the smell of her jasmine bushes, then let out a heavy sigh to relieve the stress I was feeling. Matt never did this to me, I thought. When I sign a contract, I'm not required to solve the case immediately, if at all.

"You're overestimating my investigative skills," I told her. "When Matt hires me, it's to help him and his partner understand the technical background of the victim, or the crime scene if it's at a lab. He doesn't expect miracles."

"But that's what you give him, isn't it?"

"I've been lucky."

"Right. Well, just be lucky for José and Manuel Martinez."

In a mood more fitting a shopping excursion than a potential crime scene visit, Elaine chattered about my recent successes in homicide detection.

"Remember when the solution came to you while you and I were on the phone?" she asked me. "And you hung up and went downstairs to investigate. That was pretty exciting."

I nodded, recalling that at the time she'd called it dangerous and foolhardy, not exciting.

By the time we pulled up in front of José's house, not far from Gary Larkin's in the Elmwood district, Elaine was full of confidence about the immediate future. We'd find a clue to Manuel's whereabouts, she was sure. We'd have him back today, and by Saturday evening we'd all be eating curry vegetables at Siad's Kenyan restaurant, just like old times. The bright Berkeley sun appeared to be on her side.

JOSÉ WAS WAITING with coffee and bagels, the sight of which reminded me of Matt, who had a plain bagel and cream cheese for breakfast every morning.

"I'm not your doughnut-type cop. Those are the old guys," Matt had told me with a grin.

I hoped I could stop thinking of him long enough to carry out my unauthorized investigations without guilt.

We sat at José's kitchen table, holding mugs of coffee, Manuel's room looming in the backs of our minds like an enormous envelope we couldn't bring ourselves to open. The results of a medical test. Yes or no on a job application. The verdict from the jury. A letter from a lover. Once we knew the answer, our lives might never be the same.

I stood up first. "Shall we have a look?"

José led the way down a narrow hallway lined with framed prints of high-tech graphic designs. I walked past schematic diagrams and enlarged cross sections of megajoule lasers, precision machine tools, and the domed cyclotron building of Lawrence Berkeley Laboratory—BUL's neighbor on the hill. I resolved to do something creative with my own bare walls in Revere.

"Are these your drawings?" I asked him.

"Yes," José answered, his tone lacking even a hint of pride.

Elaine swept her arm along the length of the wall. "These

won STC awards,'' she said as if she'd been given the job of publicist for her modest, creative friend. ''Society for Technical Communication.''

''I know what STC means. Remember I attended a dinner when you won for editing the annual engineering report?''

Elaine grunted as if to shrug off an impending compliment. José seemed focused on the doorknob in front of him.

Manuel's room surprised me. I'd expected to see the usual teenage tchotchkes—action figures, trophies, posters of basketball stars, rock singers, race cars. Probably because my only other recent contact with a young man was with Andrew Palmer, whose trailer home on the outskirts of Revere was covered with large prints and racing paraphernalia. The murder of Andrew's stepgrandfather had been the subject of my last investigation with the Revere PD.

Manuel's walls, by contrast, were bare except for a small bulletin board with a calendar, a schedule for band practice, ticket stubs, and about a half-dozen photos, all of them with the same couple in different settings. The young man, tall and lanky, with light brown hair, looked nothing like José.

''Manuel?'' I asked.

José's answer told me I hadn't contained my surprise at Manuel's looks with any success. ''His mother. She's a tall blonde.''

Elaine blushed as we both turned to look at her. We might as well have said ''like Elaine.'' The rare burst of laughter was a welcome relief, as if we'd opened the window to hear the normal sounds of Berkeley life outside the small room.

''Liz wanted to name our son Joshua so he wouldn't be identified as Latino. Imagine—Joshua Martinez. That's the only time I ever got my way with her. I insisted our boy would have an ethnic first name to go with his last.''

I smiled at the thought of Joshua being a nonethnic name these days. Turning back to the bulletin board, I removed a five-by-seven photograph of the teenagers in formal dress. The young woman was tiny compared to Manuel, her white wrist corsage appearing to envelop her arm. A fair-skinned redhead, she wore a black dress, off one shoulder, with tiers of sheer fabric from the waist to just above her knees. It seemed many decades ago that black was anything but a "cool" color, reserved for older women or funerals.

"I thought you said Manuel didn't have a girlfriend. Who's this girl in all the pictures?"

"That's Jennifer. She lives a few blocks away, on Ashby. The fancy-dress picture is from the Christmas ball last year. But she's not really a steady, you know. I told Manuel, school is first. That's the only important thing."

I wondered if José realized that his story had changed from 'Manuel doesn't have a girlfriend' to 'I told Manuel he shouldn't have a girlfriend.'

"Can I keep this photo for a while?"

"Sure. I gave the police a copy. I wanted to give them a shot of Manuel alone, but this is the most recent photo I have."

"This is fine," I said. I slipped the snapshot into a side pocket of my purse, wondering why I'd asked for it. Because all the TV and movie detectives do it for one thing, I decided, and because it made me look and feel productive for two others.

I pulled the calendar from the bulletin board, reading the few ordinary-sounding notations for May: a class picnic, a dental appointment, a school holiday on the day of a teachers' conference. For Wednesday, May 31, the day he disappeared, he'd written only "band practice."

"Do you know if he had any special plans for Wednesday after practice?" I asked José.

He shook his head. "No." José's voice was weak and embarrassed, as if he should have thought to install a camera in his son's backpack for such emergencies. I put my hand on his shoulder in an effort to keep him calm and clear-thinking.

"It's okay," Elaine said, probably with the same thing in mind. "Manuel plays E-flat clarinet," she added. "José was going to buy him his own instrument for his birthday." I nodded solemnly, wanting to affirm the idea that she'd given me useful information.

I took in the decor of Manuel's room. Hardwood floor, with a small multicolored rag rug by his twin-size waterbed. A comforter, black on one side, denim on the other, matching the pillowcases. An eight-shelf teak-colored case against the side wall, braced for earthquake safety, was filled with children's books, trophies from grade school sports, and neatly lined-up action figures in colorful plastic. I had the thought that Manuel hadn't changed the contents of his shelves for several years.

The only sign of disorder was a mountain of bulky athletic shoes in the corner, unpaired, a tangle of blacks and whites with colored stripes. Each shoe appeared to be two stories high and weigh more than all my pumps put together.

"It's a pretty neat room for a boy, don't you think?" José said.

Elaine nodded her head.

"It is neat," I said.

Is that a clue? I asked myself. Did Manuel's neatness get him into trouble? My head ached from lack of sleep and the anxiety of having two people looking over my shoulder, waiting for me to be brilliant, as if I were a world-renowned psychic about to receive a message from the electromagnetic aura of a teenage boy.

I went to Manuel's computer—a PC with Windows software, printer, scanner, and an external hard drive in the shape of a tower. I looked at the screen on the thirteen-inch monitor. The crystal ball, I thought, extending the spiritualistic metaphor. Surely the hard drive will give up a clue. Or the stack of zip disks in the Lucite holder. Or the brightly colored floppies spilled around the keyboard. Did everything come in black and neon these days?

Elaine and José watched me navigate through Manuel's computer system, something either one of them could have done as well. Although his files were as neat as his room, it was on his computer screen that Manuel had hung his posters. The monitor's desktop pattern was a collage of sports figures, none of whom I recognized—but then, Babe Ruth and Joe Di Maggio exhausted my repertoire of familiar faces in sports.

"Was Manuel a spectator or participator?" I asked José, pointing to the balls, nets, and gloves on the screen.

"Neither, actually," he said as if it embarrassed him that his son wasn't a jock. "Manuel was not into sports at all. I designed the desktop."

Giving Manuel two points for good taste, I turned back to the screen and perused the colored folders that lined the bottom; they were labeled GAMES, APPLICATIONS, ASSIGNMENTS, CLIP ART. Bulletin board and browser icons were arranged along the right border. The contemporary school bag, I thought. The electronic version of a spiral notebook, a dictionary, and a bag of marbles. I wondered if Manuel had a place in his computer system for snacks.

Wandering around Manuel's files, I found cards he'd created— a birthday card for his father, a Mother's Day card, a Valentine for an unnamed recipient. His Internet bookmarks listed a few game sites and, I noted with pleasure, a science site. I resisted the temptation to visit it immediately. Manuel's word-processing folder contained essays he'd written for applications to colleges, all of them local.

"He wants to stay close to home," José said of his missing son, apparently unaware of the irony in his remark.

Manuel shared an E-mail account with his father. The good news—they used the same password, so we were able to read it. The bad news—for that same reason, we knew there'd be nothing he wouldn't want his father to see.

"Was Manuel a casual computer user, or did he spend a lot of time at it?" I asked José, still struggling for a good grasp of the boy's personality.

"I don't know what's normal these days. It seemed to me he spent a lot of time here and he was very good at it. A lot of his classmates called him for help to set up their systems, and even one of his teachers asked him to install some new software."

Nothing unusual for a teenager of the nineties, I thought. Almost everyone I knew with a website had had it designed by someone under twenty. Another dead end.

At first I decided not to bother going into Manuel's homework files, but in the interest of thoroughness, I clicked on the AS-SIGNMENTS folder. Among the smaller files we found a short paper on *Romeo and Juliet,* and another on the causes of World War II. I realized Manuel and his classmates were born about the same year compact discs and the Sony Walkman came on the market, so they probably put World War II in the same category as the Trojan War.

One 60K-file, the longest in the directory and labeled CBD, caught my eye. I knew at least one meaning of the acronym—chronic beryllium disease. I opened the file and read the full title of the paper. "Chronic Beryllium Disease: Can We Prevent It: The Case for New Regulations for Beryllium Workers." I was interested to see that Manuel had indeed written a paper on CBD, the lung disease that had been in the news lately. I leaned forward and muttered a sound close to "hmmm," causing Elaine and José to gasp and bend over my shoulders. Apparently my mumbling, coupled with an attentive posture, led them to believe I'd stumbled onto a ransom note or a map to Manuel's current whereabouts.

"Looks like a term paper," I said. I read out loud from the first paragraph, smiling at the dramatic words that typically characterize a newspaper article or a student paper. "Beryllium is an extraordinary material, lighter than aluminum and six times stiffer than steel. But unfortunately, poorly regulated beryllium plants have exposed hundreds of employees to death and disease. This magical metal can also be treacherous to the small, but not insignificant, percent of the general population that have a devastating immunological reaction to it."

"Could be for chemistry," Elaine said.

I shook my head. "It says ENV I. And these subheadings—Occupational Hazard Reappears, Industry Disputes Workers' Reports, Class-Action Suits Filed—they look more appropriate for an environmental program, or even a civil law class."

"Right," José said. "That was his big project for this spring. Manuel took an environmental sciences class."

"I'm going to print it out," I said. "It looks interesting."

"Do you think it means something?" Elaine asked.

I felt my face flush with embarrassment. By "interesting" I'd meant technically engaging, not necessarily pertinent to Manuel's disappearance. How could I explain I found it hard to resist a report on a scientific topic, even one written by a seventeen-year-old?

"It might mean something," I said. At the same moment my

mind leaped from Manuel Martinez's term paper on chronic beryllium disease to Gary Larkin, the murdered beryllium expert,
and I thought maybe there was a bit of truth in my cover-up.

SEVEN

I TALKED ELAINE and José into changing their plans to take me to lunch, and instead spending time by themselves.

"A walk on the marina will do you both good," I told them.

"How would you know?" Elaine asked. Although her laugh was at my expense, a reminder that physical exercise is not on my list of preferred activities, I was glad to hear it.

"I read it in a book," I said.

José seemed resigned to my failure at divining a clue in Manuel's room, but he hadn't completely lost faith in my abilities as a tracer of missing persons. He gave me Manuel's class schedule, outside activities, and a list of some of his classmates. I promised to give the situation more thought if he'd promise to take a break from it.

I doubted José had had a minute's rest since his son had disappeared. I tried to imagine how I'd feel if we'd been unable to account for one of Rose's children, even for a few hours, when they were teenagers.

A scenario with me as the abducted child was less clear. Would Josephine have worried about me? Or would she have been furious at me for causing her so much inconvenience? I'd never know, but I was coming closer to thinking it might not matter.

Alone in Elaine's house, I took a deep breath, brewed a cup of coffee, and planned my strategy for handling the crime wave I found myself in. I rummaged through her CDs and chose a medley of Italian arias as background music.

Which case to work on first? I decided to have a look at the police reports on Gary Larkin's alleged accident, then move on to the beryllium reports and Manuel's term paper.

I settled in the rocker and adjusted my lap to hold a stack of magazines in lieu of the clipboard I'd use if I were in my own apartment. The bright cover of Elaine's *Sunset* magazine, baskets of magenta million bells and petunia blossoms hanging over wicker patio furniture, was in sharp contrast with my mood.

I put the manila envelope I'd gotten from Terry on top of the cheery porch scene and extracted the papers. Terry had blacked out certain areas, giving the reports the look of a product with a bar code, or a report declassified by the Department of Energy. I knew I had photocopies and it was no use holding the sheets up to the light.

I flipped through several police department forms. On one of them, the category "incident" had been checked to refer to Gary Larkin's death. A pretty big incident, I thought, if you're Gary Larkin. I was happy to see I had the statements, if not the names, of the technician who'd discovered Gary's body and several so-called involved persons, none of whom had a checkmark in the "suspects" block.

The summary of the medical examiner's report interested me most. She'd found traces of beryllium oxide, the compound the group worked with daily, in Gary's respiratory system but not on the mask connected to the respirator canister. She concluded that he'd inhaled a small amount through mishandling. *That's what you think,* I told her silently.

I read through the other documents quickly and put the envelope aside. If there was a clue to Gary's death embedded in forms BPD-106 through 110, it would take at least one good night's sleep for me to find it.

For stimulation, I turned to Manuel's paper, twenty-five pages long, submitted May fifth. The structure of the report was typical of a student project, with a table of contents, Roman numerals to mark the sections, and a list of references.

From Manuel's introduction, I learned details that most professional scientists and engineers don't bother with: Beryllium was discovered by the French chemist Louis Vauquelin in 1798. The nineteenth most abundant element, beryllium is present in the Earth's crust, found in the mineral beryl. It's also found in emeralds, which are a precious form of beryl, and an important commercial source of the element. Manuel listed the most common uses of beryllium: as a component of car ignition systems and as an alloy in golf clubs, bicycle frames, computers, brake discs, and space-craft.

I was about halfway through the section dealing with a proposed change in the federal standards for handling beryllium when Elaine's phone rang.

Rose Galigani, calling at dinnertime on the East Coast, was checking up on me.

"I hope you're behaving yourself," she said.

"What does that mean?"

"Well, ordinarily the phrase implies you shouldn't get drunk or max out your credit cards on fancy clothes and souvenirs, but in your case it means don't hang around the police station and don't snoop around murder scenes."

How about missing persons scenes? I almost asked, but thought better of it.

"So what are you doing?" she asked me.

"Reading a term paper on chronic beryllium disease," I said, answering too quickly. I clamped my hand over my mouth as if to take back a confession. I knew she'd ask why, and I still hadn't learned to lie on the spot to people I cared about. Without advance warning and time to prepare, I always came up with the truth first.

"What on earth for?"

"It's by Elaine's boyfriend's son. Very interesting. Only about one or two percent of the population is susceptible to the disease in its most serious form, but it's amazing how many of those people are workers in the beryllium industry. It's basically a lung disease. The primary symptoms are shortness of breath, chest pain...."

"Gloria, is this a new case you're working on?"

I should have realized my attempt to distract Rose with little-known science facts wouldn't work. I had no desire to tell her that besides what I thought of as a beryllium murder, I was also working on a missing persons case. She already worried too much about my safety. Besides, I didn't want Rose to think Elaine was getting me into trouble. There'd always been a slight tension between my two best friends. Because they'd never had the chance to get to know each other, I'd told myself.

"Not exactly a case," I told Rose.

"Not exactly. Gloria, why don't you go see the Golden Gate Bridge, Chinatown, all the little shops on Unity Street."

"Union Street."

"Whatever."

It was just like Rose to send me to San Francisco, which was much more her kind of city than Berkeley. Maybe that's a common denominator for Elaine, Rose, and me, I thought. We'd all gotten through the sixties without a multicolored crocheted vest, a tie-dyed T-shirt, or Earth shoes.

"Don't hang up. Someone here wants to talk to you," Rose said as if she were about to put a five-year-old on the phone.

"Hi." Matt sounded a bit like that same five-year-old boy who doesn't want to say Merry Christmas to his mother's second cousin from out of town. I hoped it was only because he was on display in the Galigani family dining room.

"Hello," I said. "Are you there for dinner?"

"Yeah. Rose is afraid I'll lose weight while you're gone."

I laughed, picturing a feast of Italian foods spread across the enormous Galigani dining room table.

"Her famous lasagna?" I asked.

"For starters. Are you keeping busy out there?"

"I am. How are those new cases coming along?" I asked, eager to move the topic off my so-called vacation to Matt's exciting professional life. I also hoped I wasn't missing any excitement at the Charger Street lab in Revere. As if I didn't have enough melodrama in California.

"New development in that credit card operation."

"The guys who were stealing cards from gym lockers?" I remembered the scam—thieves posed as potential health club members to gain access to the facilities, then emptied out the lockers that weren't secured. A surprising number of lockers had no locks or ones that were easily jimmied.

"Right. Homicide turned up in one case. One of the owners, Rick Chapman, was found murdered, with a bunch of other people's cards on him."

"So an owner was in on the scam?"

"Looks that way. It's the Feds' case, technically, but I still might have to testify. Are you keeping out of trouble, by the way?''

What was this new reputation I'd acquired? I was always the good girl in school. Did my homework, arrived on time, never disobeyed my teachers. Josephine saw to that. *If I ever have to come and talk to a teacher because you were bad, I'll kill you* had kept me in line. Maybe I was entering my rebellious senior years.

I cleared my throat before answering Matt. In the twenty-four hours since I'd left him, I'd wormed my way into the lab library looking for suspects in an alleged accident case, had a clandestine meeting with a Berkeley cop who gave me semi-unauthorized information, and agreed to help find a missing teenager. And I had the feeling I was just getting started.

"No trouble. I'm having a great time," I said. "Elaine and I are talking, walking around."

"What was Rose talking about? A new case?"

"Oh, you know Rose," I said lightly.

"Gloria."

"What?"

Matt laughed. "You know *what*. You're not harassing Inspector Russell, are you?"

"No. I haven't even called him." At last, a question I could answer truthfully.

We chatted a few more minutes about Rose's dinner menu, and promised to E-mail each other. Before he hung up, Matt gave me one more admonition.

"Don't make me come out there to keep you safe. I'm afraid of earthquakes."

"I wouldn't mind if you came out here," I said in a manner that could be called phone flirting.

AFTER THE CALL from Revere, I cooled down with a couple of lemon cookies from the jar on Elaine's counter. Not as tasty as the stock of Italian desserts Rose and I kept on hand, but acceptable, and probably healthier. Cannoli and tiramisu belonged to no recommended food group, and I'd never seen them on a nutritional pyramid, though I treated them as if they were.

I went back to Manuel's term paper. He'd taken pains to cite the latest occupational exposure limits and threshold values for concentrations of beryllium, the conditions under which the regulators believed nearly all workers may be repeatedly exposed day after day without adverse health effects. Without naming the company, he wrote about a class-action suit against an industry giant, the plaintiffs claiming health problems from beryllium exposure. The workers alleged the corporation ignored reports that they were being sickened by beryllium, even at minimal allowed exposures, and company officials neglected to inform regulators of the complaints.

Using a newsmagazine as reference, Manuel reported on people who contracted the disease from dust carried into their homes by beryllium workers. "Some victims were women who washed their husbands' work clothes," he wrote. I wondered if Manuel thought female victims constituted more of a tragedy than male victims, something I'd never understood. But this is not a paper on equal rights, I reminded myself.

The paper ended with an exhortation for the government to ensure compliance with beryllium exposure limits, and for companies and laboratories to adopt better methods for assessing employees' sensitivity to beryllium.

"New blood tests allow us to screen people for early signs of CBD rather than wait for years for severe symptoms to develop," Manuel wrote. "CBD is a disease that can be prevented. If modern science has given us this technology, then we should use it for the benefit of mankind."

Manuel's youth and sincerity came through in his homework assignment, and I felt a twinge of sadness at the thought of his being harmed in any way. I tried to come up with a connection between Manuel's term paper and the beryllium work of Gary Larkin's team. But I knew it was unlikely BUL was involved in safety violations; the group was research-oriented, with only a few well-trained people handling beryllium. The problems Manuel cited in his paper were more typical of those that occurred in industry, where hundreds of plant workers breathed in beryllium dust everyday.

Some of my attempts to link Manuel's paper with his disappearance resulted in scenarios so complicated they died in mid-thought, before I could write them down. Suppose someone in the unnamed, negligent company in the lawsuit read Manuel's paper, recognized the case, and kidnapped Manuel to silence him. Improbable. Manuel had no sources other than those available to the general public.

Or, suppose a product containing beryllium, a particular brand of calculator or television set, was a health threat and Manuel had discovered this. Highly unlikely. Experts agreed CBD was an industrial problem only, and that finished products like bicycles and windshield frames containing beryllium posed no threat to consumers. And besides, Manuel didn't discuss specific commercial products in his paper.

I resigned myself to looking elsewhere for clues to Manuel's whereabouts and wondered if I had the language skills necessary to interview the teenage friends on the list José had given me.

Though I didn't expect to find answers in the CBD paper, I decided to finish reading the last few pages anyway, and leave Manuel's peers to the police interviewers. His report was well researched, and I found myself hoping Manuel would be alive long enough to work in a physics lab.

In a glossary in the back, Manuel had gathered acronyms used by scientists and regulators, some of which I hadn't seen in a long time, like PEL—permissible exposure limit—and TLV—eight-hour average threshold limit value.

On the last page, he provided fifteen references, including websites on the Internet. I read down the list, starting with an impressive collection of regulatory groups: the American Conference of Governmental Industrial Hygienists, the National Institute for Occupational Safety and Health, the Occupational Safety and Health Administration, and the Registry of Toxic Effects of Chemical Substances.

One reference on that page of Manuel's homework set my eyelashes fluttering and sent a shiver through my body. "Personal interviews," it read, "with beryllium scientists G. Larkin,

S. Kellerman, L. Carver, and R. Johnson of the Berkeley University Laboratory.''

A loud ''aha'' came from my lips, though there was no one to hear it.

EIGHT

WHAT DO SCIENTISTS and detectives have in common? I asked myself. They don't believe in coincidences. Larkin, Kellerman, Carver, and Johnson. The coauthors on the five beryllium reports I'd taken from the lab library. The beryllium team of the late Gary Larkin. I walked back and forth in front of Elaine's dark brick fireplace, trying to focus again on a connection between Gary's murder and Manuel Martinez's disappearance. I'd already dismissed the likely scenarios, I reminded myself.

It wasn't as if Gary died from chronic beryllium disease. The medical examiner said he'd died suddenly, at work in his lab. CBD is a disease of the lungs taking a long time to develop, and not considered fatal, except with repeated overexposure. Although serious cases of CBD can be debilitating and shorten life expectancy, it doesn't cause sudden death.

During my walk I constructed a grand theory in which Kellerman, Johnson, or Carver kills Gary Larkin—granted, I couldn't come up with a motive. Manuel finds out about the murder while he's writing his term paper—admittedly, this was a weak link. Then Manuel is killed when he confronts the murderer—also a weak link.

Lucky I'm not a detective and can't act on my wild conjecture, I thought. Not officially, anyway. What I could do was calm down and figure out a way to meet the big three beryllium engineers who were still alive.

I went up to my room and rifled through my luggage for a notebook. That's been my problem until now, I decided, I haven't taken notes or made lists. Armed with new analytical tools, I returned to the rocker with another cup of coffee and renewed determination.

After visiting Manuel's room and reading his term paper, I felt I knew him. With no rational basis other than his father's word, plus the young man's neatness and youthful idealism about setting the world right, I thought Manuel Martinez might deserve the label Elaine had given him: "a good kid."

And even if Manuel turned out to be "a bad kid," I was determined to get to the bottom of his disappearance for Elaine Cody, one of my best friends, who'd asked for very little from me over three decades. Whether or not José Martinez would survive any longer than other men who came and went in her life didn't matter. Elaine needed me now.

The first two items in my newly organized crime-solving scheme were to read the beryllium reports and check *Who's Who in California Science* for information on the authors. It was number three, a sublist of possible opportunities for interviewing suspects, that forced me to realize how easy my Revere PD cases had been, with obvious links to serious money and big industrial partners. And most important, I'd always had a legitimate way to interview suspects without leaving my house, since the victims were waked in my building, two floors below my apartment in the Galigani Mortuary.

Let's see how well you do this time, without all that help. I heard my mother, Josephine, admonish me in her usual way. Since moving back to Revere and meeting Matt, I'd noticed her constant reprimands and castigation getting weaker, but they hadn't disappeared completely. I thought of Johnny Cash's "boy named Sue," a classic country-and-western tune that even an opera fan like me had heard. Maybe it was true that giving a child a handicap at the beginning of her life makes her stronger in the end. *Thanks, Josephine,* I told her with a specious smile.

I heard Elaine and José pull into the driveway shortly after three o'clock. I remembered how delighted we were when Elaine bought her brown-toned Tudor. Besides being suited to Elaine's elegant taste, it had enough room along the side for her car, an older version of her current Saab.

"There are approximately three houses in Berkeley with a garage, and six with a driveway, and I got one of them," she'd said, exaggerating only slightly.

I pushed the stop button on the CD player, aborting the tragic closing aria of *La Traviata.* Too late to locate happy sounds, I thought, but they didn't have to enter to music from a death scene either.

Should I tell them my hypothesis? I wondered. I didn't want to get José excited about the far-fetched fable I'd constructed, even if saying nothing meant he'd lose confidence in my ability to help him find his son. Besides that, I realized with dismay, I'd had a lot of practice keeping quiet about my suspicions, as well as my comings and goings around murder suspects.

When I saw Elaine's long face and José's tired posture as they entered the living room, I knew their marina walk had fallen far short of rejuvenating them.

"Any news?" Elaine asked.

"I wish there were. I suppose there's nothing new from your end either?"

"Nothing," José said. "I checked my messages and left one with Barnett at the police station."

At least Dennis Russell's not in charge, I thought. The reminder of Berkeley PD's inspector evoked a tingling sensation in my body, as if I'd heard a piece of chalk squeaking across a blackboard at the wrong angle. Though I'd never met him, I had a good idea of his attitude from his telegramlike E-mail to Matt, rejecting my services.

I knew the answer before I asked, but I couldn't stop myself from resorting to the traditional Italian antidote to unfavorable times.

"Is anyone interested in a snack? I brought some saltwater taffy from the Cape and a box of pizzelle." I pretended not to notice their lack of interest and arranged my fingers in the shape of a circle. "You know, those round, flat anise-flavored crispies. They're from a new bakery in Beachmont," I ended weakly.

"No, thanks."

"I'm not hungry."

I searched my brain for a way to cheer them up. In the end, I cast away my resolve to keep my improbable ideas to myself.

"I may have something," I said, acting on my short-term goal of brightening their faces.

José sat on the couch and put his hand on my shoulder.

"Gloria, what is it? You have a lead?"

"I might."

I showed Elaine and José the references in Manuel's CBD paper to Gary and to Kellerman, Carver, and Johnson, now linked in my mind like the famous team of Einstein, Podolsky, and Rosen, who wrote landmark physics papers in the early part of the twentieth century.

"Those are the authors from our trip to the library," Elaine said.

"Right. The same set of engineers show up twice."

"You think one of Gary Larkin's colleagues not only killed him, but kidnapped Manuel?" Elaine asked.

"Why would they do that?" José asked.

He and Elaine took turns addressing me.

"What's in Manuel's term paper that makes you think so?"

"Did he find out something while he was writing it?"

"He already turned that paper in a month ago. Why would they wait?"

"Couldn't this be a coincidence?"

All very good questions, ones I had no answers for. So I changed the subject slightly.

"I'd like to meet these engineers he refers to. Does either of you know any of them well enough to set up a meeting?"

"Well, I've met Kellerman, of course," José said. "Jennifer's father."

"Jennifer?"

"The girl you were asking about? In the photos with Manuel? She's Jennifer Kellerman. Her father is Sidney Kellerman."

José spoke very slowly, some phrases ending in a question mark, as if I needed special coaching to get the connection. He wasn't far off. Elaine's modest living room seemed to shrink to the size of the small grad school darkroom I'd used to develop my photographic plates. Was everyone in Berkeley connected to everyone else? A few hours ago, I'd assumed the two cases I'd taken on had nothing in common. Now they seemed like the same case—the vanished Manuel Martinez, who wrote a school paper on beryllium disease, dates Jennifer Kellerman, who is the daughter of Sidney Kellerman, who wrote beryllium reports with the deceased Gary Larkin. The same case, or part of a nursery rhyme? I wondered.

"You haven't been gone from the lab that long, Gloria," Elaine said. "Don't you remember? It's like a small town. Even our little place on the hill. You can't go to the supermarket without meeting your boss and three technicians from the print plant."

I did remember; with most of the employees living locally, chances were your neighbor and your neighbor's wife and grown children all had badges from BUL or one of the other two nearby labs. I also recalled my first years in the early sixties, when it was quite the opposite. The policy then was no two people in the same family could work at the same lab. I never did understand the reasoning behind that—if you and your husband knew the same secret weapons information, how did that pose an increased threat to national security? Pillow talk that could be overheard? A temptation to spy together? Or another general rule derived from one particular case?

Back to the business at hand, I decided.

"José, do you know Sidney Kellerman well enough to drop by his house? Or invite him to dinner or a drink?"

José's eyes dropped to his bulky gray-and-black tennis shoes, not too different in style from his son's. He drew in his breath and clucked loudly.

"We don't get along too well."

"Over Manuel and Jennifer?"

"Yes," José answered, seeming surprised at my good guess. Had he never looked at his son's bulletin board? Was he never a teenager?

"What did you argue about?" Elaine asked, joining us after a brief absence to prepare coffee and snacks.

The bit of action I'd stirred up appeared to have gotten her back on track as a hostess, and the smell of Peet's French roast and anise pizzelle told me the trip to the marina was not all in vain. I reached over the bowl of baby carrots and picked up a chocolate-covered cookie as José started his explanation.

"Jennifer's mother died about a year ago, so Sid's a single parent, like me. I guess that makes you overprotective sometimes.

We both thought the kids were seeing too much of each other. They walked or rode to school together in the morning, then after school they'd hang around, mostly at our house, using the computer. She'd go home for dinner and then they'd be on the phone to each other. Every night it seemed."

"But you told me Manuel didn't have a girlfriend."

"He didn't. He shouldn't have. I guess I didn't want to admit it."

Before I could suppress it, an exasperated sigh left my lips. "José, you're going to have to be honest with me—and with yourself—if we're going to make any progress here."

I hoped I didn't sound too severe, but apparently I was harsh enough for Elaine to come to his rescue.

"Okay, so he's upset. He's going to tell us everything from now on, though," she said as if José had been unfairly reprimanded by his day care provider.

"So Manuel was seeing too much of Jennifer Kellerman," I said. "That means you and her father agreed on that point?"

"Yes, but Sid thought it was Manuel's fault, and I knew Jennifer was the one calling all the time, stopping by for any excuse. Pitiful. She'd ring the bell and ask if she left her jacket in the hall closet." José shook his head, as if recalling the image of a tiny young woman whose love was unrequited. I wondered how accurate his impressions were of Berkeley's own Romeo and Juliet. "It was getting so Manuel didn't have time for any other friends. I had to force him into band to take his mind off her."

Nothing like E-flat clarinet to distract a seventeen-year-old boy from his girlfriend, I thought. I wondered if José's awareness of human emotions could be even more primitive than mine, or whether single parenthood had clouded his mind.

I took a long breath, taking time to talk myself out of reprimanding José for withholding information.

"When was the last time you and Sid had words?" I asked him, forcing a matter-of-fact tone.

"It's about a week ago now, I think. He was more upset than usual. I'm not sure why. He called me up and said to make sure Manuel never went over there again. He said it would be better for everyone if Manuel disappeared from the face of the earth."

Elaine's tiny coffee spoon fell onto the ceramic tray, making a clatter loud enough to startle me and send my cookie careening to the floor. In the few moments of silence that followed, I figured we were all processing José's inopportune remark in the same way—a figure of speech, something Sidney Kellerman had said in anger, without thinking, and that José repeated in the same unconscious way. Without articulating our thoughts, we sipped from our coffee mugs and moved on.

"José, is there anything else you want to tell me? Remember this is about finding Manuel. Keeping him from harm."

"We don't mean to pry, José," Elaine said. "But anything can be important."

José breathed loudly as if trying to expel the last cubic centimeter of air from his lungs. "The money," he said, biting his lower lip. "Lately Manuel seemed to have more money than he should have had."

"How much more?"

"Not a lot," he said, holding up his hand to halt further conjecture that his son walked around with wads of cash. "Not hundreds of dollars or anything. I give him an allowance because I don't want him to work. I want him to study." As José pounded his fist into his hand, I wondered if he used the same gesture with Manuel, and how effective it was.

"How much money, José?" I asked. I could feel Elaine's stare, like a warning to be kind to her friend, but I plowed on. "And how did you find out?"

"It was a matter of twenty dollars here and twenty there. I'd see he bought some software, or concert tickets for him and the girl."

"Her name is Jennifer." Cruel as I sounded, I needed José to acknowledge reality.

José nodded. I could see that I was wearing him down, and wished I didn't feel so badly about it. Did this mean I wasn't cut out for police work? Or just that I wasn't a good policewoman?

"Jennifer," José said. "And he had some new clothes, without having to ask me."

"Can you pinpoint when you started to notice?"

José bit his knuckles, a gesture I remembered from my own

childhood, when my aunts or uncles were frustrated or angry at themselves, or at the universe in general. Must be a Mediterranean thing, I thought. "He got a lot of money at Christmas, so that doesn't count. His mother, plus his uncles and aunts, everyone gave him money toward his new computer. After he bought it, he was broke for a while. Then, I'd say around February, yes, it was Valentine's Day, he bought Jennifer an expensive bracelet."

"Did you confront him about it?"

José shrugged. "Casually. I didn't challenge him, exactly. He told me he'd saved up his allowance. But I knew it was a lot more than that." José got up and started pacing. "If only I'd said something. But how hard do you push? It's so hard to know."

"José, none of this may have anything to do with where Manuel is now. We need to keep calm. And for certain, you can't blame yourself."

"She's right, José. You've been a good father," Elaine said as if she knew.

"Let's go back to our beryllium engineers. Is there anyway we can approach one of the others?" I asked. "Lincoln Carver or Rita Johnson?"

"Don't you know them?" Elaine asked. "Weren't they on that task force with you and Gary a few years ago?"

"Not that I remember. There were a lot of people coming and going on that team."

Not all scientists and engineers at the lab know each other, I wanted to remind her. As a technical editor, she'd worked with us long enough to know better. But I was also aware of my own inadequate personal network. I tried not to sound defensive, sure that Elaine hadn't meant to call attention to my shortcomings as a social being. Outside of the dinner group, I'd socialized very little, choosing to spend many hours with my long, narrow helium-neon laser, often going in on weekends.

As for this trip, I'd decided not to call the few colleagues I had sent a Christmas card to, and tell them I was in town. I realized I'd be setting a precedent. If I visited Berkeley and didn't get in touch with them, it would be harder to do it the second time I came, and then it would become more and more awkward, and finally the friendship, or whatever it was, would be over.

I'd prepared myself for that course, and I didn't think changing that decision would help my investigations. What would I say? "I'm back after a year, and just called to ask if you could help me solve a murder and find a missing teenager." The greeting didn't flow well in my mind.

During my musing, Elaine and José had come up with ideas of their own. I heard them talking about me as if they knew I'd mentally left the room for a while.

"She could call Johnson or Carver and say she's heard about their research and wants to interview them for a newspaper story," José said. He continued walking back and forth in front of the couch, forcing Elaine to exercise her neck to follow his path.

"Or, if we're willing to spread the word that Manuel's missing, and risk having his mother find out," Elaine said, "Gloria could say she's a friend of his father and wants to follow up on anyone he's talked to in the last few weeks."

"But the interviews he had with those engineers took place months ago. Why would she bother talking with them after all this time?"

"They don't have to know she knows how long ago it was."

"Too complicated," I said, raising my arm for attention. "We might as well make me a missing persons officer for the Berkeley Police Department."

"Not a bad idea," Elaine said. "Don't tell me you haven't impersonated a police officer in the past year."

I ignored the reference to my occasional compulsion to resort to fraud when I needed access to important information.

"I think the direct way is best," I said. "I'm simply going to call them and say I was a friend of Gary Larkin's and I want to know more about how he died."

"And in the process, you could learn something about where Manuel is," José said, hope returning to his voice.

"That's right," I said, checking my watch. "It's after four.

Close to quitting time. And it's Friday. If I don't reach anyone now, we'll be out of luck for the whole weekend.''

Elaine was ready with a lab phone book open to the J's. Evidently we were going to start with the woman.

NINE

I LEFT A MESSAGE with Rita Johnson's voice mail, giving my name, Elaine's phone number, and a vague sentence that she might interpret as a work-related call. I hoped that would make her more inclined to call me back than "Hi, I'm Gloria, retired-physicist-turned-crime-fighter."

Lincoln Carver picked up on the fourth ring, interrupting his own electronic voice. The recorded voice sounded deep and rich, with a slight Southern accent. The live voice of Lincoln Carver, with its quick "Yes?" sounded like he had one hand on his light switch, ready to leave for the weekend.

"This is Dr. Gloria Lamerino," I said with a rare acknowledgment of my official title. I used it only to get attention in matters I considered urgent. And once in a while to impress someone who needed to be put in his place, I admitted to myself.

I gave Carver the brief statement I'd rehearsed. I wasn't completely comfortable passing myself off as a friend who needed to come to terms with Gary Larkin's death, but it was partially true, and seemed the best way to get the information I needed.

"I don't see how I can help you," he said. "Gary was working alone in his lab that night. You probably know as much as I do if you've read the newspapers."

"I just have a few questions, about his last days and some of the things he was going through at the time." Elaine's and José's eyes widened at my fabrication, and I shocked myself, too, with that one, wondering how I came up with it. Subconsciously, I must have decided that an engineer who dies from inhaling beryllium powder must have been in trouble beforehand.

"You mean the porno stuff?" Carver asked.

This time my eyebrows disappeared into the short black-and-gray bangs that lined my forehead. I cleared my throat in response to the thrill of excitement that traveled through my body.

I made funny faces at Elaine and José in an attempt to share the effect of the lucky guess, but realized I fell short in my pantomime.

"Yes," I said simply, not wanting to reveal my delight to Lincoln Carver.

"I suppose…" Carver stopped, and I worried that he'd renege.

"I'm only in town for a short time," I told him. Meaning, you don't have to worry that I'll hound you for the rest of your life.

"Are you free right now?" he asked. "I ride my bike, so it would have to be at someplace on my way home."

"Perfect," I said. "I promise not to take up much of your time. I'm near Walnut Square and can be anywhere you say in ten minutes."

"Make it a half hour, at the café on Cedar, near Martin Luther King Jr. Boulevard."

"I'll be there," I said, noting the care with which Carver designated one of Berkeley's main north-south streets. Many oldtimers still called it by its former name, Grove Way, or shortened it to MLK Boulevard. I'd even heard it called "Milky Way" once or twice. The meeting place was within walking distance of Elaine's house. What good luck, I thought.

I looked at Elaine and José. "If one of you will drive me, that gives me twenty minutes or so to check out Carver on the Internet. Do you have a bookmark for *Who's Who in California Science*, Elaine?"

"Hardly. Unless they've gone in for personal ads," she said with a grin, then caught herself in time to rub José's back and reassure him. "Of course, I don't need that now."

"Here's the big thing," I said, addressing both Elaine and José. "Did you ever hear anything about Gary Larkin's being involved in pornography?"

The answer I heard was a combination of "no" from Elaine and "oh yeah" from José. I'd always been aware that Elaine's exclusive reading of *The New York Times* kept her out of range of much of the local gossip. She'd tried to get me to read it, but succeeded only in interesting me in the Tuesday edition, which has a science section each week.

"I don't understand why you'd want to keep up with the state of the potholes in the Bronx and not on our own Warren Freeway,'' I'd teased her, mindful that it was the *Times*'s international coverage and excellent journalism that motivated her choice. José, on the other hand, read the local newspapers, which had carried the pornography story. ''I remember reading something, but it went away pretty quick,'' José said. ''I think the lab is good at keeping things like that from the press.''

''And *Labline* certainly wouldn't have carried it,'' Elaine said, referring to the internal lab paper, which was the organ of the administration. *Labline* reported breakthroughs in microelectromechanical systems, not scandals involving pornography. ''What did I miss?'' she asked.

''I don't remember a lot,'' José said. ''Just that the lab filed charges of misuse of government property against this engineer when they found he'd been using his lab computer to download pornography routinely. I didn't even remember the guy's name was Larkin till you mentioned it.''

''I'll know more after I see Lincoln Carver, I hope. Meanwhile, we have work to do.''

Elaine went to her computer to get started on the search while I made a quick change out of my jeans and sweatshirt and into a casual gray knit pants suit. I wanted to look more like a mourner than a Bostonian on vacation. I'd brought only a few from my vast collection of pins with me and wore the first one I could put my hands on— a one-inch silver Fanueil Hall Rose had sent me decades ago.

Five minutes later I was ready, and Elaine had the basic information about Lincoln Carver on her screen. José and I were both impressed with Elaine's facility on the Net and told her so.

For me it was a reminder of the differences between my two best friends. Rose Galigani had resisted technology as much she could and still run an efficient office for the Galigani Mortuary business. She left most of the computer-based work to her assistant, Martha Franklin. Rose wasn't so bad as Peter Mastrone, however, who thought the advent of microwave ovens signaled the decline of Western civilization.

I wasn't sure why all my Revere community came flooding into my mind at a time when I was working against a deadline, except that I missed them. I missed Matt most of all and had a hard time reconciling what I planned to do—interview a murder suspect—with an image of him lying next to me again.

I focused on the screen in front of me and read through a brief description of Carver's current duties at BUL: performing beryllium implosion experiments for fusion reactors. He was thirty-one, unmarried, had done undergraduate work at MIT. No honors or awards or honorary degrees. Membership in the Institute for Electrical and Electronics Engineers and vice president of the local chapter of Minorities in Engineering. The listing gave his mailing address as a post office box number in Berkeley, plus his fax and E-mail address.

Not a lot to go on, but I might be able to count on my Boston pin to awaken good memories of college in Cambridge.

The three of us were huddled around Elaine's computer in an upstairs sun porch that doubled as her home office.

"Do you understand the work he's supposed to be doing?" José asked.

"In general. Implosion experiments are the ones where you dump a lot of energy onto a small target, and, essentially, the target collapses." I prepared my hands for a mock demonstration of a collapsing sphere and continued. "It folds in on itself and releases energy in a more useful form. I guess I know enough to keep a conversation going."

"Good for you," José said, rubbing his hands together as if I'd passed a pop quiz.

Our hastily constructed plan called for José to drop me off at the Cedar St. Café on his way home. I'd walk back or call Elaine when Carver and I were through. It must have dawned on all of us at the same time that technically, in our minds at least, Lincoln Carver was a suspect in a murder and an abduction.

"You need to be careful, Gloria," Elaine said.

José nodded in agreement.

I ARRIVED AT THE CAFÉ almost simultaneously with a tall, light-skinned black man. He was looping a heavy chain around the spokes of an expensive-looking bicycle, the kind that had never had training wheels attached. We eyed each other uncertainly.

"Dr. La—?" He shrugged his shoulders and spread open his hands, the international symbol for help.

I nodded. "Just call me Gloria." I extended my hand, but he refused with a smile, showing me sweaty palms and even white teeth. His face had the kind of short, uniform beard we used to call a five o'clock shadow, though I was sure there was a more nineties name for it. His head was clean-shaven, the total effect being that all of his hair had slid down from his scalp to his cheeks.

"Thanks so much for meeting me," I said.

"No problem. I have to be out of here by five-thirty, though."

Carver didn't have to use the phrase "Friday night date." Anyone looking at the handsome figure he cut might guess he had plans for the weekend.

In typical Berkeley style, we had to clear newspapers, flyers, and used notebook paper from a table to make room for our coffees. When we were seated, I conjured up small talk about Boston, and based on what I'd read in Who's Who, I asked a baited question about beryllium technology.

"Is it true adding copper to beryllium makes it a better candidate for a reactor lining?"

"That's exactly what we're working on," Carver said with enthusiasm and surprise. "If you use our particular beryllium design, your laser temperature doesn't have to be as high, so you minimize the instabilities." I wanted to call Rose in Revere and tell her she was wrong when she'd said I hadn't learned the way to a man's heart. "We'll be reporting our data soon. X-ray spectra, neutron yield, the works."

I listened with great attention as Carver told me about a new, better-than-ever laser they used to drive the implosions.

"Gary had spearheaded the funding," he said, turning the conversation to the purpose of our meeting. "You wanted to talk about him?"

"I was so sorry to hear about his death. What exactly happened?"

"It's hard to tell. A technician found him early one morning. A Wednesday. I remember because I'd taken the day off for a class. He'd come in from a business trip to Cleveland the night before and evidently went right to the lab."

"Gary's technician, that was Matt, right?" I asked, using the first name that came to my mind.

"No, it was Larry. Larry Pursiano, the old Italian guy that's been there for years." How handy for me, I thought, committing the name to memory.

"And he was just—dead, on the floor?"

Carver nodded. He stared past me in the direction of Cedar Street, where Friday evening traffic was in full swing. His voice was low and halting, as if the memory was painful for him. Or is he feeling guilty? I wondered.

"Pursiano said it looked like he might have been wearing a respirator mask. The canister was near him. Probably getting ready to make a cut in the brick of beryllium he'd brought from Cleveland."

"That's it?"

"That's it." Carver had turned his gaze back to me. He took a deep breath and relaxed the muscles of his face. "We all miss him. Him and his tissues." Carver smiled and made a gesture with his hands to mimic pulling tissues from a box and blowing his nose. "He had bad allergies. And they seemed to be getting worse lately. Probably the stress. He carried those little travel-size boxes around with him everywhere. The Labwipes were too rough on him."

I smiled, as if I, too, had firsthand knowledge of Gary's tissue habit. I was accustomed to sharing fond memories of the deceased on both coasts with their surviving friends and relatives.

"He was a good guy. He used to visit the local schools as part of a science program our education department developed. He loved teaching kids about beryllium, how it's a great, often underrated structural material. He even had bumper stickers made up, 'Beryllium, the Final Frontier,' and handed them out to the kids." Carver laughed. "I'm not sure they really got it."

I laughed with him. "I wish I'd thought of that," I said. "I could have done 'Spectroscopy, Stairway to the Stars.'" Pleasant as our in-jokes were, I wanted to move on before Carver's time was up. "I'm sure you miss Gary," I said. "What are your plans for the team now?"

"Good question. We're all in line for Gary's job. Me, a guy named Sid Kellerman, and also Rita Johnson." Carver sipped his cappuccino without getting the tiniest bit of foam on his lip.

"Do you know if Rita is in town by the way?" I asked as if she, like Gary, was another close friend of mine.

"I'm sure she is. She has a family wedding this weekend. Otherwise she'd be off camping. Rita's not going to be able to tell you anymore than I did, though."

"I might just want to get a woman's perspective." I nearly gagged on the words. Was I always this quick to sacrifice my beliefs for short-term gains? I looked around, checking for witnesses to my hypocrisy, but the café was empty except for us and an older couple sitting across a table from each other reading separate sections of the *San Francisco Chronicle*.

Carver frowned and uttered a soft grunt. "A woman's perspective. I suppose you mean her suit against the lab."

I gulped and covered my surprise with a dab of my napkin on my lips and made a mental note to speak to Elaine about keeping up with the local news.

"How's that coming?" I asked, shifting in my seat. I wished I had a co-conspirator across the room to give a thumbs-up sign to.

"They still haven't heard whether they'll get class-action status. She's one of the key players in the group."

"It's the women who..." I waved my left hand as I lifted my mug with my right.

"Right. The lab professional women, hoping to make a claim of widespread gender discrimination for over a thousand female employees, past and present." Carver said this in the tone of one mocking a political speech.

"I remember something like that happened a few years ago. The director put aside funds to make up for lower starting salaries for female scientists and engineers with comparable credentials and experience as males."

"This time they're going for more than that—raises, promotions, even locker room facilities. Rita's got her work cut out for her."

"Have they already filed the suit?"

Carver nodded. "Some time in March. Hey, maybe you can get in on it."

"Probably not," I said with a smile, as if I was going for the prize in a contest for most loyal employee. "But I hope I get to talk to her. I've left a message on her voice mail at work."

"She's more likely to check her E-mail. Let me give you that." Carver pulled a pen from an unlikely spot in his tight black biking pants and wrote an E-mail address on a partly used napkin. "So, did you work with Gary at one time or something? I don't remember seeing you around."

"We worked on a task force a few years ago, and then kept up the contact." I was glad I wasn't under oath to define "contact" when the truth was that I didn't have to know a person well to snoop into a suspicious death. And, these days more and more deaths seemed suspicious to me. "But it's the pornography..." I said, shaking my head in a tsk-tsk fashion. I hoped my bluff would work and Carver would fill in the blanks.

"Right. He was cleared of course. But it hurt him in a lot of ways. People remember the accusation, no matter what the facts are, a lot of times."

"Do you think his reputation suffered? Is that what you mean?"

Carver nodded. "It changed, you know, the way people thought of him. He'd always taken the high moral ground, and this kind of made everybody wonder. And it certainly wasn't great for his divorce case."

"Right," I repeated, my version of a technique TV detectives used—pretend you already know the information. "Marlene. He filed that around..."

"Just before Christmas I guess he caught her and her boyfriend at a little unscheduled celebration."

"That must have been hard on him."

"Yeah, but he moved fast. Gary made a big deal of how she was fooling around. Wanted to keep all his money away from

her. Then when it looks like he's been getting his jollies..."
Carver cleared his throat. "You see what I mean."

"I do see," I said, beginning to feel like a second-rate therapist, repeating everything the patient says. "Was there actually
a trial on the pornography charges?"

"No. The charges were dismissed before things got too far in
the courts. And they should have been." Carver's vigorous nod
showed a sense of loyalty, whether out of respect for the dead
or genuine belief in his colleague, I couldn't tell. "Gary's lawyer
showed that anyone could have hacked into Gary's computer,
from inside or outside the lab. We certainly make it easy to do
that since we leave our systems on twenty-four hours a day."

"And all this happened, let's see, around..." I began.

"The hearing was about a month ago, end of April. I think
the charges had been filed in early February."

"I don't suppose anyone knows how the money settlement
turned out," I said, with a casual stir of the last of my cappuccino
foam.

"Not specifically, but from the way Gary acted, I'm sure Marlene got more than he thought she deserved. He had a lot of
money from patents he'd filed before he came to the lab, and in
spite of the community property law, there's always some negotiating that goes on."

"Lawyers," I said, with a shake of my head, taking the easy
way to keep our rapport going. Who couldn't agree that lawyers
were ruthless negotiators?

Carver nodded. "It's awful to say now, but Gary was pretty
hard on us. He accused me, Sid, even Rita of being responsible
for the porno. I guess the downloads showed equal parts male
and female."

We both laughed at the double meaning in his description of
Internet pornography.

"Why do you think he would accuse you?"

"We knew a couple of his passwords. We had to, to access
the data files. And it had to be scary for him. Besides the moral
thing, and the monkey wrench it threw into the divorce proceed-
ings, it's no joke to be accused of misuse of government property."

"Let me make sure I have this straight. They traced the downloads to his computer—how did they know to look in the first place?"

"Just through random monitoring. The lab has a special group for computer security, and they're always on the alert, and not just for spy stuff, for anything from leaks of proprietary information, to general misuse like this. Anyway, in the end Gary was cleared. I'm glad of that."

"Did they ever determine who the hacker was?"

Carver shook his head. "Never did. Probably some eight-year-old from Nebraska."

"Probably."

Lincoln Carver was so charming, I nearly forgot he was a suspect in two cases. Before it was too late, I brought up my other reason for the meeting.

"Speaking of kids—do you remember meeting Manuel Martinez—a high school student writing a term paper on chronic beryllium disease?"

Carver leaned back until his wrought-iron chair was on two legs. I worried about its stability on the tile floor, but figured Carver had orders of magnitude more agility than I'd had even in my prime.

"No," he said. "I don't remember meeting anyone like that."

I placed the photograph of Manuel and Jennifer on the table between us, and turned it to face Carver. I put my finger on Manuel's tuxedoed chest. "It would have been a few months ago, during the last school term, probably right around the beginning of the year."

Carver looked at the photograph, but not as carefully as I would have liked. He picked it up and held it by one corner. He seemed to be staring past the edge, instead of focusing on the image. "Nope. Never met him," he said, flipping it back to me as if he were dealing cards.

Carver checked his watch, an enormous timepiece with a wide black fabric strap and a keypad with more functions than my first calculator had. "Sorry, but I have to run. Nice meeting you. I hope the rest of your trip is good."

We stood up. Before I could collect my jacket and purse, Carver was out the door, leaving only a pleasant trace of after-shave in his wake.

TEN

SINCE THE WALK to Elaine's would have been uphill most of way, I gave in to my laziness and called her from a phone booth on the corner after Carver left.

In the car, I briefed her on my first suspect interview, as I thought of it.

"Do you think he...*has* Manuel?" Elaine asked. Her simple word choice seemed to strain her considerable powers as a professional editor. "Why else would he lie to you and say he didn't recognize him in the photo?"

"I don't know. Maybe he really never met him. Without a motive, we can't be sure about anything. There's hardly a strong connection between Manuel and Carver, other than his name's appearing in the reference section of Manuel's term paper. Carver has a lot of publications. I'm sure he's referenced all the time." I lowered my voice during my next offering, knowing it would not be welcome. "Maybe Manuel cheated. He might have talked to only one person and decided to impress his teacher by citing three interviews."

I shifted in my seat and caught Elaine's expression. She'd raised her eyebrows and half turned to look at me. "Don't tell José that."

"I wouldn't dream of it."

I told Elaine what I did get from Carver: the name of the technician who found Gary's body, more information on the pornography case and the date of the hearings, and some insight into Rita Johnson's political leanings.

"I can't believe you didn't hear anything about the lawsuit," I said, trying to keep a nonaccusatory tone.

"I did, come to think of it, but I don't remember that name. I'm sure some other tech editors are involved in organizing the case. Just not me."

In all our years together, Elaine and I had never pursued the topic of gender discrimination. Maybe it was time. "Are you paid the same as men with similar education and experience?" I asked her.

She shook her head. "The salary printout is in the library for anyone to look through, as you know. And now you can buy your own copy, for about a dollar. But I've never bothered to check. Is that awful?"

"Not necessarily. I'm just curious." No more than it was awful for me to skip the sixties, I thought. Like Elaine, I'd never stopped to question whether I was being treated on an equal level with my male counterparts. I'd always considered that if I did the best job I could, I'd be rewarded accordingly. My experiences with women or other groups who claimed discrimination had been unfavorable. To me they appeared to substitute stridency for competence.

"I can't wait to meet Rita Johnson," I said.

RESTING MY NOTEBOOK on my knee as Elaine drove, I added to my To Do list while my interview with Carver was fresh in my mind. Call the technician, Larry Pursiano—he might be working a weekend shift. E-mail Rita Johnson. Get Elaine to look on-line for back newspaper stories on *Government v. Gary Larkin,* and *Rita Johnson and Friends v. Government.* These cases get bigger every hour, I thought.

We'd agreed to stop for a take-out dinner, saving our gourmet appetites for Saturday evening at Siad's. Elaine didn't spend anymore time at her range top than I did at my little stove in Revere. I still had reading I wanted to do, and I was eager to get started. Not to mention I was tired. I'd read that it takes one day per time zone change to get your biological clock in sync. I was only one third there, and my first twenty-four hours had been anything but restful.

"Italian okay?" Elaine asked with a grin.

"I'll make do. Especially if there's more Peet's coffee around."

A half hour later, we spread out our buffet on Elaine's coffee table: a liter of linguine alfredo, a large tossed salad, and a loaf of garlic bread.

"This meal's designed to keep me awake and working," I said. "Did you do this on purpose?"

Elaine's face fell, her chin quivering as if she were going to cry.

"What's wrong? I was only joking."

"It's a lot of things. For one, I've been feeling guilty, practically forcing you to deal with José's crisis."

"I don't feel forced, Elaine. Don't worry about it. Let's take a break and enjoy this feast."

"Let me finish."

I stopped filling our plates and listened. Elaine grabbed tissues and held them at the ready, though her eyes were dry. For some reason, she made me think of Carver's depiction of Gary Larkin, carrying tissues with him wherever he went.

"Here's what makes it worse," Elaine said. "I'd been feeling a little used, thinking you came out here because you thought there was a murder to solve, not to visit me." She held up her hand to indicate she wasn't ready for my comments. "And then, I turn around and use you to solve this case for my boyfriend. So, now I'm doubly guilty."

Though I didn't follow Elaine's math, I knew what she meant. I'd thought about the strange timing of my trip myself. I'd planned to visit Elaine after one year in Revere, and not before, to be sure I'd make a good decision about whether to stay in my hometown. I suppose if I'd had my tickets before I found out about Gary's death, it would have been easier to convince myself that it was a grand coincidence. As it was, it came out to fifty-fifty—half visit, half curiosity about what I saw as a beryllium murder.

"Maybe we can call it even," I said. "We're using each other, but only in the way friends are supposed to use each other. Maybe if I hadn't heard about Gary's death, I'd have waited till July or August to visit you. Who knows? But as long as I'm here now, I'm happy if I can help José, too."

By the time we finished our intense dialogue on friendship, interspersed with a few tears and hugs, the once creamy pasta was an unappetizing, cold lump of noodles stuck to the bowl. The smell of garlic had also run its course. We picked at our salads and called it a night.

I LOOKED AT the digital readout on my bedside table and told my body it was indeed only nine o'clock, not midnight. But even on the West Coast it was too late to try Marlene Korner again. I settled myself on the bed, spreading out beryllium articles, redacted police reports, and the lab phone book. I was used to this arrangement, except it was even easier to play office on Elaine's queen-size guest bed than on my own full-size one.

Since Elaine had volunteered to look up Kellerman and Johnson in *Who's Who in Science* and print out the pages for me, I started by calling Larry Pursiano's number at the lab. I was so surprised that he answered in person, it took a moment for me to come up with, "Good evening. I'm Dr. Gloria Lamerino, a former colleague of Gary Larkin."

Pursiano told me he was on a break, working swing shift, and only had a minute to talk. I gave him the same story that had worked with Carver, and got a similar response.

"There's not much to tell. I found Gary on the floor, and I called the police."

I regretted not having looked at the police statements. It wouldn't have been too hard to pick out Pursiano as the one who'd discovered the body. In lieu of homework to rely on, I brought out my most desperate voice.

"I just want to talk to someone who saw Gary in his last days. I live in Massachusetts now and it's been so long since I've seen him."

"Okay," he said, his pronunciation leaning slightly toward "hokay," like the way my Italian uncles said the word. Other than that, I detected no accent in the man Carver had called an old Italian. Thinking back on the young black man, I realized Pursiano might be all of fifty years old to rate that description. "I'm working straight through till seven in the morning. We're doing data runs and everyone's doubling up shifts. I can meet you then, but I won't be very awake."

"I won't keep you long. Where shall I meet you?"

"I usually get breakfast in the lab cafeteria before I go home to bed. Can you come there?"

"I certainly can. I'll see you there at...?"

"Seven-fifteen."

"Thank you, Mr. Pursiano."

I hung up the phone in time to answer Elaine's knock.

"You don't have to knock on your own door."

"I couldn't be sure Matt hadn't sneaked across the country and climbed up a ladder to your room."

"I wish."

"Oh?" Elaine's eyebrows went up as if to say, tell me more.

"Never mind. But this is exciting—I have a seven-fifteen meeting with Larry Pursiano."

"You also have a nine o'clock with Rita Johnson."

"What?"

"It's on my answering machine. I forgot to check it when we came in. She says she got your phone message and she'll meet you at nine at the café on Cedar. Sounds like the same place where you met Carver. Your West Coast interview room. I didn't erase it, in case you want to hear it."

I was out of bed and into my robe and slippers before Elaine finished her last sentence.

Bent over the machine, I heard Rita Johnson's voice, another young one.

"I won't be home tonight, but you can E-mail me at rkjohnson at bul dot gov to confirm, nine o'clock Saturday morning at the café near the corner of MLK and Cedar. I have to be somewhere at eleven. Bye for now."

"Does that sound like the voice of a raving feminist?" I asked Elaine.

She shrugged her shoulders.

"Or a killer?"

She shrugged again.

WE SAID GOOD NIGHT for the second time that evening, dividing the chores again. Elaine took on the task of E-mailing a simple confirmation message to Rita, over my name. I spent as much time reading as I could before I fell asleep.

I read the printout on Johnson first. Her current duties at BUL were not much different from Carver's except that she'd been responsible for the evaluation of sputter-deposition, a coating process that produces a clean, uniform film on a fusion target. Johnson was thirty, unmarried, had done undergraduate and graduate work at Stanford.

I wondered when I'd started thinking of people in their thirties as young, and decided it was when I realized I could have a child that age. I thought about fifty-something Gary Larkin, working among the young Ivy Leaguers, but Kellerman's bio evened out the age range. Sidney Kellerman, almost sixty and a widower, had also gone to school at MIT, another shining light in engineering education.

In an effort to organize my data, I made a grid with names down the side, categories across the top. I wasn't sure what this would accomplish except that at a glance I'd be able to run my finger across to Kellerman and down to honorary degrees and see that he had none. I felt I should be making a column for weapons and another for locations—Carver with beryllium powder in the lab, for example?

I put my board-game matrix aside and picked up the police statements. Terry had blacked out names, addresses, and telephone numbers wherever they appeared, reminding me of how news shows overlay black rectangles on the eyes of people being arrested, or protected witnesses. The space on the form for NARRATIVE was available to me, however, and I had no trouble finding Pursiano's.

The officer's notes for the technician's story had details I was looking for. Pursiano had reported to the beryllium wing at six-fifty Wednesday morning, May 17, to start his shift. He unlocked the door, which was always secured, and noticed that the lights were on. This was not unusual since experimental runs were often made all night. He worked for about a half hour at his bench in the main bay of the facility before walking down the hallway to get coffee and finding Gary's body.

I'd passed through the beryllium wing while I was a regular lab employee and remembered the setup: one cavernous room in the center, with rows of workbenches and tall stools looking like a schoolroom, except for the stiff mats at each station, bordered in yellow-and-black safety stripes. The room was lit by giant fluorescents along the ceiling. Clean rooms and glassed-in offices lined three walls, the fourth being dedicated to a set of vending machines and a few tables. An unlikely spot for a watering hole, but that's how it worked out. A four-foot fabric partition separated the vending area from the enormous safety-glass zone.

Gary had been working in a corner room that held benches and equipment for sectioning slabs of beryllium. I knew the engineers at BUL had the special task of determining how much radioactive material was contained in bricks of beryllium that came from JET, the fusion reactor outside Oxford in the UK.

Pursiano had said he happened to be walking by the room and saw a respirator mask on the floor. The door was open, he walked in, and saw Gary Larkin's body.

Although there was no specific box for "alibi," I noticed Pursiano had woven his into the narrative. He told police he'd gone to bed early Tuesday evening because of his early Wednesday shift. His wife was home with him.

Pursiano described Gary as "curled up like baby."

"I thought he was taking a nap," he'd told the police.

A shiver ran through my body as I read the account. For no apparent reason—other than that murder made me nervous—I got out of bed and checked the burglar alarm pad in the hallway to be sure the red light was blinking.

I FELT I HAD enough energy for one more report and shuffled through the pile to see if I could identify Rita Johnson's police statement. On one of the forms, in the category "involved persons," the box for "sex" was not completely blackened and I saw the top of the letter F. I suspected Terry had done this deliberately, to make it easy for me to sort through the statements. I thought about writing her a thank-you note, but didn't want to call attention to her unorthodox support. For all I knew, Inspector Russell screened everyone's mail at the station.

It appeared Johnson qualified as "involved" since she was the second person to see Gary's body. Unless she killed him, I noted. She showed up for work right after Pursiano had called 911 and the lab's emergency team. Neither she nor Pursiano had touched anything, except to check Gary's pulse. They closed the door to the room and stood outside and waited for the authorities. Johnson told police she'd last seen Gary on the Friday before, May 12, as he headed out the door for a plane to Cleveland. She'd met him at the lab to give him paperwork he'd need when he met their beryllium supplier at the Ohio plant.

It was also Rita Johnson who later helped identify the substance Gary had inhaled, beryllium oxide, a combination of beryllium and oxygen. Her alibi: on Tuesday evening, she'd been at a meeting of women planning the strategy for their lawsuit. The meeting didn't break up until close to midnight. She went straight home, but since her roommate was out of town, no one could verify that. Gary Larkin's death was estimated as sometime after eight-fifteen in the evening when he logged in at the lab, and early the next morning when his body was found. Not exactly a small window. And not an iron-clad alibi for Rita Johnson.

It occurred to me that Johnson had shown up pretty early for a professional who was free to keep her own hours; if Pursiano's time line was correct, she was there shortly after seven-thirty. Although the official lab hours were from eight to five, it was only the administrative personnel who kept that schedule. Scientists and engineers came and went at all hours, and were more likely to come in late and stay late.

I wrote that question as number one, the start of a list of queries for Pursiano and Johnson in the morning. I fell asleep while writing the number two.

ELEVEN

On Saturday morning, for my two meetings I dressed in a burgundy suit with matching flats. Elaine frowned at the combination and embarrassed me into changing to black pumps.

"It wouldn't be so bad if you had pants or if your skirt were black, but having wine-colored shoes that match your skirt is too cute," she'd said. She knew me well enough to predict that that word would motivate me to climb the stairs to my luggage and find an alternative. She approved of my pin at least—a stylized compass with a tiny red garnet as the symbol for north.

Elaine seemed happy to chauffeur me to the lab cafeteria at seven, and to be on call to shuttle me to the Cedar St. Café afterward for my nine o'clock meeting with Rita Johnson.

"Just like a regular workday," she said in a breezy tone. "Back-to-back meetings."

I suspected Elaine's mood was lighter because she hadn't checked in with José yet, and also because of our heart-to-heart the night before. She planned to sit in the cafeteria with me until Pursiano showed up, then excuse herself and wait in the library.

Neither of us could bear the thought of lab coffee. Government-issue food and drink are no better quality than its furniture, we decided, and settled for bottled water. Today's generic cafeteria smell was that of greasy sausage with hash browns. The decor didn't vary much in such institutions from coast to coast, I'd noticed, and I envisioned millions of gallons of the same dull green paint brushed across miles of federal walls.

I was surprised at the number of patrons at the early hour, most of them with full breakfasts on their trays. The sight of lab-fashioned omelets and bacon at seven in the morning made me slightly queasy. Seeing a table full of women in polyester pants, ruffled blouses, and high heels had nearly the same effect on me and I was glad I'd had Elaine around in the seventies to convince me to skip that fashion trend.

We took seats side by side, facing the main door, and spotted Pursiano a few minutes later. He had the earmarks of a technician in my mind—small build, worn jeans, baseball cap, metal lunch box, and punctual to the minute. As with Lincoln Carver the day before, Larry Pursiano and I seemed to identify each other immediately. I wondered how retired lady physicists were stereotyped in Pursiano's mind.

We stood up to greet him, Elaine combining the move with a graceful exit.

"You must be exhausted," I said as Pursiano deposited his lunch box on a chair next to mine. "I'm really grateful that you'd see me."

"It's okay. I'll get some breakfast and be right back."

As I feared, he came back a few minutes later with the Saturday Breakfast Special—waffles swimming in butter and maple syrup, a slab of ham on the side. A paper cup filled with orange juice was the only palatable item on the tray, and even that was more the color of hospital gelatin.

I took a gulp of my carbonated water, imagining it to be an alkalizer.

"So were you a friend of Gary's?" Pursiano asked me.

Why did everyone assume that? I wondered. Wasn't there room in this world for people like me who just wanted to put things right when someone died under suspicious circumstances, even if he was only a casual acquaintance? I gave Pursiano the standard speech for the week, about my being on an energy task force with the deceased, then launched into my questions.

"Do you remember what you did when you found Gary's body? Did you check his pulse right away?"

Pursiano shook his head. "Nope. I could tell he was dead. I called 911, plus the lab's emergency hot line. When Rita came, she said we should check his pulse, so she went in and put her finger on his neck."

"Did you look for any signs of disorder around him, to see if there might have been a struggle?"

Pursiano looked up from his waffles. "Nope." His voice was low, as if he'd just been put on guard.

"Was there a phone in the lab, or did you call from outside the room?"

"There's a phone on the wall right outside." Pursiano squinted his dark eyes at me and tilted his head to the side. "You sound more like a cop than a friend."

"I'm sort of both," I said, incredulous of my own words. I thought I was doing so well during my trip to California, not impersonating law enforcement or mortuary staff, my two staples on murder cases in Revere. Pursiano's features seemed to take on those of another semi-old Italian, Sergeant Matt Gennaro of the Revere Police Department, with the same dark face and droopy eyes. I felt my cheeks flush, no less intensely than if Matt had been sitting at the next table witnessing my scam.

"I thought the police were finished. They said it was an accident, didn't they?"

"They did…uh, we did. But there's always that chance it wasn't, and we need to be thorough. So, if I could just ask a couple more questions."

"Shoot," he said, apparently satisfied with my explanation. He arranged a multilayered heap of waffles on the prongs of his fork.

"You told the officer at the scene you saw a respirator mask on the floor as you looked in from the corridor?"

"Right. The door was half open."

"Was the mask right near Gary's face?"

Pursiano looked up and to the left. I tried to remember the pop psychological meaning of the gesture. Introvert or extrovert? Visual or kinetic? Left-brained or right-brained? No wonder I'd never been any good at humanities, I thought. The chart of the fundamental particles of physics is much simpler.

"No," Pursiano announced at last. "The mask was closer to the door than to the body, over by the sink as a matter of fact." He used his sticky fork to point to the notes I was taking, probably assuming I wrote down only meaningful information. "Does that mean anything?"

"It could," I said in the solemn tone of a serious investigator.

I tried to re-create Gary Larkin's murder in my mind. Someone tampered with the mask, I theorized, putting beryllium oxide powder on the inside half of the canister it was connected to. Then, when Gary inhaled, he'd pull the powder directly into the mask and into his lungs. Where's the problem with that? I asked myself, using an old research trick—first design armor that no bullet in the world could penetrate, then design a bullet that could penetrate any armor in the world.

I found the problem in my theory very quickly. Beryllium oxide powder comes in different grain sizes, anywhere from metal chunks to a material similar to talcum powder. No matter what the size, there would be material left in the mask and around Gary's face. But the medical examiner had found only the slightest trace of powder in Gary's respiratory system, and the police lab had found none at all on the mask. Would the killer have knocked Gary out, put beryllium oxide on his nostrils, then awakened him so he could breathe it? Not likely, I decided, frustrated that the "means" part of motive, means, and opportunity would not be as easy to figure out as I'd first thought.

I concluded my self-contained debate in time to see that Pursiano's plate was clean, except for swirls of maple syrup that looked like tire marks in the sand at Revere Beach. I leaned closer to him. "Do you know anyone who might have wanted to hurt Gary?"

Pursiano shook his head. "Not hurt him like that." His hands were folded in front of his empty plate, like a schoolboy behaving himself so he could leave soon. His fingernails reminded me of my father's, which never looked clean, no matter how hard he scrubbed them.

Lost in another reverie of Revere, I almost missed the rest of Pursiano's answer. "When Gary was promoted, there was a lot of jealousy. It's different with the scientists and engineers. With us technicians, we have levels, one to five. You do your job as a three and you get moved to four. There's no competition."

"Was there a lot of rivalry for Gary's new job?"

"They all wanted it. Carver, Johnson. Maybe not Kellerman so much. He's almost ready to retire anyway. But would they kill him over it? I don't think so. You'd have murders everyday around here.''

I nodded. I tended to agree with Pursiano's assessment of laboratory politics. ''Just one more thing,'' I said, sensing he was ready to go home to a well-deserved sleep. I took the photograph of Manuel and Jennifer out of my purse and laid it on the table between us. I put my finger once again on Manuel's pale blue tuxedo shirt. ''Do you remember seeing this young man around? Maybe even in this cafeteria with Gary or someone in his group?''

''No, I don't think I know this boy,'' he said, forming his mouth into a pout, as if he might be missing something by not recognizing the handsome teenager.

I was ready to let Pursiano go. When I scribbled Elaine's number on my card and asked him to call me if he thought of anything that might be useful, I realized I'd crossed a line I hadn't crossed with Carver. I knew I'd given Pursiano the strong impression I thought Gary had been the victim of foul play.

As he left, Pursiano smiled and gave me a salute. What did he have in mind with that gesture? I wondered. A police chief? The National Guard? A drill sergeant, I decided.

I FOUND ELAINE IN the library, looking through a newsmagazine. ''Look at this,'' she said, holding out the periodical. ''It's two weeks old. You can get this information up to the minute online.'' She put it down and brushed her hands, as if shaking off the dust and mildew of centuries. ''How did it go?'' she asked.

I gave her a synopsis of my meeting with Pursiano. I knew she'd been hoping for some connection to Manuel, and I hated to disappoint her, but I wasn't about to mislead her, either.

''Maybe Rita Johnson will remember him,'' she said.

''Maybe.''

We headed for the door and for Rita Johnson. The life of a busy detective, I thought.

IN FIFTEEN MINUTES, I was back at the Cedar St. Café, which was doing a thriving business this time. The Saturday morning crowd seemed to be a dog-walking troupe, and I struggled to maneuver around drooling pooches leashed to the outside tables.

Once inside, I ordered a cappuccino at the counter and took it to a table by the door, with a view of Cedar Street. I had about a half-hour wait, and no preconceived idea of what my visitor would look like. I had a feeling Rita Johnson would spot me right away, however; I was the only person in the café wearing panty hose.

I took out my small notebook. Carrying it was a new habit I'd been trying to cultivate, in imitation of Matt. I was having withdrawal pains from my large briefcase, a source of amusement for him. I'd decided this trip was a good way to separate myself from it. At the moment the thin spiral-bound notebook seemed inadequate to the task of two criminal cases.

I'd also stuffed the beryllium articles in my oversize purse; giving up a briefcase required moving up to a larger shoulder bag, I'd reasoned. I smoothed out the article and prepared my environment for study—notebook, red pencil, neon-orange highlighter. I was ready for the first report, on sputter-deposited beryllium films, by Larkin, Kellerman, Carver, and Johnson.

What better way to spend a Saturday morning, I asked myself, than with a good coffee and an interesting technical article? One great benefit to my contracts with the Revere Police Department was the motivation to keep myself abreast of the latest in science and technology. My new career had thrust me into the center of activity in the metallization of hydrogen, the helium reserves held by the federal government in Texas, and new designs of lithium batteries. In the last year, I'd given myself crash courses in the first three elements of the periodic table.

My mind strayed to the tutorials I'd given to Matt on the technical topics that pertained to our cases. I found myself planning a lesson even in his absence. Beryllium, I'd say, the fourth element of the periodic table, is noted for its high permeability to X rays, and its high-speed sound transmission, making it useful for X-ray machines and for diaphragms in stereo speakers.

I considered seeking out the science teacher at Revere High School and offering to give lectures to her or his advanced classes. Not that I was running out of Italians or Italian Americans for Peter Mastrone's class, but it was time to move on. I had an idea that Peter would lose interest in my guest appearances anyway, once he acknowledged to himself that we had no future together except as friends.

The report in front of me consisted of three pages of text and four of illustrations. The core of the beryllium team's expertise appeared to be their work on coating fuel capsules for use in fusion research. The capsules, only about two millimeters in diameter, were the ultimate target for the lab's high-power laser. They needed to have the strength to withstand extremely high pressures. Larkin and his group had systematically studied different ways of coating the targets to give them the desirable properties of strength and smoothness.

I had tipped the report sideways to examine a horizontal layout—a photograph of the vacuum chamber used for the coating procedure—when a shadow fell over the paper, accompanied by a thunking sound.

Rita Johnson had settled on the chair opposite me. She was wearing a navy Cal sweatshirt with a hood, a black fanny pack, and a cast up to her elbow.

TWELVE

"I'M HOPING YOU'RE Dr. Lamerino," she said as she adjusted her seat with some difficulty.

"Yes. And it's Gloria." I extended my hand across the table, aiming for her good left arm.

"I'm Rita."

"Can I get you something?" I asked, although I noticed several men who would have gladly taken on the task of serving the beautiful, helpless-looking woman who'd joined me. I wondered if they could tell she was one of the lead plaintiffs and an organizer in a gender discrimination suit.

"Decaf anything, please," Rita said. She breathed heavily and let out a sigh. "I'm not used to carrying this load around." Rita lifted her arm and banged it on the table as if to demonstrate its unnatural condition.

"Are you tired of telling the story of how it happened?"

"Not yet. It was just a couple of days ago. I've been trying to think of a great story to tell about it, but the truth is I was doing high dusting in my living room and fell off a ladder. That'll teach me to do housework."

"I'll remember that," I said as we both laughed. "I'll get you a drink."

I stood in line for Rita's coffee, glancing back at her now and then. She'd moved her sunglasses to the top of her head and her fanny pack to the table. She rubbed her cast, as if her fingernail could penetrate the plaster to scratch an itch. Rita had what Rose Galigani called bedroom hair—long, wild, tightly curled, and messy, as if she'd just gotten out from between the sheets. Rita's hair was tinged with red, reminding me of the snapshot of Jennifer Kellerman, Manuel's girlfriend. I fingered the photograph in my purse, thinking of how I'd present it to Rita.

I saw her checking out the papers spread at my place. I'd

meant to pack them up but became distracted by her dramatic entrance. I tried to guess what she'd think about my casual café reading. That I was trying to flatter her? Scientifically literate? Nosy?

"Light reading?" she asked me as I returned with a decaf latte for her, and another cappuccino for me.

I gave her my best retired-lady smile. "Always interested in new technology. Looks like you've carved out a niche for yourselves in beryllium coatings."

"We're just beginning the studies in that report you have. Very exciting. But you wanted to talk about Gary Larkin? Did you know him well?"

This time I was ready with something closer to the truth. Because I was more comfortable sharing my feelings with a woman? Because I was tired of my fake intimacy with the victim? Or because it was time to either get serious about solving a murder or accept Inspector Russell's conclusion that there wasn't any. "I didn't know him well at all," I said. "I'm just suspicious about how he died."

"Well," she said with a long, breathy sigh. Rita stirred sugar into her latte. I felt a twinge of envy that her body—exceptionally fit, except for the temporary setback of a broken arm—showed no signs of extra sweetener. Mine, on the other hand, was a living testimony to all the biscotti and Girl Scout cookies I'd ever consumed.

"I understand you arrived on the scene right after Mr. Pursiano discovered Gary's body?"

"I did. I actually went up to him and felt for a pulse." Rita shuddered as if the thought of touching a dead body repulsed her. I wondered what she'd think of my living above a mortuary and counting an embalmer and his wife among my best friends. "I don't know how long Pursiano had been there." She sipped her latte and avoided my eyes. "I thought the police determined it was an accident. Are you working with them?"

I was ready for this one also. "I'm retired from BUL, as I told you in my message. I've been working with the police back in my hometown in Massachusetts. Helping them whenever a death involves a scientist or someone at a lab."

Rita shifted in her chair and winced as her foot hit the base of the wrought-iron table. The light spray of freckles across her nose seemed to disappear as her face paled. Apparently she was sore all over. But I was wrong if I thought my nonresponse would get by her, pain or no pain.

"So are you working with the Berkeley police also?"

I clamped my lips together and shook my head. "No," I said, unable to come up with another mental reservation and unwilling to lie blatantly. "No, I'm not. You certainly don't have to talk to me."

"Oh, I don't mind talking to you. I just wanted to know where we stood."

Do we know now? I wanted to ask her, but I resisted in the interests of keeping on her good side.

"I realize I'm going to sound like the police, but I'm wondering if you can think of anyone who'd want to hurt Gary?"

"Let's see. For starters, me, Carver, Kellerman."

This case was full of surprises, and this latest required another napkin-to-lips maneuver on my part.

"Just kidding," she said, showing me perfect teeth, matching most affluent adults of her generation. "But we all had good reasons to dislike him, when you come right down to it."

"Do you care to explain?" I asked with a calmness I didn't feel.

"He accused us all of hacking into his computer and downloading pornography, for one thing."

"I've heard about that."

"The only one that gained from that little episode was his ex-wife."

"Marlene Korner?" I asked, up-to-date with her name, thanks to Elaine. "How did the pornography charge help her?" Like a good investigator, I wanted to hear a second opinion on the connection between Gary's divorce and the pornography that showed up on his computer screen.

"Well, Gary was the one filing, claiming infidelity. Marlene was getting it on with a guy who sells computers. Gary met him first and introduced them, of all things. Of course he thought her adultery gave him the right to keep all the money."

"And then the pornography suit made him look even worse than she did," I said, using my recently acquired information. "But what about no-fault California divorce?" I asked as though I'd been through a few myself.

"Well, even with no-fault, there's some leeway. A lot of Gary's money had been tied up because of his patents and so forth. Anyway, I think he got nervous, because when that story broke, he settled."

"Sounds like anything but an amicable divorce."

"Isn't that an oxymoron?"

Rita's tone lead me to believe she had firsthand knowledge of how to terminate a marriage, but I decided not to pursue the topic any further.

"You implied there were other reasons Gary wasn't a favorite in the group?"

"He wasn't great at human relations. Got along better with beryllium, if you know what I mean."

"I heard he volunteered in the schools."

Rita nodded. "He did, but that was more to promote beryllium than to teach kids, if you ask me. He was on this campaign to get funding for nonmilitary uses of beryllium. He wanted the government to explore peaceful applications. Transportation systems, building structures, that kind of thing."

"Isn't it already used that way?"

"Not as much as it could be. Gary claimed beryllium was discriminated against because of some overrated toxicity. Like he was fighting for the civil rights of beryllium. Ironic, isn't it?" Rita had lowered her voice at the last phrase, stirring her latte with great care.

"That he should die from it? It certainly is."

Rita sat up, apparently finished with her private memories. "And the rest of his problem was not his fault. He couldn't help being male." Rita pronounced the word as if it referred to a genetic disease. "He got promoted over all of us. I'm working on a lawsuit that covers that little game. But you've probably read about that, too."

"I have, a little."

"It's heating up. Since we filed in March, we've had hundreds of new plaintiffs come forward."

I held my breath, hoping she wouldn't realize she had a potential plaintiff in front of her. Rita reattached her fanny pack around her waist. A first movement to leave, I figured, grateful she hadn't solicited my participation in her lawsuit. "Oh, and let's not forget his tech."

"Mr. Pursiano?"

"Right, Larry. He's been complaining for a month about the poor raise Gary gave him."

"Gary supervised his salary?"

Rita nodded. "He was assigned to our group, so Gary wrote his performance appraisal and submitted the request to salary committee. Larry isn't the swiftest guy around, and Gary was a stickler on merit. More irony. If the lab went on merit and not testosterone, Gary Larkin wouldn't have been promoted."

I raised my eyebrows, involuntarily, and Rita took on a sheepish look.

"Sorry," she mumbled, but rather than contrite she sounded annoyed that she'd been caught speaking ill of the dead. "Shouldn't have said that. He was okay in his own way. He loved his work, that's for sure." She shook her head and smiled. "I know it sounds weird, but he was always talking about beryllium. He had this sexist metaphor for women—maybe he just did it for my benefit because he knew it would drive me crazy." She mimicked a man's voice. "'Women, they're like beryllium—brittle at room temperature but soft and pliable when heated.'"

Rita had a rapid clip to her speech that I associated with the East Coast, not a California native. I'd read that she'd been at Stanford since starting college and assumed she was from the Bay Area, but after meeting her I questioned it. She also finished her latte in record time, drinking as fast as she was talking. I wasn't inclined to keep her any longer.

"Well, you've given me a lot to think about," I said.

"What makes you think Gary was murdered, anyway?"

I thought she'd never ask. Besides Matt, no one else had. "He was an expert in handling beryllium. I can't imagine he'd make a fatal mistake."

"Excellent swimmers drown. Highly skilled skiers and mountain climbers have fatal falls. It happens."

"Good point."

"Well, good luck. Nice to have met you. I have to run." Rita pushed her chair away from the table and stood up to leave. She pointed to her cast. "It's going to take longer than usual for me to look good for my friend's wedding."

I wanted to tell her she could show up in her sweats with a soiled cast on her arm and still turn heads. She had one last comment for me.

"In case I didn't say it—I do miss the old guy."

She was halfway down the street before I realized I hadn't shown her Manuel's photograph.

IT MIGHT HAVE BEEN Rita's extra-fit body that inspired me; when I left her, I had a rare desire for physical exercise and decided to walk to Elaine's. Invigorated by the weather of a typical Berkeley morning—still a bit of fog, cool, and breezy—I went at a good clip and approached Walnut Square just before ten o'clock. I looked up at the brown wood multilevel structure with about a dozen shops and restaurants and realized it offered a painless way to pick up a few souvenirs for Matt and the Galiganis.

It also offered a rest room, which I would need if I weren't going straight home. I remembered exactly where it was, up a flight of stairs on the Walnut Street side, behind one of the coffee shops.

I walked up the old wooden steps to the public facilities. Just as I'd left them, I noted—unheated, cracked cement floor, ill-fitting door to the outside—more like an outhouse but adequate for the purpose.

Soon after I'd locked myself into the center of three empty stalls, I heard someone enter the area. The person walked to my door and stood there. I couldn't tell from the heavy black athletic shoes whether a male or female was facing me on the other side. I detected a faint, sweet scent that might have been perfume, but I couldn't be sure the aroma hadn't already been there as part of the mix of smells in the room. What I did know was that he or she was not waiting for a stall since there was an empty one on either side of me.

I sat there, all bodily functions suspended, my heart pounding in my chest. The shoes didn't move. I could hear no breathing but my own, louder than a vacuum pump.

It's broad daylight, I told myself, and there are shops opening all around me. If this were an attacker, why wouldn't he break through the flimsy lock on the door? Or shoot through it. Or throw a bomb over the top. Why just stand there?

I shuffled my feet on the floor and rattled the toilet paper holder as if to tell my would-be assailant I was going about my business unaware of his presence. I knew I couldn't yell loudly enough for a shopkeeper to hear me, and the street traffic was a whole story below me. I didn't want to alert my stalker that I was aware of the threat with a useless scream. I swallowed hard and thought, but my head seemed empty except for the echo of my heartbeat.

I reached into my purse for a weapon of some kind, opting not to go down easily. I wished I'd been in the habit of taking care of my nails—at least I'd have a file in my purse if I did. The half-eaten roll of peppermints, the calculator, and the small flashlight I fingered on my way through the contents weren't going to be much help.

At the bottom of the bag, I found my cell phone. I'd forgotten to leave it home in Revere. I knew it wouldn't work after all the hours away from its charging base, but I had an idea how I could use it, if it had enough power to make sounds when I pushed on the numbers.

A fake call. Is that the best I can do? I thought. The unfortunate answer was yes. Who shall I pretend to call then? 911? The attacker would know he had enough time to spare before a response team could get to me. Whoever it was still hadn't moved or cleared his or her throat, leaving me with no clues about gender. The sweet odor faded in and out as I sat there.

I made my decision. A fake call it would be. I abandoned the idea of "Rocky" as too obvious for a strong man and "Bill" or "Bob" as too wimpy. I chose Mike. I punched seven numbers at random, as if I were making an ordinary call within the area code. I was thrilled to hear the sound of the connection at each button. After a moment, I said in as loud a voice as I could summon, "Mike. Come up the stairs. Into the ladies' room. Quickly."

The unisex shoes turned in the direction of the door, giving me hope for a moment. What followed, however, was a ghoulish jig, the bulky shoes stopping, turning back to me, then finally shuffling out the door like a dancer uncertain of his steps. I breathed out and listened intently. No further sound. Had my bluff worked, in spite of the uncertainty I'd sensed at the end? Had the person left or was he or she waiting for Mike?

I could hardly believe my pitiful scheme was effective, but I knew it was my best chance to leave the stall. I tugged at my clothing, took a few breaths and went outside, rushing down the stairs to the sidewalk. I looked around and saw no one who looked like an attacker—and no one who could have passed for Mike.

What I did see on the ground at the bottom of the stairs was a ski mask. A navy blue ski mask, in Berkeley, in June. I glanced up and down the street, as if I'd be able to spot the owner and compare shoe sizes with those of my pseudo-stalker, but the only people in view were a noisy family of four alighting from a teal blue minivan.

I shivered and walked away.

THIRTEEN

LUCKY FOR ME, Berkeley has more coffee places than any city I know. I ducked into the nearest one and took my third cappuccino of the morning to a high counter along the side wall. My head throbbed, and I was still slightly out of breath from racing down the stairs and around the corner.

I climbed onto an empty stool facing a side street now busy with traffic, hoping the mundane world of shoppers and students would calm my nerves. A small placard on the counter advertised a new Chinese herbal drink, with the slogan Relax With Chai. I considered abandoning my coffee, but only briefly, since I'd never gotten much value from tea except a pleasant aroma.

After about ten minutes of sipping chocolate-laced foam, surrounded by chatter about the latest books, final exam grades, and movies—Berkeley residents called them "films"—I'd convinced myself that the person in the rest room had only the most innocent of intentions. A woman who thought she left her jacket in the very stall I'd taken. A young girl taking a breather from her boyfriend for a minute or two. Someone waiting to use the middle spot because the other two were messy or out of paper.

Then why had she run at my pretend SOS? And who'd been wearing the ski mask? I admitted one negative scenario into my brain, to account for the fleeing athletic shoes: someone waiting for the chance to reach over the door and steal my purse from the hook. That's it, I told myself. A petty thief. My new habit of snooping, which I'd developed in the past year, had put me in threatening situations, but I didn't think I'd done enough to deserve stalking or an attack during my two days in California.

I tried to think of the pleasant evening ahead, at Siad's with friendly faces from the dinner group of many years. Although I'd had a lot to drink, I hadn't yet eaten anything, and I had a sudden craving for East African curried chicken, even at ten-fifteen in the morning.

Needing one more distraction before I could face Elaine with equanimity, I pulled the next two beryllium reports from my purse, those written by Gary Larkin with Sidney Kellerman and Rita Johnson. I'd resolved not to mention the ladies' room incident. Elaine had enough to worry about.

The focus of these articles was precision grinding of beryllium oxide and other brittle materials. To get it in a solid form that can be machined, beryllium has to be compressed as a powder under intense heat and high pressure.

I suspected Larry Pursiano had a lot to do with the operation of the special tools described. The components machined for laser applications had to meet stringent specifications, often requiring tolerances of less than one micrometer—about one thousandth the thickness of a dime. Turning to the end pages, I found an acknowledgment of Pursiano's work. The reports contained photographs and diagrams of the machine setup, one of them including Pursiano in his overalls and wide safety goggles.

I was impressed that Gary's group covered a wide range of specialties in the area of beryllium research, but I wondered what else I'd expected to find in the reports. Surely if I thought there'd be a clue to Gary's death, it wasn't there. I packed up and headed for Elaine's.

THE SAAB WAS NOT IN Elaine's driveway, so when I heard the phone ringing, I rushed in to answer it.

"Gloria?"

Matt's voice. I caught my breath and ran my fingers through my hair, as if he could see its disarray through the fiber optics that connected us. During the last few blocks of my walk it had started to sprinkle—unusual for early June—increasing the curl in my hair by a factor of three.

"How are you?" I asked.

"Okay. In the middle of Day Two."

For a moment I didn't know what he meant. When I realized he might have meant the second day without me, my heart gave a little leap. I felt a confusion of emotions, from delight that he missed me to guilt that I hadn't been counting the hours since I'd left him. I'd thought of him often and hoped that mattered. I wondered how long it would take for me to be comfortable with the new level of intimacy we'd reached just before I'd left for California.

"Only eight to go," I said finally, finding relief in numbers. "Have you been busy?"

"Not more than usual. I'm sure once the bad guys find out you're out of town, there'll be a lot more activity. I hope you're keeping out of trouble. I'm relieved to hear your voice. At least I know at the moment you're safe while you're on the phone with me. Unless—you're not being held hostage or anything are you?"

"Funny."

Sergeant Matt Gennaro, man of few words, I thought to myself, how come you're so chatty today? I made a note to talk to Elaine, the expert in romantic relationships, if you based the judgment on number of separate experiences rather than longevity of anyone alliance.

"I've been putting in extra hours. You know, to pass the time. Berger's thrilled, because it gives him less paperwork to do. He's thinking of taking a long weekend with the family. What's new there?"

Take a breath, I told Matt silently.

"Not much." Just reading police reports, interviewing murder suspects, following leads on a teenager's disappearance, and faking out a stalker in the ladies' room. "We're going to a Kenyan restaurant for dinner, with the old group I've told you about."

"The one Eric Benson belonged to?" he asked, referring to the hydrogen researcher who was the victim in the first case I'd worked on with him. "You'll be a celebrity for solving his murder."

"I guess that means you're a celebrity everyday."

"Well, that's just my job. But if you think I am, I'll take it."

I felt another satisfying shiver. Amazing what two days of separation will do, I thought. And it wasn't that we saw each other everyday when we were in the same city. Something was definitely different. I could hardly wait for Elaine to come home.

AFTER MY CONVERSATION with Matt, I was out of the mood for crime solving. I wanted to sit and relive some of the wonderful moments with him a couple of days before I left. We'd gone to an old colonial-style bed-and-breakfast in Chatham on Cape Cod after my anniversary party at the Galiganis'. My mind had drifted three thousand miles, back to the Atlantic Ocean, when I heard Elaine pull in. I hoped she'd have time for a talk about the facts of life.

She seemed in no better spirits, however, and I decided to forgo my own needs for a while longer. "Still no word?" I asked.

"No. José finally called Liz, Manuel's mother. She's driving up as we speak. I offered to stay home with him this evening, but he insisted I keep our date with the group. He promised to call Siad's if he heard anything." Elaine kicked off her shoes and stretched out on her couch, her arms across her chest. I shook away the image of a floral chintz casket.

"I'm so sorry about all this, Elaine."

"I know. I'm just glad you're here."

"Not that I've been any help."

"You have," she said, and fell asleep.

IT WAS CLEAR I'd have to wait awhile to discuss my love life with Elaine. Ironic, since she'd been hoping for years that I'd have one.

I covered her with the pale blue throw I'd given her one Christmas and went back to work. I called Marlene's number, got no answer, and periodically redialed it. In between tries, I read the last two beryllium reports, by Larkin, Kellerman, and Carver. From the combinations of authors and topics in the five reports, I figured Kellerman to be the modeling man, the computational engineer who used a computer program to simulate the experiments the others did in the lab.

The reports on my lap had interesting graphs showing comparisons between data from the experiments and the theoretical results from the computer code. All five reports were technically pure in my mind, lacking shady undercurrents of skewed results. I was reminded again of how my immersion in the fourth element

was different from the first three. This time I found no potential
motive related to science—no opportunity for fraudulent data, no
controversy over a national science policy, no high-tech patents
worth millions of dollars, nothing of a proprietary nature.

I shuffled the last bit of paperwork to the top of the pile: police
interviews with Kellerman and Carver. Once more Terry had
provided me with a clue, not quite blacking out the race and sex
boxes at the top of the form. The partial C told me I was reading
the statement of a white man—Sidney Kellerman, by process of
elimination, since Lincoln Carver was black. Kellerman hadn't
been near the scene at all but was "an involved person," in
police parlance, since he was part of Gary's team. He seldom
went to the shop area, he said, since his work was mainly with
the computer, confirming my guess that he took care of the sim-
ulations. He'd last seen his new boss on the Friday before at an
afternoon meeting. He'd been home all evening on Tuesday with
his teenage daughter, Jennifer.

Carver's statement was no more revealing. He'd taken
Wednesday off for a lab-sponsored class on vacuum technology.
His pager went off about nine o'clock in the morning, his sec-
retary calling to tell him of the discovery of Gary Larkin's body.
He'd been home in his apartment by himself on Tuesday evening,
but remembered several calls he'd made and received. I wondered if the police had followed up on the calls, since technically
this was an inquiry into an accident, not a murder investigation.

I looked at the one-inch stack of papers on my lap as if they
should be telling me something. Instead they might as well have
been blank sheets, like a brand-new laboratory log book.

I tried my next problem-solving trick: make a narrative out of
what was available, and maybe the connections would appear.
On a Wednesday morning, a beryllium engineer is found dead
of poisoning by beryllium oxide; two weeks later, on a Wednesday morning, a teenager who'd talked to the engineer and members of his research team and then wrote a paper on chronic
beryllium disease, leaves his house and doesn't return. No connecting story emerged except a serial killer who operates on
Wednesdays, killing anyone who wrote about beryllium. I dismissed the idea as not plausible, unless Johnson, Carver, or Kell-

erman were killed next Wednesday. I moved on to another favorite device, list making.

Elaine slept soundly, even as my intermittent dialing of Marlene Korner's number came through the speaker phone. I wondered if Marlene had the special telephone company feature that would reveal how many times someone named Elaine Cody had tried to reach her. Some uses of technology can cause embarrassment, I decided.

I made a list of what I knew about all the principals in my cases. I made a column for Larkin, Johnson, Kellerman, Carver, Pursiano, Korner, and Martinez, and Other, in case a new participant popped into my head. As I thought of this, I realized how narrow my investigation was—what made me think the murderer, if there was one, was a member of Gary's team or his wife? There were hundreds of other employees at BUL, for one thing. And I had no idea what Gary's hobbies were, outside of his beryllium campaign. For all I knew, someone killed him for his rare coin collection or his season tickets to hockey games. As a detective you make a good retired physicist, I told myself.

I ran my eyes along my chart, looking for a match, and found a couple, but I couldn't make any sense of them. The first connection was Gary Larkin's computer. A hacker got himself into Gary's files. Manuel was into computers, and could have been a hacker, as far as his father knew. What if Manuel had got into Gary's virtual space and was responsible for the pornography on his computer? Then what? I asked myself. It could account for Gary's killing Manuel, but that's not what happened. And who kidnapped Manuel after Gary's death? I was glad José wasn't listening in to this part of the theory, where his son did something criminal, especially since the idea didn't last long.

Another connection—Jennifer Kellerman. Manuel's girlfriend, daughter of Sidney Kellerman, who worked with Gary. Could Kellerman have killed Gary because of the promotion he didn't get, and kidnapped Manuel because he was getting too close to Jennifer? Too convoluted. My scientist's brain needed things to be neater than that. The symmetry of the universe required that the cases be related more closely, the way the electromagnetic and weak forces can be combined into electroweak.

I worked my way through motives for Rita Johnson and Lincoln Carver. Gary was promoted over them. Say they both met Manuel through his CBD paper; how was that connected to their alleged motives for murdering Gary?

I was at a dead end. In my frustration, I shifted in my seat, knocked the pages off my lap, and accidentally hit the redial button on the way to retrieve them.

Marlene Korner picked up on the first ring.

FOURTEEN

UNPREPARED FOR a human voice, I stuttered my way through an introduction.

"Marlene, this is Gloria Lamerino. I was an acquaintance of Gary's, and I wonder if I might talk to you."

"About what?" Marlene sounded tired, as if my call were the eighth unsolicited ring-up of the day, following ones for aluminum siding and alumni fund-raising.

I reverted to my story about the need for closure as I passed through California and out of her life forever. I wasn't proud of my pretend grief, but I seemed to have no other option. I was slightly intimidated by Elaine's waking up and tuning in to my part of the conversation. It was harder to be devious with my friend in attendance.

"I suppose I could see you, but not today," Marlene said. "I have plans for the evening."

"How about coffee tomorrow morning?"

"I could do that. I live on Cedar. There's a café..."

"Near MLK Boulevard. I know it."

"I thought you were passing through."

"I used to live here," I said in a lame voice, holding back the exact number of years. I thought she might be suspicious of someone who claimed to have left her home in Boston for Berkeley as a young adult, lived there thirty years, then suddenly retired and returned to Boston. She might think the story too strange to be true. Most of my friends would agree with her.

"I'll meet you there at ten," she said with such reluctance I wondered why she didn't simply refuse. Did she have a hard time saying no, like many women? Or was she curious about someone who was onto her murderous ways? I couldn't wait to find out.

"Perfect," I said.

"MARLENE?" ELAINE ASKED.

"The same. Coffee at ten tomorrow morning."

"Terrific," Elaine said, stifling a yawn. She neither looked nor sounded refreshed, and I thought I'd cheer her up with tea and a change of pace. I instructed her to stay put while I concocted a predinner snack and organized my presentation on my love life.

I put a tray of sweet-smelling orange tea, grapes, crackers, and Brie on the coffee table.

"This is wonderful. I'm saving my wine allocation for dinner," she said.

"Remember I can drive and I won't be using up my quota of alcohol," I said, reminding her of my status as a teetotaler.

"Thanks. I just might drink your share."

"Matt called this afternoon," I said in a casual, by-the-way tone.

"Again?"

I saw that I was right about what would distract her—Elaine's face brightened considerably, whether from the hors d'oeuvres or the topic, or both, I didn't care.

"I think he misses me."

"You think he misses you?" Elaine put extra emphasis on "think" and cocked her eyebrows.

"I'd—uh—like to talk to you about this. His latest behavior, I mean. He talked a blue streak on the phone, which is unlike him. And he appears to be counting the days I'm away."

Elaine gulped her tea. I knew her well enough to see the workings of her brain as she figured out how to enter this new territory with me. After years of avoiding her questions and advice about my dating habits, or lack thereof, I was handing her a gilt-edged invitation. I could tell she didn't want to squander the opportunity.

"Interesting" was all she said out loud. *Tread lightly,* I heard her say to herself.

"Is this normal?" I asked, grateful that she was letting me set the pace. We both laughed at that until I could clarify what I meant. "I mean is everything different after...?"

"I know you don't want to use the S word, Gloria, so I'll try to keep this PG-rated. But, yes, things change after...it happens."

We continued to carry out the everyday motions of slicing cheese, taking sips of tea, and eating fruit while Elaine explained the facts of life after...it.

"It's good and bad," she told me as if she were a mother instructing a preteen—about the right level, given my lack of experience. "There's this new sensitivity to the other person, which is wonderful and exciting. But there's also this possessiveness that comes in. As if, after you've...after it happens, the expectations change."

"But we've never discussed new expectations."

"You don't have to. It's implied."

"What are these expectations?" I popped another grape into my mouth. "Maybe I have them and don't know it."

Elaine shifted on the couch, her face a picture of concentration. I had the fleeting gratification that at least for the moment she wasn't thinking of José and his sad plight.

"Suppose you saw Matt having lunch with another woman."

"Lunch?"

"Just lunch. Middle of the day. Say she's even a cop. Could be business."

I tried to project myself into the scene. I looked up at Elaine's ceiling, momentarily distracted by the sparkling swirls in the pattern. I pictured Matt sitting across from a woman at Russo's, where he and I had had our first meal together. I mentally stood in the doorway and watched them talking, sharing a joke. How did I feel? I needed more data.

"Is she young and cute?" I asked Elaine.

Elaine smiled. "Doesn't matter."

I went back to my scenario, as if it were a mural, like the elaborate graffiti decorating many of Berkeley's buildings.

"You're right. It doesn't matter. I don't like the picture. But I'm not sure I would have liked it even before..."

"But now it feels more like a betrayal, right? Even though you haven't promised each other not to have lunch with others of the opposite sex...oops, sorry, opposite gender." I had a schoolgirl urge to smother her with her own pillow, but settled for a light slap on her wrist.

"Okay. I think I get it. That scoundrel. I'll tell him a thing or two. Having an unauthorized lunch while I'm out of town." I banged my fist on the arm of the rocker for emphasis. My napkin full of grapes, which was resting precariously on my lap, fell to the floor, and one second later got crushed under the rocker.

Although it was at my own clumsiness, I was thrilled to hear Elaine's laugh.

AFTER A PROMISE TO each other to pick up the conversation later, we abandoned our college dormitory atmosphere and got ready for dinner. Elaine left a message on José's answering machine and we strutted out the door with a "show must go on" attitude.

We parked several blocks from Siad's Restaurant on University Avenue. As we approached it, we had a full view of the flag of Kenya hanging from an upstairs window, a large rectangular banner—black, red, and green with crossed spears in the center. Leave it to Berkeley, I thought, to have one of the few establishments featuring East African fare instead of the more popular Ethiopian and West African menus.

Elaine peered in the window, checked her watch, and opened the door for me. Curious gestures, which became clear as soon as I stepped inside. The small room was filled with silver Mylar balloons, overshadowing the Kenyan decor. A cacophony of cheers drowned out the African music. I heard a mixture of whistles, "Welcome back, Gloria," one or two noisemakers, and at least three amateur baritones singing "I Left My Heart in San Francisco."

Elaine escorted me to the head of a long table, lined with about twenty people, and sat me in front of a stack of presents.

I was touched and embarrassed, wishing I'd kept more in contact with the dinner group over the past year and trying to remember which ones I'd sent Christmas cards to. I saw several new faces, plus a few old ones whose names I couldn't recall. I focused on the ones I could identify, and gave them each a nervous smile.

"This is quite a surprise. Thank you all for this great welcome." Very creative, I thought, hearing my own weak voice. I was sure only the first two people on each side heard me.

"It's a combination bon voyage and welcome back," said a

woman halfway down the table. I recognized her as a regular for many years, one of the lab's first female chemists. I was vaguely curious to know if she was part of Rita Johnson's lawsuit, but dismissed the question as inappropriate to the party environment. What was wrong that I was more comfortable in an investigative mode than in a party mood? Was I really disappointed there was no one at the table who'd made my suspect list? Maybe that was the next topic I should bring up with Elaine.

Siad's brown tile floor did nothing to aid conversation, but my ears sifted more greetings and comments out of the noise.

"We never had a chance to do this before you left."

"Yeah, you know we love an excuse to party."

"Are you really going back to that awful weather?"

Someone pointed to the Old North Church pin I was wearing. "I'll bet there's not a single Kenyan restaurant in Boston," he said.

"You mean 'Bah-ston,'" his partner said in a poor imitation of a Back Bay accent.

"You didn't even give us a month's notice," I heard from another guest.

Elaine rescued me from that remark. "She didn't even give herself a month's notice," she said from her seat on my immediate right.

I did my best to smile through all the attention. I wished Matt were with me to enjoy the company. I missed Rose and Frank Galigani, too, and succumbed to the realization that I'd never be able to live with all my friends at once.

Elaine took a few minutes to explain José's absence, ending on a positive note I hadn't heard from her in a while. "He's probably home by now," she told our dinner companions, who visibly relaxed and returned to their festive mood.

Siad's came through with authentic curry dishes and no silverware. One of the waiters gave us a demonstration on how to use the injera, a doughy bread, to scoop up our food. This time I accepted a drink of hot, milky chai.

At one point Elaine leaned over to whisper, "Hope you don't mind too much. It wasn't my idea. Tell you later."

"I can hardly wait."

I obeyed a suggestion from Elaine that I open the presents between dinner and dessert. I struggled through wrapping paper and ribbon, and, worst of all, having everyone's complete attention. I smiled and said thank you for a subscription to *California* magazine and heavy mittens with a note that read "for the tough New England winters."

"Where did you find these in June?" I asked.

"REI," the female chemist, whose name I still didn't remember, informed me.

"Of course."

A laugh at my "Of course" rose from those at the table who knew of my aversion to serious sports and that I probably had no idea where the famous Berkeley store for the outdoors was. What my party guests couldn't see was the image the reference brought to my mind—a navy blue ski mask and heavy athletic shoes in front of a rest room stall. For a few moments I was distracted as I tried to remember what I might have done to bring on a threat, if that's what it was. As far as I could recall, before the ladies' room incident, I'd had conversations with only Lincoln Carver and Larry Pursiano.

Once the focus turned back to food—a rich mango pudding—I relaxed again and enjoyed the company.

Until Elaine's purse rang.

FIFTEEN

ELAINE DIDN'T HAVE TO explain her phone call from José. Her face reverted to the haunted look I'd seen on and off since Thursday evening. I left Siad's with her, after pocketing several business cards, scraps of paper with E-mail addresses, and a napkin with directions to an amateur performance of Gilbert and Sullivan that I knew I'd never attend. I expected I'd be writing thank-you notes; I wasn't sure how much else I'd be doing to acknowledge my party and its guests.

I met no resistance as I plucked the keys to the Saab from Elaine's hand. In the quiet of her car, we turned toward each other on the front seat.

"Do you have any details?" I asked her.

She shook her head and sighed. "Just that he's dead. They found Manuel's body. From the way José said it, I assume he was murdered." I reached over and took her hand. "Poor José," she said.

We sat for a few moments, the urgency of getting to José's house conflicting with the heavy sadness filling the car. I didn't know exactly why the age of a victim should matter to me. Murder was murder. And I knew children and teenagers were killed everyday, but I felt I'd known this particular seventeen-year-old.

We drove toward José's house on Parker Street in the Elmwood district, silent for most of the trip, though my mind was racing and I had a long list of questions. Where was his body discovered? When? By whom? Any suspects? Any signs of an accident as opposed to foul play? I focused on finding my way through once familiar streets, happy for the light traffic. At eight-thirty on a Saturday evening, I figured everyone was already where they wanted to be. Except for us.

A COUPLE OF HOURS after the discovery of Manuel's body, José's house was filled with friends and neighbors, his dining room table spread with food and drink as if there were a wedding. Or a funeral. I was amazed at how quickly someone could whip up a casserole.

In the brief conversation I'd had with José before the mourners crowded his house, I'd learned that Inspector Dennis Russell of the Berkeley PD had delivered the news in person to José—Manuel's body had been found in an abandoned battery pit just outside the lab's fenced-in property.

"How did everyone else find out so quickly?" I asked Elaine.

"The announcement was on local TV."

"And people just came over?"

"This is a close neighborhood. They pull together at a time like this. I've seen it before, when the woman two doors down died of leukemia. Even if a bike gets stolen, they're on the move. This is very hard for everyone."

"If Inspector Russell is involved in this, they must consider it a homicide," I said, half to myself, half to Elaine and José.

"His body is very bruised," José said, and then stopped abruptly. He'd gone to the morgue to identify his son's body, and I suspected he didn't want to get specific in case Liz was within earshot.

Liz had arrived from Bakersfield, with the sad look of Michelangelo's *Pietà*, a mother who'd lost her only son. She wore jeans, sneakers, and a long-sleeved T-shirt with a pattern of tiny strawberries and leaves. As advertised, she was a tall, slim, gray-blond woman like Elaine, except that Elaine would never wear a shirt decorated with fruit. A "little-girl's print" is what she would have called it under more normal circumstances.

I offered Liz my condolences, at the same time shouldering my own burden of guilt—after all, Liz hadn't been recruited to find Manuel alive. She hadn't failed. I had.

I found myself holding on to a shameful wish that Manuel was already dead before I arrived in California, perhaps while I flew over the Sierras. Even more frightening to me was the growing conviction that I had to find his killer, as well as Gary Larkin's.

"What is that anyway? What's a battery pit? Why was Manuel near a battery pit?"

Liz's soft, wailing voice sent shivers through me. She'd had José repeat the story three or four times. She clutched her tissues and banged her fists on her knees as if someone should have warned her little boy not to wander into an open pit.

Elaine knelt beside her and tried to answer her questions. "It's what they call this huge crater where they used to dump batteries and capacitors—things that hold electricity." Elaine waved her hands as if to indicate they were nothing to worry about. "They don't do that anymore because the acid would leak and ruin the soil, but they still call it by that name. And it's not strictly on lab grounds anymore, so anyone is free to go up there."

I'd been impressed by Elaine's explanation, though I doubted the excellent tutorial did much to help the dead boy's mother. I remembered Elaine had been one of the editors for an environmental impact statement in the late seventies when the pit was declared one of the government's Superfund projects, eligible for cleanup money. I pictured the site, with its Dumpsters, tankers, and endless rows of fifty-five-gallon drums, glad Liz didn't have a clear idea what the pit looked like.

ALL THAT WAS MISSING was my Galigani Mortuary staff ribbon as I tried to make myself useful answering the door and washing dishes. As I refilled glasses, I looked at each person, asking myself if he or she could have murdered Manuel. Once I eliminated all the people with red-rimmed eyes and voices hoarse from crying, I had no one left. Not a very scientific method, I realized.

My mind was also busy building a more objective plan to investigate Manuel's murder. I considered eliciting Officer Terry Spender's help again, as well as locating Sidney Kellerman and making follow-up dates with Carver and Johnson.

One trip to the front door provided its own reward—a middle-aged man and a young woman stood on the threshold. Half of a photograph come to life, except that the girl's bright smile was gone, replaced by a look of anguish rarely seen in one so young, and rarely necessary.

"I'm Sidney Kellerman. This is my daughter, Jennifer."

"Come in, please," I said. "I'm Gloria, a friend of Elaine's. José's friend." I hoped my greeting didn't sound like "I've been dying to meet you,'' which was the truth. I stepped aside for the Kellermans and pointed to where José and Liz were sitting on a couch. The two occupied either end, separated by an entire pillow, no doubt a good metaphor for their marriage, I thought.

I hurried to get a tray of assorted hard and soft drinks and arrived back in time to overhear Sidney Kellerman's words to José.

''We've had our differences,'' Kellerman said, ''but I want you to know how sorry I am. This is a terrible thing.'' Kellerman had the look of a distracted scientist, considerably overweight, with wild and curly red-gray hair and thick glasses with a piece of masking tape over one of the hinges. His shirt and pants, both maroon, were a few wavelengths short of matching and bore the stains of many meals.

José stood up and took Jennifer in his arms. She wept silently. It was a good guess that everyone's heart went out to this teenager who should have been at the movies with Manuel on a Saturday night, instead of at what I could only call his wake.

I offered Jennifer a glass of water and walked her to the kitchen, which was slightly less crowded. I hoped I wouldn't sound insensitive, but after settling her on a stool by the counter, I went about my self-appointed job.

''Jennifer, when was the last time you saw Manuel?''

''Wednesday in school.'' She shrugged her shoulders, her deep brown eyes sad and watery. She pulled her hands into the sleeves of her oversize 49ers sweatshirt as if I were the school principal about to rap her knuckles with a ruler because she misplaced her boyfriend. The prom queen had been turned into a waif by events beyond her control.

''Did he mention any kind of trouble he might be in? Anyone he made angry for some reason?''

''No.'' She shook her head, her voice so low I had to strain to hear her.

''It's very important that you try to remember. Did he have a fight with someone at school?''

''No.''

I thought a minute before asking the next obvious question. ''Did anyone ever try to sell him drugs?''

"No," she said louder than I'd heard her so far, as if to nip in the bud any smearing of Manuel, a guy so pure no one would dare even offer him a controlled substance.

I thought of telling Jennifer about Al and me, that I knew how it felt to lose someone you thought you were going to marry. But I figured I was too old in her eyes for a love life, and I didn't want her to think I needed sympathy.

"One last question, Jennifer. I know it might be hard for you to think about, but did you and Manuel have any kind of argument or disagreement lately?"

Jennifer looked at me. She played with her red hair—a finer, brighter version of her father's. "We never fought," she told me. "But..."

"Yes?" I rushed to rescue her voice from the black hole it seemed headed for.

"Something was bothering him. He wouldn't tell me. He used to always tell me everything."

"Jennifer?" Her father startled me, though he was most likely speaking at a normal volume.

Jennifer slid off the stool immediately. I had a hard time picturing her as a rebellious daughter sneaking out on her balcony for a visit with Manuel.

I took a card from my purse, and quickly edited it with Elaine's address and phone number. Next time I'll print up a California version, I thought.

"Please take this, Jennifer. And call me if you think of anything that could help us find who did this to your good friend." I watched her put the card under her enormous sweatshirt, and could only guess that there might be a pocket under all the fleece.

Kellerman glared at me, apparently too polite to voice his opinion of my action. I felt compelled to explain my dealings with his daughter.

"Mr. Kellerman, I was asking Jennifer if she had any idea who could have done this to Manuel," I said, hoping at the same time to win his cooperation.

"How could she know that?"

"I'm just trying to help. I know everyone wants to see Manuel's killer caught."

He took his daughter by the shoulders, and turned her away from me, leading her back into the living room as if she were blind. "Well, that's not our job, is it?" he said.

I couldn't argue with him.

BY TEN O'CLOCK, several people had already left. There was one more task I had to do before the crowd thinned out too much. It was time to make my move.

I walked down the corridor away from the living room, past the bathroom, past José's award-winning high-tech graphics, and into Manuel's room. I had nothing in particular in mind, except to take another look, thinking something might pop out at me if I didn't have Elaine and José looking over my shoulder. I figured the police would have taken anything useful already, but it seemed a more practical thing for me to do than mingle with people not likely to be Manuel's killer. I knew Russell was working that angle, anyway.

I closed the door behind me and opened the blinds. Not much light came in from the streetlamp, but I didn't want to give away my position. I walked to the closet and peered in, nearly tripping on the shoe boxes stacked on the floor close to the edge of the door. I remembered seeing them last time and assuming they held shoes. This time, it registered that his shoes were piled in a corner of his room, leaving the shoe boxes available. For what? I flipped open the tops of several of them and saw an assortment of comic books, music programs, and flyers.

One box held receipts of purchases, seemingly from a variety of sources, the print too small for me to read in the dark space. I didn't think José would mind if I took a few off the top to check out Manuel's spending habits of late. I stuffed a handful of the thin papers into my jacket pocket.

Absorbed in reordering the shoe boxes, I didn't hear the door open. But I did hear the deep, throaty voice.

"Dr. Gloria Lamerino, I presume."

I jumped at the sound echoing off the blank walls.

In spite of my increased heart rate, I reasoned no murderer would call me by my full name, and so politely. I decided I'd already be dead if that had been his intent, and I was able to answer in a normal voice. "Yes, I'm Gloria Lamerino."

"I see you've been busy, interviewing people."

Not a question, I thought, no need to answer. The man was tall and lean, in an ill-fitting brown suit. He stood in the doorway of Manuel's room rocking on the heels of his shoes, as scruffy as the brownish mustache that drooped over his upper lip.

"Did you learn anything from Kellerman or his daughter?" he asked.

This time I thought I'd try answering a question with a question.

"Are you also doing some investigation?"

"Well, that's my job." He reached into his jacket pocket—causing a slight stirring of my heart—and pulled out his badge. "Inspector Dennis Russell, Berkeley Police Department."

I should have known, I told myself, mentally slapping my forehead. From the suit and the shoes.

"How do you do," I said with a smile, feigning pleasure at meeting the man who'd rejected my services, denying me an opportunity to bring a murderer to justice.

"Now would you care to answer my question? What did you learn from Sidney and Jennifer Kellerman?"

Russell's attitude did nothing to inspire me to share. I guessed he wouldn't have done well in day care. Before my experience working with Matt I might have been intimidated to the point of apologizing and telling Russell everything I'd learned in my two days in California, little as it was. But after a few months "on the job" I'd become more comfortable treating police officers like any other professionals—almost. As for Inspector Russell, it was easier than I'd have thought to view his pitifully dressed figure only as someone in my way.

"I didn't learn a thing," I said.

He looked down at me and crossed his arms over his chest. "Is there anything you'd like to tell me about this case?"

"I'm a friend of Elaine's. Manuel's father's friend. That's why I'm here." I hoped it would take him a minute to decipher the convoluted relationship. Meanwhile, I walked past him, my fingers pushing Manuel's receipts farther down into my pocket as if it were contraband. It probably is, I thought, wondering if the police had searched the room yet.

I left Manuel's room without another word to Inspector Russell. In spite of my bravado, however, I wouldn't have been surprised to have him come after me with handcuffs and read me my rights.

I was happy to see José near the front door, helping Elaine on with her jacket, and quickly joined them.

"I'm ready to leave," Elaine said to me.

"Just in time."

"I'm sorry. I know it's late." Elaine seemed to interpret my comment as an expression of displeasure, as if she'd kept me against my will.

I tried to explain through a pantomime, raising my eyebrows and jerking my head back to where Russell was emerging from the corridor. I caught a glimpse of Russell out of the corner of my eye and realized he was the only person in the room who knew what I was trying to say. I knew he'd never choose me for his charades team.

ONCE IN THE SAAB, Elaine let out a heavy sigh. I rubbed her shoulder with my free hand as I steered us toward home.

"This was a tough night for you," I said.

Elaine nodded, and then a tiny smile crossed her lips. "You're a bad influence, Gloria. I found myself eavesdropping."

"So? What did you pick up?"

"Well, Kellerman was the one who let the police into Gary's house the day of the accident—uh, murder. I got this from the neighbor on the other side. It seems Jennifer did occasional cleaning and chores for Gary, and took care of his house when he was on travel. So they had a key."

"Interesting."

"But no big deal, huh?"

"Well, we knew Kellerman and Larkin were neighbors from the newspaper item, remember? It said something like 'his neighbor on Ashby.'"

"You don't miss much."

"At the moment, I feel I'm missing a lot."

"Another thing, a guy named Witte from the lab was there and he started talking about Gary and Marlene and her new boyfriend. Evidently he's a salesman for some big discount computer company."

"Interesting," I said again with little enthusiasm, since I'd heard as much from Rita Johnson. "Did you get his name?"

"Ted something. Maybe you can ask Marlene tomorrow."

"Maybe I can."

I didn't have the heart to tell Elaine she had a long way to go to excel at eavesdropping.

SIXTEEN

SUNDAY MORNING appeared normal, by all outward appearances, once we'd put aside the local newspapers, with their stories of Manuel's murder on the front pages. Elaine had insisted on buying them, though she usually eschewed local news.

"So I'll know what everyone else is reading about Manuel," she'd said.

I considered José's pain at seeing a grainy likeness of his murdered child on the doorstep and hoped his neighbors would have gone around before dawn and cleared all lawns of the sight. After the showing of the night before, I wouldn't have put it past them to buy every copy from the local newsstands and hide them from Manuel's parents.

Elaine and I sat in her living room looking though old photographs, still wearing our robes—hers a rich, creamy chenille, mine a gray flannel with frayed sleeves. I wasn't happy with most of the pictures that included me. We sifted through albums from the annual lab picnics, holiday parties, and retirement luncheons, plus many weekend excursions and vacations we'd taken together.

"I only look good when I'm wearing a lab coat," I said with a whine that set Elaine laughing.

"Not true," she said, holding up a snapshot of Rose, Elaine, and me on Maui in the late eighties. How I'd been talked into posing in a bathing suit between the two of them I couldn't imagine. I made a move to tear it to shreds, but Elaine yanked it away.

"About the party last night," Elaine said. "I hope you didn't mind too much."

"Not really, once I got over the surprise."

"It was Florence Hoover's idea."

"The chemist?" I asked, embarrassed that I wasn't sure of the name of a person who'd organized a party for me. I hoped she'd made my short list of Christmas card recipients. If Rita Johnson thought Gary Larkin had poor social skills, it was because she hadn't examined mine.

At eight-thirty, the morning fog still shrouded the bay, leaving the room gray and chilly. Or maybe it was the knowledge that we had a rough day ahead of us. Elaine was waiting to hear from José about what she could do to help. The police hadn't released Manuel's body, forcing his parents to wait before they could make funeral arrangements.

I noticed Elaine's eyes drifting past our conversation.

"Are you wondering how José and Liz are doing together?"

"Yes. Isn't that awful? What kind of person am I?"

"A normal one. This kind of event can either bring people closer together or drive them farther apart. But I've never heard of a case where it undoes a divorce and a remarriage, if that's what you're worried about."

"José told me he'd finally called Liz to tell her Manuel was missing, and by the time she drove up here, his body had been found."

I shivered at the horrible circumstances. "How awful."

"Her husband's coming up tomorrow. José was careful to tell me she's staying with some friends in El Cerrito. I'm embarrassed that he thought he needed to reassure me about our relationship at a time like this."

"I'm glad he's sensitive to the situation. He obviously knows it's hard for you to be on the outside of this."

"That's it exactly. I'm like a stepmother, or even less. And I feel bad that I didn't try to get to know Manuel more."

Is there ever a death without regrets? I wondered. I wanted to run to my room and make a list of people I should be nicer to, in case either they or I should die soon, but I brought my attention back to my friend.

"Just focus on doing whatever helps José. Never mind anything else for the moment. You're good at suspending your own needs when the occasion calls for it. This is one of those times." Take this advice from someone who couldn't make her own mother happy, I thought. The world's expert on love and family relations. Good friend that she was, Elaine didn't bring up my lack of credentials.

When the phone rang, Elaine picked it up before the first ring was completed. From her side of the conversation I gathered it was not José, but someone offering sympathy. After a couple of minutes, she handed me the phone.

"It's for you, too," she said. "It's Terry Spender."

I took the phone, hoping for good news, like, Officer Spender had just been promoted several ranks and was now Inspector Russell's supervisor.

"Hi, Gloria. I'm calling to give you a heads up."

The remains of Siad's curry dishes made themselves known in my stomach. A warning from a police officer was not a good way to start the day.

"Something wrong?"

"Not sure. But Russell came in right as I was leaving my shift this morning. He was...annoyed."

"I suppose my name came up."

"Not specifically."

"But there was little doubt who he meant, I suppose." I imagined my cherished Italian name couched in terms fit for the streets, punctuated by words I referred to by their first letters only.

"Yeah. Ranting and raving about a snoopy woman obstructing a police investigation."

"Is that the sanitized version?"

"Kind of." Terry laughed, reminding me of the pleasant meal we'd shared, watching the sun set in the west and passing information under the table. My own Deep Throat affair. "I don't know what he's going to do about it, if anything. But I thought I'd warn you."

"Thanks, Terry. I can't tell you how much I appreciate it."

"Those reports I gave you..."

"Don't worry. I'll burn them if it will make you more comfortable." After I commit them to memory, I added in silence.

Terry made a sound that sounded close to "pshhh," as if Russell's opinion of her mattered no more than the eighteenth decimal place in a calculation. "In fact, I have a couple more things for you. I have some photos of the scene at the lab and also at Gary's house.''

"Photographs of inside his house?'' I sat up straighter in the rocker, nearly repeating the grape fiasco of the day before, this time with my mug of coffee.

"Right. Just a formality, even though it wasn't a crime scene per se. I guess they went to look at his place after they found him—you know, to make sure no more victims and such—and they took photos for completeness.''

"Does that mean they thought it was murder at first?'' I could only hope.

"Not necessarily for very long. It's always something to consider for SC. Suspicious circumstances. It's really just to cover all bases.''

"What would I do without you?''

"Glad to cooperate. I could also get you a few things from the Manuel Martinez file if you want.''

I drew in my breath. A good news day after all. "I owe you, Terry. Is there anything I can send you from Boston?''

"How about a Bruin?''

"A what?'' I asked, but immediately connected her request to the nine—or was it ten?—rugged men who played hockey at Boston Gardens. "I'll see what I can do.''

"What if I drop the package off in a few minutes? I'm on my way home.''

"Wonderful. We'll have some coffee ready.''

I WAS DRESSED in ten minutes, back in my dark green airplane outfit, which Elaine had already washed and dried for me.

"If you're going to wear these fake materials that don't need dry cleaning, we might as well take advantage of it,'' she'd said when I told her not to bother.

Terry arrived before either Elaine or the second pot of coffee was ready. I greeted her as warmly as I could without bruising myself on the hardware at her waist. Thanks to Matt, however, I was used to hugging someone packing a gun.

"I've never seen you in uniform, except in a photograph. Very impressive.''

"I usually change before I leave the station, but I have another official call to make this morning before I'm really through." Terry put a plain brown envelope on the coffee table, at least as appealing to me as a box of pastry would have been. "There might be something useful here. Are you getting anywhere on these cases?"

"Thanks for asking. Not very far, I'm afraid." I served coffee and warmed-over scones I found in Elaine's freezer while I briefed her on my lack of progress. I'd heard the phone ring again and assumed Elaine's failure to appear had to do with a call from José.

My attempts to link Manuel Martinez's term paper on chronic beryllium disease with Gary Larkin's inhaled beryllium oxide, and then to Manuel's death seemed even more far-fetched when spoken out loud to an officer of the law.

I was ready to admit defeat and send the envelope away with Terry, when the doorbell rang. Since I had the benefit of an armed woman in my presence, I skipped my usual look through the peephole.

I opened the door to Sidney Kellerman. He was wearing the same maroon pants and shirt he'd had on the night before, or their identical twins with the same stains.

"I'm sorry to bother you this way. But I wanted to apologize for my behavior last night. You wrote this address on the card you gave to my daughter."

"Come in," I said. "Although there's no need to apologize. Everyone is on edge at the moment."

I ushered Kellerman into the living room and introduced him to Terry. I wondered what he thought of my casual breakfast party with a uniformed police officer.

"Are you working on Manuel's case?" he asked her.

"In a way, we all are," Terry said in a pleasant tone, but without further explanation.

"I hope I'm not interrupting anything."

"Not at all." Terry checked her watch. "In fact, I was about to leave. Nine a.m. It's getting near my bedtime."

Terry left, and I turned to my latest guest. Elaine still hadn't come downstairs.

"Can I get you some coffee?"

"No, no thanks. I want to get back to my daughter. I just wanted to tell you that I'm happy to cooperate. If I can be of any help..."

I could hardly believe my good fortune. I wondered if I should take the time to run upstairs for my notes or wing it. I decided in favor of spontaneity, considering Kellerman's desire to leave quickly.

"I appreciate your coming. I wanted to ask you about a paper Manuel wrote last term, on chronic beryllium disease. He made a reference to interviewing you, plus Gary, Lincoln Carver, and Rita Johnson. Do you remember talking to him about the project?"

Kellerman scratched the gray-red stubble on his face and pushed his heavy eyebrows together. "Yes, I think so. I wouldn't call it an interview exactly. He just E-mailed me and asked a couple of questions about beryllium. Then we had one or two chat sessions. His interests were more political than technical as I recall. Did I think workers should be informed if they were handling toxic substances? Should the regulations be more strict? Should companies be liable when a worker got sick from work-related tasks? Things of that nature. Why do you ask?"

"I'm trying to follow a few leads. This may not even be relevant." I was reluctant to disclose my theory that the Larkin and Martinez cases were connected. Kellerman was, after all, a suspect in my book. At least he didn't deny talking to Manuel about his paper, I thought, remembering Carver's dismissal of Manuel's photograph.

"I'm also doing some follow-up on Gary Larkin," I said.

Kellerman laughed, his face taking on a more normal look. "I heard that."

"I guess it's still a close community, isn't it? It would help to know when you saw Gary last."

"Well, I guess it was that Friday before he left for Cleveland. We had a meeting sometime in the afternoon." Kellerman smiled and shook his head and I could feel another Gary Larkin anecdote coming on. Sure enough, he took a minute to reminisce about

Gary's playfulness and tendency to bore people with information about beryllium.

"He'd pull this stunt in the airport all the time. It's a wonder he didn't get arrested. He'd have a brick of beryllium with him, perfectly harmless, but he'd wrap it in wire just to draw attention at the X-ray machine. The security people would call him aside and ask him to explain. Of course that's just what he wanted." Kellerman ran his hand around his face, using his fingers to squeeze his eyes shut, as if the memory moved him to tears. I pushed a box of tissues in his direction, just in case, but he waved it away. "He'd go on and on about how useful beryllium is for frames on bicycles and windshields."

"I've heard about his need to proselytize about beryllium."

Kellerman nodded. "It was his pet project. Have you met his ex-wife, Marlene's boyfriend, by the way? Ted Gernich."

"No, I haven't."

"Computer salesman. Gary introduced them. Not a happy outcome."

"Yes, so I've been told."

Kellerman shook his head, seemingly out of pity for the troubles of his deceased colleague. "Yes, Gary certainly had his problems. I suppose you also know his technician, Larry Pursiano, had filed a grievance because of the poor raise Gary authorized for him?"

"I heard something about that, too."

"Well, it sounds like you're well informed. I'd better be going anyway. I hate to leave Jennifer alone very long."

"Please give her my best," I said as I walked him to the door. And please be a little more subtle the next time you want to throw suspects my way, I thought.

ELAINE CAME DOWNSTAIRS at nine-thirty, surprised to hear she'd missed two rounds of company. She'd put on a navy blue outfit, as if to be ready for a serious day, but her face was relaxed.

"José?" I asked, pointing to the telephone.

She nodded. "We talked it out. Thanks to you I was able to offer support without asking for anything. For the moment."

"Are you going over to his house?"

"A little later. The police said they were ready to release Manuel's body, so José and Liz will be at the funeral parlor this afternoon. The wake will be tomorrow evening, then private burial on Tuesday morning. I have a list of people he'd like me to call, and a few chores."

"I'm glad he's having you help."

"Me, too."

I was about to offer my services when the doorbell rang. Elaine and I gave each other quizzical looks and uttered simultaneous comments about the busiest of Sunday mornings. Since Elaine was pouring herself a mug of coffee, I went to the peephole.

I jumped back as if a megajoule laser had been trained on my good eye. I swallowed hard and ran my hands through my hair. My gasp must have been audible, because Elaine was at my side, a touch of panic in her voice.

"Who is it?"

By way of an answer, I opened the door to Matt Gennaro and his luggage.

SEVENTEEN

MATT WAVED HIS TAXI away, his grin as wide as the United States, and stepped inside. Elaine was patient through a long hug, then stepped in.

"Okay, guys, it's hardly been three days."

"How did you find us?" I asked him. "I don't remember giving you this address."

"I'm a detective. It's what I do." Matt's attempt to imitate a tough guy, with an imaginary cigar between his fingers, sent us all into tension-shattering laughter. For me, the relief it brought was enormous, although the big question "Why are you here?" hadn't come up yet.

A pleasant shiver ran through my body as I considered that he'd traveled all the way across the country to hug me. Until I remembered what I'd been up to in his absence. For a moment, I was back in Revere. My mind turned to its customary task when Matt arrived at my apartment unannounced—I looked around the living room for incriminating evidence. As usual, I had something to hide.

On Elaine's coffee table was the manila envelope from Terry Spender, the seal of the Berkeley Police Department larger than life, as if it were backlit by a bright blue bulb. At least the crime scene photos aren't spread out, I thought.

When I shifted to the present again, I heard Matt and Elaine's conversation.

"I figured you'd miss her, but this is something else," Elaine said, shaking her head.

"I was in the neighborhood." Matt was apparently still not ready to be serious.

"Let's get you some coffee." Elaine poured the last bit of Peet's into a mug. "You must have taken the red-eye."

"I came stand-by on a one A.M. flight into Oakland."

"And you're just getting here?"

"We stopped in Chicago, with an hour layover. I didn't want to show up in the middle of the night, so I hung around the Oakland airport for a while." His corduroys and brown tweed sports jacket bore the marks of an all-nighter in cramped seats, but he couldn't have looked better to me if he'd stopped for an Armani suit and a makeover on the way. If it weren't for Elaine, who wouldn't have minded, I'd have leaned over and rubbed my cheek on his graying stubble.

Matt had settled on the couch next to Elaine, both of them looking at me as if it were my turn to speak. I took a seat on the green-padded rocker, stretched my neck, and took a deep breath. My eyes landed on the mantel clock, and I heard another involuntary gasp from my throat.

"Nine-fifty," I said. "I'm going to be late."

My meeting with Marlene Korner had edged its way into my consciousness just in time. I could barely stand the déjà vu of keeping an appointment with a murder suspect while Matt looked on with disapproval. He doesn't know where you're going, I told myself, but I knew I detected a frown on Matt's brow.

"You have to be somewhere?" Matt asked.

"I have a ten o'clock meeting. I'm so sorry."

"A meeting on a Sunday morning? During your vacation, when you should be shopping?"

Although Matt's words were playful his tone told me he knew what I was up to and didn't like it. My stomach lurched as I swallowed a mixture of feelings, like incompatible liquids in a laboratory dewar—surprise and pleasure at seeing him, embarrassment that I might not be worth the trouble he'd taken to get here, and annoyance at his borderline patronizing tone. Like a freshman lab gone bad, I thought.

"I won't be long. It's just down the street, and you probably need a nap anyway."

Matt leaned forward, his head low, hands on his spread-apart knees.

"Gloria, if this is about the Larkin case, I have to tell you, Russell is on the warpath."

Russell. Inspector Dennis Russell. The reality exploded in my brain, sending blood to the far corners of my face. That's why Detective Matt Gennaro is here. Russell sent him, the way the school principal tells a parent to have a heart-to-heart with a delinquent fourth-grader. I had the irrational desire to reverse any pleasure I'd felt at seeing Matt, as if I could run the whole film of the past ten minutes backward, and unhug him at the end.

"Russell is why you're here? You flew three thousand miles to check up on me?"

"Gloria, I wanted to see you. You know that." Matt stood up and started toward me. I stepped back and rubbed my forehead, clearing it for receiving information.

"Did Russell call you?"

"Yes."

"And tell you to have a talk with me?"

"Yes."

Matt had his hands in the pockets of his open jacket, his chin hanging, his eyes nearly closed. I thought I could discern the outline of his gun, holstered under his arm.

"Am I under arrest?"

Elaine's head snapped up from its neutral position. Her eyes widened as she looked at Matt, as if to say "not in my house."

Matt sucked in his breath and shook his head. The corner of his mouth twitched and I could tell he didn't know if he should smile. He bit his lip and chose a noncommittal expression.

"No, you're not under arrest."

"Then, if you'll excuse me, I'm going to my meeting."

I GOT INTO the Saab, happy I'd kept the keys from the night before. I hoped Elaine would forgive my rude exit. I hadn't even asked what time she'd need her own vehicle back. I leaned my head on the steering wheel. A large percentage of me didn't care what Matt thought of my plans, the rest hoped he'd followed me out to the driveway to apologize—as if I were sure which of us was in the position of needing forgiveness. The ghost of Josephine sat on my shoulder and told me, *If you weren't such a busybody, he wouldn't have had to trek all the way out here to keep you under control.*

My shoulder twitched. I put the car in gear and prepared my

mind for a meeting with Marlene Korner. The ex-wife of a murder victim, I told myself, as if to reinforce the need for my involvement.

Several times on the way to the Cedar St. Café I looked in the rearview mirror for signs of a taxi. Or a police car, sirens blazing, Dennis Russell at the wheel. But the streets of Berkeley proved quieter than my own insides.

THREE VISITS in three days seemed enough to qualify me as regular to the counterman at the Cedar St. Café. He gave me a big smile and a warm greeting, his lip ring moving with the rhythm of his words.

"Double cap, regular milk," he said.

"Right. How can you remember that?"

"It's what I do."

I groaned. Did even the soda jerk have to remind me of Matt? I deposited a generous tip in the glass mug on the counter in spite of the corny hand-lettered sign in front of it which read Can't Accept Change? Leave It Here.

I took my drink to a table by the window. Lucky for me, the fog had partly burned off and most of the dozens of customers preferred to sit outside, looking like a club of sun-worshippers, either after, or instead of church. The outdoors was never my first choice for any activity, especially eating, sleeping, and weddings. I'd had to bend my rules often while becoming acclimated to the California lifestyle.

It occurred to me that I'd only seen Marlene once or twice in my life, and many years ago at that. Another essentially blind date. Assessing my green knit pants suit, I decided that if she came in looking for a retired female physicist in the crowd of cutoff jeans, khakis, and Cal sweatshirts, she'd have no trouble picking me out.

I waited fifteen minutes, made longer by my lack of reading material. I'd intended to stuff the Berkeley PD envelope in my purse, but my hasty departure precluded that. The best I could hope for was that Matt hadn't shoved it through Elaine's home-office size shredder. I sipped my double cap and thought about what I'd ask Marlene if she ever showed up and what I'd say to Matt if he hadn't already flown home.

A moment or two before I would have given up, a couple walked toward me. Younger than me, I decided, but older than almost everyone else, though their nearly matching clothing fit the fashion of the clientele more than mine did. I stood up to greet them, glad I was getting two for one, with no doubt in my mind that Marlene's male partner was Ted Gernich. He looked like everyone's image of a salesman: a long gait with a hand stretched out ten yards too soon, and a wide smile that said "I want to be your friend and sell you things." I had the feeling he was going to use my first name often.

"Gloria?" he asked.

"Yes. And you must be Ted. And Marlene." I extended my hand. I could play at sales, too, I told myself.

"Now I do remember seeing you at various lab functions, years ago," Marlene said.

I thought of my interviews with Lincoln Carver and Rita Johnson, both of whom implied there'd been a divorce-inspiring affair between Marlene and Ted. Marlene seemed so naïve and carefree, it was hard to imagine her in a rendezvous with a salesman at a low-rent motel. Maybe at the tennis club, I reasoned.

Both tall and lean, in matching khaki shorts, Marlene and Ted showed they took fitness after forty seriously. Unlike their Sunday morning date. It was clear that cafés were only brief stops on their way to physical activity—biking, tennis, jogging around a suburban reservoir, hiking in the woods—whereas for me, getting to the café was the exercise.

"Gloria, I've heard a lot about you," Ted said, his midwestern accent elongating the greeting. "I'm telling you, Gloria, this is a sad time for our little community."

"It is sad, and I'm grateful for your willingness to meet me."

"Ted and I talked it over after you called. We decided we really wanted to meet you. We'd like to be neighborly and cordial with all Gary's friends. I apologize if I was short with you yesterday."

"Not at all." First Kellerman, now Marlene. A change of heart seems to be going around, I thought.

"What are you drinking, Gloria?" Ted asked, giving Marlene a neck rub at the same time.

"I think I'll switch to decaf, thanks."

"Be right back." Ted snapped his fingers and headed for the counter.

Marlene smiled at me, tilting her head in his direction. "He's something," she said, as if her child had just made honor roll.

I smiled back, like an approving friend. "I hear he has a background in computers." I said, following the pattern of "I understand your little boy won first prize at the science fair."

Marlene waved her hand as if to fan away a bothersome insect. "Oh, Ted's not technical at all. He was a poli sci major at Georgetown. He sells computers, but he isn't married to them." She covered her mouth as if to take back the words, but I heard a nervous giggle instead.

I imagined Marlene Korner's decision-making process. If her marriage to a beryllium-lover failed, she'd try someone who had no genuine interest in anything technical. I supposed Ted was not even a computer user, just a computer salesman.

I tried to remember when my opinion of salespeople changed. There'd been a time when I'd loved one; my uncle Johnny had sold insurance when I was a child. I'd looked forward to his visits to our house every Friday morning to collect the premium. My mother would have coins ready for him on the kitchen table, next to "coffee and," which meant a shot of whiskey, instead of cream and sugar. Looking back, I wondered if the reason I relished those memories was that Josephine seemed happy when her brother was there, and her attention was focused on someone other than me.

"Young lady, here's another cap for you." Ted's milky voice interrupted my trip to the Revere of the 1950s, and I prepared myself to resist a good deal on a used printer.

Somewhere between Uncle Johnny and Ted Gernich I must have had more negative than positive sales experiences, I decided.

"I know you don't have a lot of time, so let me just ask a couple of questions."

"We should probably wait." Another tilt of the head toward

the counter, where Ted had gone back for napkins and silverware. Marlene's headband, a leopard skin design, held her shoulder-length hair off her face and gave her a young, bouncy look, in contrast to the tiny wrinkles at the corners of her eyes and mouth.

"Certainly." How about small talk, I wanted to ask her, or does that have to be chaperoned also? Meeting prep for Marlene and Ted had turned into a bigger production than I'd anticipated. Or maybe it was its inauspicious beginning with a door-slamming exercise at Elaine's house. I struggled for another safe topic, but Ted was back with a supply of place settings Rose Galigani would be proud of, if they'd been sterling silver instead of white plastic.

"What exactly are we looking for here, Gloria?"

Was that the editorial we or the papal we? I wondered. The sales we, I decided, reminding myself that sarcasm would not win me the information I needed.

"I'm tying up a few loose ends," I said, a phrase I'd picked up from TV's *Columbo* series. I hoped Marlene and Ted wouldn't realize I was the only loose end in the minds of some. "When was the last time you saw Gary?"

"We had our final meeting with the lawyers about six or seven weeks ago, right after Easter."

"So that would be around the middle of April?"

Marlene nodded. "We met at my lawyer's office in downtown Oakland. After that we shook hands and went home." She cast her eyes down and stared at the surface of her latte. "I never saw him again until the funeral."

I cleared my throat in preparation for a touchy question. "I assume there were no nasty fights during the divorce?"

"Of course this is a private matter, Gloria," Ted said. I couldn't disagree, though if I'd had my way, divorce settlements would be public record. "But, yes, everything was quite satisfactory."

"I understand your reluctance to talk about it. And I know I appear to be prying, but an investigation sometimes requires delicate questions." I folded my hands in front of me on the café's wrought-iron table. "Please be sure that anything we say here is strictly in confidence." Was I impersonating a priest now, too? I asked myself.

"It seems we misunderstood the purpose of this little get-together. I hope you'll understand that we'd like to keep that information close to home, if you know what I mean." Ted flashed me a smile in direct contradiction to the harshness and finality of his tone.

Both Marlene and Ted were becoming increasingly agitated, perilously close to gulping their drinks, and I sensed my time was almost up. I'd expected the familiar pattern of a Gary Larkin anecdote—the omnipresent tissues, a beryllium joke, an airport stunt—but none was forthcoming.

I took my last shot.

"Did you know Manuel Martinez?" I asked. "The boy from the Elmwood district who was murdered?"

"No," they said together, heads shaking in rhythm.

"Didn't know him, but what a shame," Ted said.

"His poor father," Marlene said.

"I thought you might have met him since his girlfriend did chores and a little housework for Gary. Her name is Jennifer Kellerman. Does that sound familiar?"

Marlene pursed her lips. "That must have been at his new place on Ashby. Gary was allergic to dust—and everything else—so I'm not surprised he didn't do his own housecleaning."

Ted slapped Marlene's knee. "Time to go, sweetie."

We said good-bye, thoughts of my own alienated sweetie flooding to the front of my brain.

EIGHTEEN

FACING MATT AGAIN. That would be the hard part, I thought, as I drove back to Elaine's.

We'd disagreed about the level of my involvement in police matters before, but this time I felt we'd crossed some threshold; I'd never stormed out of a house before. My move seemed more dramatic coming after he'd flown three time zones to see me. To stop me from completing an investigation, I told myself, and felt a flush come to my cheeks.

I thought of calling Rose Galigani in Revere, as if she'd know Matt's motivations more than I did. Happily married for more than forty years to her mortician husband, in my mind Rose epitomized expertise in male-female relations. If anyone could tell me what was in Matt's mind—other than himself—it would be Rose.

I pulled into a gas station on Shattuck, walked over to the battered pay phone, and pushed cracked, rusty buttons for Rose's number. I wondered if the Nikki and Benito whose names were carved on the metal counter of the semi-booth had as much trouble with their love life as I did.

I wouldn't believe this scene if it were in a movie, I told myself: a gray-haired woman standing in a service station lot, reading the graffiti in a pay phone stall, calling long distance to find out if her boyfriend still likes her. When the Galigani answering machine came on, I hung up, grateful that I'd minimized the embarrassing incident.

Still not quite ready for the reality of Elaine's newest houseguest, I felt trapped. I'd left all my resources at her house, but I was reluctant about returning and having to confront Matt. I was anxious to look through Terry's envelope, plus all my notes. And I had a sudden memory of the receipts I'd taken from Manuel's closet. My run-in with Russell had put them out of my mind until this moment, and I had the irrational daydream that they were becoming more and more illegible as they lay wrinkled in my jacket pocket in Elaine's guest room.

I decided to take a drive, determined to find an isolated spot to review my cases, with my mind my only resource. Three cases, now, I thought—Larkin, Martinez, and Gennaro.

I searched my memory banks for a familiar lookout, and came up with several along Grizzly Peak Boulevard, a two-lane, winding road leading up and away from the campus. I'd gone there often as a Berkeley resident, and knew I could find a good spot without a map.

I headed for the hilltop, driving up Hearst. I felt compelled to edit the signs along the way, deciding the yellow Narrow Road warnings were redundant. If you'd gotten this far, you wouldn't need the signs.

I passed the lab buildings and the Lawrence Hall of Science. Although their parking lots offered a perfect view of the bay, they were too crowded for my purposes. As I swerved around a man in black spandex on a bicycle, pedaling up the steep grade, I marveled that we were the same species. Even at the peak of my physical ability, I wouldn't have been able to make the trip without an internal-combustion engine at my disposal.

And at the moment, I was beginning to question the wisdom of the trip in a car, finding myself out of shape for negotiating the sharp curves. I thought about counting the number of tailgaters I'd already seen on the narrow road, glad none were on my tail.

I drove with the windows down, allowing the aroma of the eucalyptus trees to soothe my senses, trying not to think of the thousand-foot drops, alternating to my left and right, and continued on until Cragamont became Grizzly Peak Boulevard. When I reached the top, I pulled over to the right, onto a flat area of gravel, dotted with a few candy wrappers and crushed soda cans. The lookout could accommodate about a half-dozen cars, but I had it all to myself, complete with the breathtaking view of the bay I'd hoped for.

I wondered if I'd be able to concentrate in the midst of the spectacular hills, looking out on the San Francisco Bay. I could almost hear the strains of a symphony, as if I were part of a documentary or a travel video. I thought of a quote I'd read on a poster in my dentist's office. ''Certain aspects of human reason do not seem to function in the presence of a view.''

I had a sudden desire for Matt's presence, and wished I could have taken him here. Setting up a self-debating mode, I reasoned that he'd come to California only because I'd misbehaved; if I'd been playing the agreeable tourist, he'd still be in Revere catching real troublemakers.

So much for the Gennaro case.

With my back to the road, Tilden Park and a lush ecological study area all around me, I pushed my seat back and enjoyed the vista, but only for a few minutes. My fingers and brain itched to get back to work. I rummaged in my purse and found a pen and a postcard I'd taken from Siad's restaurant on Saturday night. The brown-toned photograph of the small dining room reminded me of my surprise party a little more than twelve hours ago. It could have been twelve months ago, given all that had happened since.

Except for the address in the upper left corner, the back of the card was blank, ready for my fresh start on Larkin and Martinez. This time I thought I'd study the chronology, recording all events for both cases, whether I considered them related or not. With the postcard oriented vertically, I made a list of everything I knew, and the approximate dates.

1. Late December—Gary catches Marlene with Ted, files for divorce.
2. January—Manuel buys a new computer with Christmas money.
3. January or February (ask teacher)—Manuel starts term paper on CBD.
4. Early February—charges filed against Gary in the pornography case.
5. February 14—Manuel buys bracelet, starts showing has more money.
6. March—Rita Johnson files lawsuit.

7. Mid April—Gary and Marlene meet with lawyers to settle divorce terms.

8. Late April—Pornography charges against Gary dismissed.

9. May 5—Manuel submits term paper on CBD.

10. May 17—Gary murdered.

11. May 31—Manuel disappears.

12. June 3—Manuel's body found.

I wanted to add number 13—June 4, Gloria walks out on Matt. But I had to keep focused, and I was running out of postcard.

I made another list, squeezing it into the slot for the addressee, of things left to check out: Terry's envelope, Manuel's receipts. Now all I needed was a new highlighter to draw the connecting lines. In my dreams, I thought.

After an hour I realized I'd hardly looked at the view. Was I so driven that I couldn't take a few moments for meditation? Why was I doing this in retirement? I asked myself. Unlike for my Revere Police Department contract work, I wasn't even getting paid for this self-imposed assignment. I should be home in a pear-scented bubble bath, reading *Gone With the Wind* or *The Philosophical Foundations of Quantum Mechanics.*

I moved the seat of the Saab forward to the driving position and started down the hill. I'd figure out what to say to Matt when I had to, I decided.

I'd barely left the turnout when I noticed a dark-colored sport utility vehicle in my rearview mirror, too close for comfort. Although I'd owned a Jeep and driven extensively on back roads while I lived in California, my year behind the wheel of the Galiganis' hand-me-down Cadillac had dulled the edge I needed to navigate the Berkeley hills. While Massachusetts drivers were legendary, the fatality rate in my home state was very low, fender benders being the main cause of high insurance rates. In California, there were few low-stakes accidents. On the freeways and roads like Grizzly Peak Boulevard, it was usually all or nothing.

I knew fatalities were not what I should be thinking about while the SUV kept close behind me. I tried to get a look at the license plate, in case I decided to lodge a complaint later, but in my anxious state, I registered only a couple of digits. I looked for a turnout to let the vehicle pass, and nearly made it into one or two, but couldn't get to them in time. I focused on the road, tapping my brake periodically to alert the driver that we were coming to an S curve, posted at fifteen mph. It did no good; he kept closing in on me until I was sure he was going to hit me.

I was right.

The first time the car hit the Saab's bumper—only a tap—my immediate, irrational thought was how would I explain this to Elaine? A fine houseguest I was, one who should have taken the bus. But in another minute, I realized a scratched bumper was the least of my problems.

The SUV came at me again, this time smacking my rear bumper on the right edge. The Saab moved into the next lane, mercifully empty of oncoming traffic, and my heart moved into a strange place in my chest. I held on to the wheel and steered back into my lane, evaluating my options. Go faster to get away? I didn't like the risk of spinning out and landing at the base of a young redwood tree a quarter of a mile below. Turn at an angle to bounce the SUV off my bumper? I'd need computer-aided modeling to get that one right. A U-turn? Out of the question in the tiny roadway.

What I needed was a relatively straight stretch of road with no traffic in the other direction—I could steer across the south-bound lane into the hillside and take my chances with the eucalyptus trees. Although the traffic was light, it wasn't zero, and my hopes for a more friendly path were dashed by the next black-and-yellow sign—the symbol for curves, over the words Next 1.5 Miles. At least I know exactly what I'm in for, I thought. Too bad I don't have the luxury of checking the odometer.

The SUV seemed undaunted by the curves, although the laws of physics dictated that I had the advantage. The Saab's wide wheel base and low center of gravity made it more roadworthy than an off-road vehicle like the one attacking me. I reasoned that the SUV driver knew that and was merely trying to intimidate me, not kill me. Little comfort as the monster hit me again.

My palms had turned to sweaty masses, slipping off the wheel as if there were a layer of wax on the dark green rim. My only choice for the time being was to push the Saab as fast as I could to keep ahead. At each bend a new vista presented itself, sometimes to my right, sometimes to my left. On this trip, the views inspired me not with their beauty but with the hazard they represented. I wondered how far down I'd drop, how many spins per minute down to sea level. I felt the impact in my chest as if I'd already slammed into a tree.

After five or six more curves in the road, and useless calculations on my part, I saw an opportunity. With a short, straight stretch in sight, and no cars coming from the north, I knew I had to take the one shot, and act quickly.

I jerked the wheel to surprise the SUV driver, and steered the Saab into the opposite lane. Then I hit the brake and headed for a manzanita bush. I wished I could have achieved one of the useful out-of-body experiences I'd heard about, but unfortunately, I was never more in my body than the time it took to deliberately drive my car into the sturdy bush, its spring leaves ready to envelope me and my car. Although I'd tried to slow down considerably, the impact activated my airbag, pressing me against the seat. My breathing seemed to stop and bright lights of all sizes flooded the insides of my eyelids.

My jaws and stomach muscles ached from holding my breath. I finally let the air out of my lungs, and looked up in time to see the SUV roar away. I thought I saw its brake lights and had a momentary fear that he'd come back to me, winding up the hill in reverse, to finish the job he'd started.

Except for an unbearable pain in my neck, I felt intact. Coffee had spilled onto my lap and Elaine's box of tissues had somehow landed on my head. No blood, nothing broken. I was so happy to have the SUV off my tail, I almost relaxed and took a nap on the balloon-shaped pillow wedged in front of me. I knew I should get out and check the damage to Elaine's car, but I felt pinned to the dashboard, not by the airbag, but by a greater weight—a heavy question. Was this just another rude California SUV driver, or had someone deliberately tried to kill me?

"Ma'am, hold still and we'll get you out of there. Backup's coming."

The voice seemed to come from far down the canyon where I'd narrowly missed spending my last moments.

I looked out my window at the handsome California highway patrolman in his two-tone-brown uniform and high boots, his friendly motorcycle a few feet away, and cried.

"I'M REALLY FINE," I said to Elaine and Matt. "I told you, I didn't even need an ambulance, but they wanted to take me here for tests." What I kept to myself was how hard I'd tried to leave the emergency vehicle and walk home without ever breathing a word to anyone about the Grizzly Peak incident.

"And now we're waiting to see if you passed those tests," Elaine said.

I was in a wheelchair, just a formality, the paramedic told me, facing Elaine and Matt in the waiting room of St. Leander's Hospital in North Berkeley. I felt one hundred years old, my legs under an olive green lap robe, and bandages on my arm where the needles had penetrated my skin.

The other groups of people in the waiting room were considerably less active than our little family—no undercurrents of arguments, no stubborn refusals to sit still. Maybe patients at that end of the room were sedated, I thought, happy I'd been able to talk my paramedical team out of drugging me.

My reunion with Matt when he and Elaine arrived to claim me had been purely physical. A long hug, damp eyes, no words for a while. But he couldn't leave his job behind for too long.

"Were you able to give the CHP a good description of the vehicle?"

I screwed up my face. "I told them as much as I could remember; it was a dark color, blue or green. And I know I saw a 767 together. And something else about the license plate was strange, but I can't put my finger on it. Otherwise..." I shrugged my shoulders, sending a pain shooting up my arm. I did my best to cover the grimace. "I was concentrating on keeping the car on the road."

"You did better than I would have," Elaine said.

"What about your car?" I asked, afraid to hear the answer.

Elaine shook her head. "Not to worry. You somehow steered into the softest spot on Grizzly Peak Boulevard. I'll take it in this week, but it's completely drivable."

I took a long breath. The big question in all our minds, I could tell, was whether this had been a deliberate attack on me, or just another conquer-planet-Earth driver out for Sunday fun. I was voting for the latter, but common sense told me otherwise. Apparently my friends had the same thoughts.

"Gloria, I know this isn't the best time, but Matt and I have been talking," Elaine said.

How nice for you, I thought, as I shot them a silent look, knowing I wasn't going to like the direction the conversation was headed. I made a move to leave the wheelchair, but everything hurt, and I wasn't exactly in sprinting form.

"There's no use trying to second-guess all this," Elaine said. "Which means I know you won't let me blame myself for dragging you into Manuel's case, but it's time to quit. Everything." She spread her hands out as if to wipe my slate clean, or call me safe at first base.

Matt screwed up his face at the mention of quitting—a word he knew would never work with me—and clearly thought it was his turn.

"Not quitting, more like turning over whatever information you have, whatever good ideas you've come up with..."

I rolled my eyes, as if to tell him not to bother. "You're saying Inspector Russell will accept my help?"

"I can't speak for Russell, but we could give it a try."

"And if he refuses, you'll agree to let me do this without him?"

"I can't promise that."

"Then why would I bother?"

Matt shook his head and let out an exasperated sigh.

The next round of dialogue consisted of two words, spoken simultaneously: Matt's "Gloria" and my "Matt," both at a higher-than-normal volume.

Elaine looked around at the others in the waiting room, as if to disclaim knowledge of the two of us. "I think I'll go check on your status," she said.

Her escape left me facing Matt. With nowhere else to look, I studied his worried countenance, the droopy eyes I'd grown to love, and asked myself if I really wanted to lose him through stubbornness. Did I have an extra responsibility to keep myself from harm now that we'd become close? Maybe more important for my psychological health—was I determined to sabotage a relationship that brought me wonderful companionship and great pleasure?

"I didn't think you'd still be here," I said.

"I'm not going anywhere."

"I mean there, in my life," I said, compelled to explain.

"So did I."

NINETEEN

WE WORKED OUT a treaty over Elaine's coffee table, agreeing to brainstorm all the facts of the cases.

"You don't have do this if it's too hard on you," I told Elaine, knowing half her attention was with José and Liz making arrangements for their son. "I'm happy to have something to do," she said. "I've made all the phone calls on the list José gave me. And it was a good distraction. I can see why you're so caught up with investigating. This would be intriguing if I weren't so personally involved."

Happy to be out of a wheelchair, I submitted to being served dinner. I'd eaten nothing but cappuccino foam all day, and apparently my friends had fasted also. We had our choice of takeout from among Berkeley's innumerable ethnic menus.

"I can't believe we chose pizza for our first meal in twenty-four hours," Elaine said.

"I'm happy. Let's see if it's as good as Russo's in Revere," Matt said, reminding me how narrow his taste in food ran.

The combined smells of pizza, coffee, and Matt's light aftershave gave me such a warm feeling, I decided to be magnanimous and share the contents of Terry's package. But not before exacting a promise from Matt.

"You can't mention her name in front of Inspector Dennis Russell."

"I can live with that."

We looked through the photographs of Gary Larkin's house, unremarkable in layout and decor. The police photographer had been thorough, and we were able to piece together Gary's life, or at least his house, room by room. I wondered about the significance of his bedding's having the same leopard skin design I'd seen on Marlene's headband. Perhaps they were more compatible than they thought.

His home office space consisted of a multipurpose computer desk ensemble, the kind that comes with directions for assembly in several languages. Gary's was a dark fake-wood structure, overflowing with the usual clutter of papers, disks, and CDs. The photography was sharp enough to be able to read the labels on Gary's binders.

"Look at this," Elaine said. "What kind of person has a library like this? Beryllium 1, Beryllium 2, up to Beryllium 10."

"Good bedtime reading," I said.

Matt and Elaine shook their heads and clucked their tongues at me, but I was used to being misunderstood by my nontechnical friends.

We shuffled through the dozen or so photographs several times each. We made a great effort to keep the pictures pepperoni-free and to refrain from mentioning how unhelpful they were. Once or twice, I thought I saw something—or didn't see something—I thought was important, but when I tried to pinpoint it, it went away.

"On to the police report on Manuel. Are you ready for this, Elaine?" I asked.

She nodded. "As long as José and Liz never have to see it."

The police had told his parents simply that Manuel died of asphyxiation. The report had more interesting details, which I read aloud. I read the first paragraph quickly, half expecting to see the phrase "by beryllium dust," but the conclusion was the killer had used ether on Manuel to subdue him, then suffocated him using a fabric with wool threads, such as a jacket or blanket.

"Did you say ether?" Matt and Elaine asked simultaneously.

"Ether is used as a solvent, most often to clean glassware. But it doesn't mean it was a lab person. It's like acetone," I said in a lame voice. My friends knew my reluctance to accuse scientists of criminal behavior, and were kind enough to bear with me as I reminded them how ether could be a garage staple for someone with a stubborn lawnmower, for example.

The police report mentioned an attempt to cover Manuel's body with debris from the pit. He was discovered by the lab's waste handlers making their usual Saturday rounds.

The time of death was not pinpointed with any degree of accuracy. Essentially, the coroner said it was sometime between when he was last seen and when he was found dead, much like the conclusion on the Gary Larkin report.

"What about the way they do it on TV?" Elaine asked. "Can't you get a little more information from body temperature, stiffness, the presence of...insects?"

"Not every police district will do that," Matt said. "It's not an exact science, and a good defense attorney will pounce on it. So some counties won't even venture a guess."

Elaine shook her head, as if the intricacies of the criminal justice system were beyond her grasp. "What else is in the report?" she asked me.

I laid out a hand-drawn sketch that identified the exact spot where Manuel had been found, in the northeast corner of the battery/capacitor pit, just off the road, by the gate. A symbol for a wheel marked the position of his bicycle, near the fence that enclosed the waste area. We leaned over the coffee table to look at the drawing, but nothing inspiring came of the exercise.

"There's not much more," I said. "The report says waste is delivered to the fenced-in area beyond the pit on Wednesday and Saturday mornings only, which means Manuel could have been killed as early as Wednesday, the day he disappeared."

After my recitation of the cold facts of the death of a teenager, the room fell silent, as if we all needed a private moment before continuing our own lives. Although I'd never met Manuel, I felt a sense of loss and a renewed determination to find the person who'd taken his life.

"Anything else to share?" Matt asked, bringing us back to work.

"I have one more thing," I said, producing the pile of receipts I'd taken from Manuel's shoeless closet.

"Where did you get these?" Elaine asked, prompting a nudge and a nervous glance from me. "Never mind," she said.

Matt made no comment, although I was sure he didn't miss the interaction.

We sorted the thin slips of paper of various sizes, arranging them by date. Except for one video game bought in December, the earliest pile was for January.

"Okay, what do we have?" Matt asked. "What's the first purchase?"

"January fifth," Elaine said, smoothing out an eight-by-ten sales slip with perforated edges. "Nine hundred ninety-nine dollars, plus tax, for a new computer at the Plug Strip."

Matt gave a low whistle. "That's a lot of spare change for a kid."

"José already told us about this," Elaine said. "Manuel got the money from his mother and aunts and uncles for Christmas. The Plug Strip is a discount store, so I'm sure he got a lot for his money."

"A discount computer store?" I felt as if I'd been zapped by one hundred and twenty volts of alternating current.

"Have you heard of the Plug Strip?" Elaine asked. "Are they on the East Coast?"

"No, it just sounds like a store with obnoxious salesmen," I said, my mind racing back a few hours to my last meeting with a representative of the species. "Quick, what's the telephone number? It's not quite six o'clock. They might still be open."

I punched in the numbers for the Plug Strip, my hands trembling as if I'd cracked an international code. Or a murder case. "Is the salesperson identified on that receipt?" I asked Elaine, who was still holding the paper as if it she knew it was important but not quite how.

"Let's see. There's a number at the top under 'Sales Associate.' It's 73454."

After at least ten rings, someone picked up. Another perky California voice.

"Is Ted Gernich there?" I asked.

"He's not working tonight."

I gave Matt and Elaine a smile and a thumbs-up, though I wasn't sure they knew the significance.

"No problem. I'm from payroll working at home. I'm just trying to verify his ID number—is it 73454?"

"Hold on."

I gave my friends a crooked, apologetic smile, as if lying in their presence was worse than fibbing privately. Matt was wide-eyed. Elaine shrugged her shoulders and poured refills all around.

I had a few bad moments on hold, as I imagined the young woman asking her boss if payroll worked on Sundays. Or tracing the call and dispatching Russell's men to my door. But the cheerful clerk had no such concerns, evidently.

"Yep. That's Ted's number," she said. "Anything else?"

"No, thank you. Good night."

I hung up the phone. "Bingo," I said, surprising us all.

MY EUPHORIA was short-lived as Elaine and Matt tried like good scientists to beat down my theory.

"Just because Ted sold Manuel that computer, it doesn't mean he lied about not knowing him. Imagine how many customers he sees in a day."

"And that was back in January, the peak of the season, most likely. Everybody's got Christmas money and a New Year's resolution to become computer-literate," Matt said.

"Like you?"

"Like me," he said, sending me a smile that almost knocked my thinking off its track.

"There's another thing," I said. "Hear me out. Something wasn't right in my conversation with Marlene and Ted, but I couldn't put my finger on it at the time. When we were talking about Manuel's death, Marlene said, 'his poor father.' How would she know Manuel lived only with his father? The paper didn't have that information, did it?"

"I don't think so," Elaine said. "I think it just said 'his parents.'"

"Right. So why wouldn't Marlene have said 'his poor parents'?"

"What's the difference?" Elaine asked. "A casual remark. It can't be that significant."

"No, Gloria's right," Matt said, to my delight. "Especially a woman. She'd be more likely to say 'his poor mother.'"

"Unless she knew Manuel lived only with his father."

"Okay," Elaine said. "So, then what does it mean that she might have known him and lied to you about it?"

I remembered the time line I'd written out on Grizzly Peak Boulevard. "Think about this," I said. "Manuel buys a computer from Ted. There's a lot of interaction while they figure out the system he'll buy. He realizes the kid is very good at computers, a potential hacker. Gary has filed for divorce and is about to take all his money with him. He and Marlene have been looking for a way to discredit him."

"Don't forget California's no-fault divorce," Elaine said.

"There's always room for negotiation when lawyers are involved. And maybe they don't even expect money from a judge. They just want to hassle Gary, give him grief. It happens."

"Don't I know it," Elaine said with a wry smile, but not loudly enough to stop me from delivering my punch line.

"So, they pay Manuel to break into Gary's computer and upload pornography."

Elaine shook her head, giving me an immediate verdict. "Far-fetched."

Matt hadn't voted, so I persevered. "The timing is perfect. Say it takes Manuel a couple of weeks or so to work it out. He's done by early February, which is when the pornography is discovered and charges are filed. Then Manuel buys his girlfriend an expensive bracelet for Valentine's Day."

Matt scratched his chin, a sign he was thinking things over, but Elaine still held out.

"How would they know the pornography would even be discovered?"

"There's constant surveillance on the lab's system. You know that. It was bound to be picked up sooner or later. And they had discretion as to when the divorce hearings would take place."

"José won't like it," Elaine said finally.

IN SPITE OF her reluctance to accept the idea of Manuel's being a criminal, Elaine stayed with us while we worked out the pros and cons of the theory.

Matt's contributions were about motive. "Marlene and Ted could have murdered Manuel—say he got greedy or threatened to expose them. But it doesn't give them a motive for killing Gary, unless he found out they were behind the charges against him."

My problem was how Marlene and Ted could have obtained

beryllium oxide, and how they could have gotten into Gary's lab. Big questions still, but I felt we were making progress for the first time.

Not surprisingly, Elaine focused on Manuel. "José said Manuel continued to have this extra money. But this sounds like a onetime thing. Once the divorce papers were signed, there'd be no need for Manuel's...services."

"Unless, as Matt says, he got greedy."

"What about Manuel's term paper?" Elaine asked. "Didn't you say it was well done?"

So? I wanted to ask. But I knew Elaine was grasping at ways to get Manuel's name back on the honor roll. How can we suspect criminal behavior of a kid who writes an excellent research paper, with lofty goals for health and human welfare?

I cleared my throat, unhappy about throwing another dart at Manuel's good record. "Actually, the term paper turned out to be an effective way to start the hacking process. You get into people's E-mail. Manuel had a good excuse to write to the beryllium engineers."

"He could have done that without doing a term paper," Matt said. "Yes. I'm not saying he didn't really want to write a good paper on CBD. It's just that it made it more convenient. He, or even his teacher, could demonstrate that he had a legitimate need to obtain E-mail addresses, and get the engineers into a chat session. And while he was communicating with them, their lines were open."

"And that's how you hack?" Matt asked.

"Essentially. It's like cruising the streets looking for an opportunity to commit a crime. An open window. Keys left in a car. A wallet hanging out of a pocket."

"So the hacker cruises the Internet looking for an opening."

"Right. And since it's a brute-force, trial-and-error process, the more time you have, the better. So the idea would be to keep the engineers talking. Naturally Manuel had to do his homework, too, to have something to talk about."

"Could you do this?" Matt asked, scratching his head. "Could you hack into someone's computer?"

"Not a chance," I said, rushing to assure him I was neither a computer genius nor a white-collar criminal. "I know the theory from reading about it, but I could never do it myself."

"You just read the right things? *Hacking for Dummies?*"

I gave him a big smile. "Something like that."

We were on the verge of retreating to our own private world again, when Elaine's voice broke in.

"I don't like it," she said, severely dampening my exhilaration at coming up with a plausible theory. "You're saying Manuel operated his own one-kid blackmailing ring from his computer."

I'd been so thrilled to be back in tutorial mode, as well as on friendly terms with Matt, I hadn't noticed her discomfort.

"It doesn't mean he was a hardened criminal. But it's possible he saw this as an easy way to make a few dollars. Didn't you say José wouldn't let him have a job?"

Matt checked in to support my thesis. "Guys try things when they want to impress a girlfriend. And kids think they're invincible. They think they'll never get caught. There won't be any consequences." Matt's voice trailed off and I imagined he was remembering any number of specific examples he could give of teenagers who turned out not to be invincible.

Elaine bit her lip, a sign of the severe stress she was under.

"I'm sorry, Elaine," I said. "This might be all wrong. It's just an idea. And even if it's right, it doesn't make it any less awful that Manuel was murdered."

"It's not perfect," Matt said. "But it's something to take to Russell."

I bristled, throwing my shoulders back as far as they could go in my still-painful condition. "Why talk to Russell? He's never been interested in my help."

"Because he's local law enforcement, that's why."

"He hasn't done very well so far. We started with one unsolved murder, and now we have two."

"You can't blame him for Manuel's death."

"You're right. That was unfair. But I'm upset that you'd ask me to drop my involvement in these cases."

"What do you want to do? Arrest Marlene and Ted yourself? Take them in for questioning?"

I shot him a look of annoyance. "No, I don't want to be

deputized, thank you. I'd like to follow through on the big questions, that's all. We need to find out if they have alibis for Wednesday night. And how they could have pulled off murdering Gary in his lab. Neither one has a badge."

Matt shook his head. "You've done some good work here, Gloria, but these are Russell's cases."

Our deliberations were as intense as those of two scientists debating hot versus cold fusion, until we were interrupted by a phone call. Elaine jumped up to answer it.

"It's for you," she said with a grimace. Not José, was the unspoken regret.

"Gloria, Lincoln Carver. Do you have a minute?"

"Of course." I'm in the middle of a fight with my boyfriend, I imagined telling him, but I'm glad you called.

"About that photograph you showed me the other day. The one of that kid?"

"Manuel Martinez."

"He's the one they found in the pit, right?"

"That's right. Do you remember talking to him now, about chronic beryllium disease?"

"Yeah. I didn't actually meet him, though. That's why I didn't recognize him in your photograph. He E-mailed me, asking some questions for his homework, and I E-mailed back."

"Just once?" I remembered that Sidney Kellerman had also referred to E-mail and a chat room visit or two with Manuel.

"A few times. We had a couple of chat sessions. He wanted some stats on what percent of the population was sensitive to beryllium, that kind of thing. And he used an E-mail moniker, a strange combination of letters and numbers, so I didn't put two and two together until today. When I saw the picture in the paper was the same kid you showed me, I thought I should call. Not that I know squat about how he died or anything."

"Did you ever talk—uh, E-mail—about anything personal?"

I heard Carver clear his throat, and wished I could see whether he was squirming. "No. Like I said, it was about beryllium. Unless you mean, how I personally felt about the new regulations for workers?"

"No. I meant personal, such as finding something on your computer that shouldn't have been there."

"Look, I didn't call to be grilled again."

"I understand that, but your contact with Manuel Martinez could be important. Have you talked to the police?" I smiled at Matt as I said this, as if to remind him I was sometimes capable of following procedure—sending my source to the proper authorities.

"No. I haven't talked to the police. I don't know anything," he said, emphasizing each word. I had the feeling Carver regretted his call to me, but I'd figured out his motive.

"So this phone call is to clear yourself with me, in case I found out later that you lied to me in the café?"

"Look, I didn't have to call you. I thought you might like to have things tied up is all."

"Tied up, as in 'neat'?"

"Yeah."

"Well, it's anything but neat here, but thanks for calling, Lincoln." I came close to slamming the phone down onto its cradle. "He's hiding something. I'll bet he was being blackmailed by Manuel, too," I said to the room at large. My friends had amazed looks on their faces.

"What?" I asked.

"Since when did you become such a hard-boiled interrogator?" Elaine asked.

"Since no one will listen to me, and since my physical being has been threatened twice."

Matt put his cup down. "Twice?" he asked.

"Two times?" Elaine asked, as if to help me understand the question.

With great reluctance I told them the story of the athletic shoes in the ladies' room, and the ski mask on the sidewalk. "It was probably a random flasher," I said.

"The fact that this happened today makes it more likely targeted," Matt said. "I'd think this'd be enough to make you step back."

Elaine nodded. "It would do it for me."

"Is 'step back' the new euphemism for 'quit'?" I asked.

It was Matt's turn to storm out of the room. But he went only as far as the kitchen to warm up a slice of pizza.

THE NEXT TIME the phone rang, it was for Elaine. She took it upstairs, and came down a few minutes later, carrying her jacket and a small leather tote.

"I'm out for the night, probably, if you don't mind," she said. "You have José's number."

"I'm glad he's allowing her to give him support," I said to Matt. We stood in the doorway, waving Elaine off. "I don't imagine it's going to be a fun night."

"It could be for us, though."

I laughed. "It certainly could be," I said, leaning back into his chest.

For the next few hours, we dropped all talk of murder and abduction.

TWENTY

MONDAY MORNING brought a new bargain between Matt and me. He'd go to the station and talk to Inspector Russell about our theory of Manuel as junior-level electronic blackmailer.

"It has enough merit that I think police resources should be brought to bear."

"Well, when you put it that way," I said, insinuating his flattery had worked.

I got something in return for my generosity in obeying the law—permission to continue to investigate in any way that wouldn't impede Russell's cases or put me in danger. Ambiguous enough to be acceptable, I'd decided.

Matt and I agreed on one thing: He'd go to the Berkeley police station without me, even claiming the theory was his if he thought it would help Russell's mood and inclination to follow up. He put on his blue suit, which he wore every Monday—apparently no matter which coast he was working on—and called a taxi.

"And what are you going to do today?" he asked me, grinning broadly, as if he were giving me a test he knew I could pass if I were so inclined.

"I'm going to stay home and think. And try to get the goods on Sidney Kellerman, Rita Johnson, and Lincoln Carver. And the technician, Larry Pursiano." I hoped my attempt to use forties detective language would diffuse the gravity of my plan, but Matt wasn't easily distracted.

"How are you going to do that?" he asked.

"I could try to hack into their computers."

"Ha," he said. His tone was light, but his facial expression, with its frown and screwed-up nose, indicated he wasn't sure whether I was joking or not.

Our good-bye kiss, and my promise to take care of myself,

embodied a picture of the fifties so vivid I could almost feel pearls at my neck. But I had more to do than vacuum and dust, and it was unlikely that Matt would come home to the smell of a roast in the oven.

I went upstairs to work on Elaine's computer. It took me about five minutes to concede I didn't have the skills for hacking. I decided instead to log on to the lab's website and see if I could find anything that would help either case. I typed in the URL and scrolled through the latest information on funding levels for major projects, internal awards for technical excellence, engineers who'd been made fellows of professional organizations, and cafeteria offerings for the month of June.

I was about to search elsewhere for inspiration when I saw an icon for WOSE, the lab's Women of Science and Engineering Organization. I'd never been a member, having a firm belief in the separation of professional associations and support groups. Ordinarily, I would have scrolled past WOSE, but I thought it might have something on the lawsuit Rita Johnson was involved in.

As I'd guessed, there was a long article on the progress of the suit, plus interviews with key personnel. A call for more female participants was issued, stressing the importance of a large number of women coming forward. For class-action status, the piece reminded us, the plaintiffs had to prove the problem was too pervasive for each case to be tried individually.

I clicked on the listing, RITA JOHNSON INTERVIEW. Fortunately, Elaine's system was up-to-date with real audio software, so I was able to access the taped meeting. The picture quality was poor—jerky, like an old-time silent movie, but I was interested only in content anyway. I settled back to watch Rita being interviewed by Janelle Bly, the president of WOSE, who looked not much older than Courtney the librarian, Terry the policewoman, and Brianna the waitress. Janelle had her back to the camera. Her long, straight hair acted like a blond curtain next to Rita's face, and seemed to be the source of the questions.

The question-and-answer session was mildly interesting. Rita explained that the suit sought unspecified financial compensation. "But the most important part," she said, "is a reform of the payment and promotion systems of the lab. We're looking at discrimination in hiring, awards, and promotions, plus inclusion in important committees and allocation of valuable resources like laboratory space and access to research funds.''

Rita presented her case with an energy and intensity that came through even though her presence was confined to a two-inch square in the upper left-hand corner of my monitor.

I found one fact particularly impressive, and wondered if it were true: that women represented only 8 percent of high levels of management in scientific institutions, a number that hadn't changed in twenty years.

"This is not a case of individual cases involving special circumstances," she said, making her plea for class-action status.

"Any last message you'd like to leave us with?" Janelle the president asked her.

"I'd like to emphasize that it's not only money and promotion we're seeking, but a certain dignity that comes with having our professional abilities recognized fairly. At times it seems I offer the women who clean my house more respect than laboratory management offers its female employees.''

I sat back in Elaine's ergonomically correct office chair. Had I heard right? Could I take it at face value? Had Rita Johnson given me exactly what I needed to tie her to Manuel's murder?

I played the interview again, sitting through the rhetoric I seemed to know by heart, waiting on the edge of the chair for the last quote. It was as I'd remembered—a reference to the women who cleaned her house—as good as an admission that Rita never did high dusting, and therefore didn't break her arm while attacking cobwebs from a ladder in her living room. Not that I was surprised Rita Johnson didn't do her own housecleaning. I simply wondered why she'd lied to me about how she broke her arm.

I moved away from the computer and stretched my legs. While I wandered around Elaine's house, I formulated a summary of what I'd just learned that might help me solve the puzzle of Gary Larkin's and Manuel Martinez's deaths. I constructed my theory with care, giving great consideration to how Inspector Russell might respond to a connection between a fib about housekeeping and a double murder.

Suppose Rita was being blackmailed by Manuel, I mused, half out loud to the empty house. Say he found something that would upset her credibility as a chief architect of the lawsuit. I played the scene, as if it were being acted out in front of me. Rita lures Manuel to a face-to-face meeting. There's a physical confrontation—I remembered hearing that Manuel's body had bruises, indicating a struggle before he died. Rita breaks her arm in the skirmish. I interrupted the action with a question—would Rita be able to overcome the well-built teenager? Maybe, if she had a weapon, plus the element of surprise on her side.

I was fairly happy with the script, although I couldn't work things out to include Gary Larkin yet. But that would come, I told myself.

Or, I thought, recognizing the narrowness of my hypothesis, Rita broke her arm lifting weights beyond her capacity and doesn't want to admit weakness. Or she has an abusive boyfriend. Or girlfriend. Not likely, but I made the point to myself that there were any number of ways to break an arm other than in the act of committing murder. I couldn't even count on Matt, let alone Russell, for support with this one unless I had more evidence.

My only recourse was to call Rita.

I WAS ALMOST DISAPPOINTED that I had Rita's telephone number handy. Maybe it was the influence of a night with Matt, but my commitment to take care of myself reared its head as I picked up the phone to arrange a meeting with a suspected murderer. Before the voice of reason took over, I remembered I hadn't shown Rita the photograph of Manuel during our interview at the Cedar St. Café. The perfect excuse to get back to her.

"Rita Johnson."

"Rita, this is Gloria Lamerino."

"Good morning," she said, sounding distracted. I heard muffled voices in the background, as if I'd interrupted a meeting.

"I can tell you're busy, but I have a couple more questions to ask you. Can we meet again briefly?"

"I'm really swamped this week."

"I wouldn't bother you if it wasn't very important."

"Maybe you could E-mail me, and I'll try to get to it as soon as possible."

"It's about Manuel Martinez, the young man who was murdered." My effort to make my voice sound ominous seemed to have some effect, if Rita's long, heavy sigh was any indication.

"All right," she said. "But I'm tied up all day."

"His wake is this evening. Were you planning to attend?"

"Why would I go to his wake?" Rita's clipped speech forced me to speed up my own.

"I was hoping you were ready to tell me how you know him," I said, shooting the remark back like a second round from a semiautomatic.

Another deep sigh. My own breathing rate increased as I pictured Rita Johnson walking into Inspector Dennis Russell's office, arms outstretched—one regular, one broken—saying, "Gloria Lamerino figured it out. Arrest me."

"Look, I can't talk now."

"When?"

"I have to be at the lab in Livermore for a meeting at four-thirty this afternoon. Meet me in the parking lot at three. We can talk there for a few minutes before I leave. I park in B-4, north-side."

"Where the old World War Two victory gardens used to be?"

"Right. That's the only lot with any spaces left by the time I get here."

"I'll see you there."

Excitement took over my body—the thrill of closing in on the solution. I was sure Rita was involved somehow. Otherwise, why would she have agreed to a meeting at the mention of Manuel's name? I pictured the Larkin and Martinez murders as a two-sided puzzle, one crime scene on each side. Every time a piece fit into a slot on one side, the other side became a little more clear also.

Another thought flashed through my mind as I mentally replayed the call with Rita. On the phone, she'd implied her usual arrival time was too late for her to park in the close-in lots, but on the day Gary died, she'd arrived just after seven-thirty in the morning. What was so special about that day, except that Gary's body needed to have its pulse taken?

I had almost two hours to get to Rita's parking lot of choice. Without a car, it might take that long, I mused. I decided to walk to the campus and take the shuttle from there up to the lab, hoping the local service still operated as I remembered. I'd have plenty of time to get back and be ready for Manuel's wake in the evening.

I changed out of my sweats and put on comfortable oxfords, dark pants and a light jacket, suitable for the sixty-degree weather. Though it was still early, just after one, I thought I should leave the house. I didn't want to risk having to deal with Matt if he came home before I left. Although technically, I wasn't breaking any promises, I told myself. I wasn't impeding Russell's investigation by seeing Rita, and I certainly wasn't putting myself in danger. It was broad daylight. As bright as on the day I was stalked in the ladies' room, and on the day that I was pushed off the road, I thought, with a painful tightening of my muscles.

About fifteen minutes into my trip, I realized I was out of shape for walking in the sun. After a year in Boston, I'd gotten used to a consistently higher level of humidity—not always comfortable on hot summer days, but a pleasant filter for electromagnetic radiation. In the dry California climate, the full power of the sun was often hard to take, defeating the best sunglasses and sunscreening techniques.

As if in defiance of the memory, I rejected my initial inclination to cross to the other side of the street when I approached Walnut Square. I even stopped for coffee at the same café where I'd recovered from my stall incident. Brave as I was, however, I was glad I didn't need to use the rest room again. I used my break time to review my notes, but I couldn't concentrate; my distractions ran back and forth between excitement for the upcoming meeting with Rita and curiosity about how Matt was making out with Russell.

At the northern edge of campus, I saw the familiar shelters for the special shuttle bus that cruised Berkeley, circling around the campus, the laboratories, and the neighborhoods. I reached the stop as the two-forty bus pulled up. Perfect timing.

"Not too many people want to go way out there this time of day," the driver told me. Randy, as his name tag read, looked to be a student—a young Asian, with dark, almond-shaped eyes and a black ponytail longer than I'd seen on any of the waitresses who'd served me over the weekend. He wore a blue-and-gold nylon jacket with a patch on the sleeve that identified him as a University Transit driver. "You better believe there'll be a big rush a couple of hours from now, though."

"I'll bet," I said, wondering how Rita would make the trip. Probably by bicycle or on foot, I thought, remembering her well-conditioned body.

For the second time in a few days, I was treated to the dazzling view of three of the bridges that spanned the bay. I twisted my body to match the road winding up to parking lot B-4, keeping the bay in my sights.

"Nice view, huh?" Randy said.

"Beautiful. And you get to see it everyday." Just as I did before I chose a view of St. Anthony's Church in Revere instead, I thought.

"We're here," Randy said. "Whereabouts is your car?"

"No car. I'm looking for a woman who may not be here yet. I'll get out and wait."

"Sun or shade?" Randy asked, endearing me once again to Generation X.

"Shade."

Randy drove over to the shelter at the edge of the lot. In the next moments, the magnificent blues of the ocean and sky were superseded by a more compelling sight. A neon-green jacket, lying on the ground, came into my field of view, below the window of the bus. I gasped as I looked at the form under the jacket.

Long, curly red hair. Arm in a cast.

"Stop." I gave the order with such force, Randy hit his brake immediately and I banged my head on the pole in front of me. "Someone's hurt," I said even before I was off the bus.

Rita Johnson lay sprawled on the gravel next to a tangled bicycle, in the middle of an aisle of cars. With great calmness and presence of mind, Randy used his radio to call for help, carrying it to Rita's side.

"She's breathing," he said both to me and the dispatcher. "But you'd better come fast."

I was relieved that Randy seemed to have profited more from first-aid classes than I ever did. Once the session was over, I quickly forgot whether to use hot or cold, to raise or lower a head or a foot, to touch or not to touch a body part.

Randy took off his jacket and placed it under Rita's head, mumbling soothing words. I knelt beside her, hands folded in front of me, useless even as a prayer leader.

When the paramedics arrived, I was in the same position, one question recycling itself in my head. How could this have happened in the middle of such a bright day?

TWENTY-ONE

I COULDN'T CONVINCE the paramedics to let me accompany Rita to the hospital in the ambulance. They scooped Rita, her helmet, and her briefcase from the ground and sped away, sirens blaring, leaving Randy and me to be questioned by a uniformed officer who'd arrived in a patrol car. Once again I was surprised at the number of people pressed into service by one call to 911.

I looked at the dark-skinned young policeman, Garcia, according to the embroidery on his chest, and hoped the difference in our ages would give me a credibility I didn't deserve.

"You had a three o'clock meeting scheduled with Dr. Johnson?" he asked me. I assumed Rita's identity had been the subject of the huddle Randy and I weren't invited to when the emergency crew first arrived.

"Yes."

"Any particular reason you were meeting out here instead of in an office?"

"She was very busy today. She had to be at meeting in Livermore and thought it would be faster for me to meet her here." I noticed I'd been wringing my hands and made an effort to relax. I waved my arm around, encompassing the rows of vehicles. "She had to come here for her car."

Garcia nodded and took notes. "And the subject of your meeting?"

"She was going to give me a report," I said, my voice cracking. I hoped he thought it was from old age. For the first time in my life, as far as I could recall, I was deliberately withholding information from the police. My eyes hurt from squinting as I faced the sun to talk to Garcia, but I was afraid if I put on my sunglasses I'd look even more suspicious.

"A report."

I nodded, afraid to open my mouth, lest the truth spill out onto the gravel where Rita's body had lain. I'm meddling in a police matter, I imagined myself saying, trying to solve two murders single-handedly, and that woman was one of the suspects I'd planned to confront.

"What kind of report?" Garcia asked, thankfully unable to read my mind.

"I'm a retired scientist," I said. I took a breath, relishing the opportunity to say something truthful, but it didn't last. "She was going to give me material on a new process I was interested in, on beryllium coatings for fusion reactors." Dazzle him with jargon, I thought, switching from the helpless-little-old-lady persona.

I watched him write and wondered if he could spell beryllium. I had an odd desire to give him a tutorial, like the kind Gary Larkin was famous for. The kind I often gave to Matt, I thought, with a twinge of regret that I'd betrayed his trust by setting up the meeting with Rita in the first place.

When Garcia turned his eyes on me, tapping his notebook on his wrist, I was ready to hold out my hands for cuffs. But he gave no indication he didn't believe every word I'd said.

"Okay," he said. "At the moment, there's no reason to think of this as anything but an accident, but I'll keep this information, just in case it does turn out to be a police matter."

Just in case, I thought.

"We'll call you if we need anything else. This is the number where you're staying?" Garcia read back to me the basic identification I'd given him.

"Yes, that's correct," I said half under my breath. Lying is its own punishment, I decided, as I struggled with my dry mouth and queasy stomach.

Randy, who didn't have to lie, told Garcia his side of the story, and gave him his address and phone number. Then he returned to his job as bus driver to the guilty. On the way back to Shattuck Avenue, I let him ramble on about what might have happened to Rita, the crime and accident statistics on campus, and whether today's incident would make the campus newspapers. In his excitement, he didn't seem to notice I was hardly participating in the conversation. He seemed pleased when I asked for his supervisor's name so I could write a commendation for his performance in a crisis.

"Gosh, thanks," Randy said. "You held up your end. Too bad there's no one I can write to for you."

There's no one who'd be happy with my behavior, I wanted to tell him. I had only myself to blame for Rita's attack, even if no one had discovered me yet. I hoped I wouldn't be writing Randy's letter from jail.

The emergency personnel had refrained from guessing how Rita came to be unconscious in the parking lot, a large, bloody bruise on the top of her head, upsetting the beauty of her lovely hair. I guessed the presence of the wrecked bicycle from the laboratory fleet went a long way to persuading them Rita had fallen from it, perhaps thrown off balance by the heavy plaster cast on her arm. Government-issue bicycles were notorious for being poorly maintained.

"We won't know until we have a good look," the person in charge had told me.

I walked back to Elaine's from the bus stop, conscious of my disheveled appearance, but not inclined to refresh myself at the Walnut Square rest room, my own personal crime scene. I'd had enough excitement for one day. My hands were dirty, and my black slacks were soiled from my fruitless exercise on the parking lot gravel.

I was unable to enjoy the beautiful June day as my mind wandered from the tree-lined streets in the charming old neighborhood. Instead, I gave myself a quiz. Who knew Rita Johnson was coming to meet me? If it was the person in her office when she took my call, why would he go all the way out to a remote parking lot to stop her? And why not wait for me and get us both? Furthermore, if Rita knew her attacker, wouldn't he have made sure she was unable to identify him later? I held on to any thread that would make the attack on Rita a random act of violence, though it was thinner than a single fiber-optic strand.

BY THE TIME I reached Elaine's house it was nearly six-thirty. The only sign of life was a note from her and Matt on a yellow lined pad—"Gone to wake, 11000 San Pablo. Call if you need a ride. Check answering machine. Message for you."

The electronic greeting, which had been logged in at about the time I was supposed to meet a live, conscious Rita Johnson, was from Rose Galigani.

"I hope you're behaving yourself," Rose's voice said. I looked around, as if she might be hovering in an upper corner of the living room, or sitting on Elaine's mantel among her Hummel figures, shaking her finger at me as she sometimes did when she disapproved of my choices. "I hope everything is going well." Rose's emphasis on each word in the sentence told me she knew the purpose of Matt's visit, knew we'd argued, and hoped we'd made up—a lot to read into a few words and a tone of voice, but Rose and I had been friends since grammar school and I was sure I was right.

I called Alta Bates hospital, but wasn't surprised that no information on Rita Johnson would be released over the telephone.

Nothing to do but change into some nongravelly clothes, call a cab, and go to Manuel's wake. Maybe the taxi driver could help me come up with a good story about how I'd spent my afternoon. Shopping wouldn't work, neither would a movie, two of my least favorite ways to spend free time, and Matt and Elaine both knew it. It's what I should be doing at nearly sixty years old, I told myself. I imagined Rose's criticism of my rounding up my age from fifty-six, but at the moment I felt older than last year's software.

WHEN THE CAB pulled up to the blue-canopied walkway of the Bayside Chapel on San Pablo, I still had no idea what I'd tell Elaine and Matt. The truth seemed my only option, though I knew it would send Matt and me off on another argument. For the first time since my arrival in California, I wished Matt were three thousand miles away. From the number of cars in the Bayside parking lot, I had reason to hope it might be too crowded for them to notice me. I paid and thanked my driver, and entered the funeral parlor.

I got my wish for a wake, I thought, with great regret.

Every mortuary in every city reminds me of Galigani's parlors, and the Bayside was no exception. In the woman arranging wreaths of flowers, I saw my dear friend Rose, who went to work one Christmas morning to dress a stillborn baby that had been sent to her by the Revere hospital. The mother had also died in childbirth, and although they were strangers to Rose, she'd called me in California, overcome with grief.

In the distinguished-looking man greeting guests at the door, I saw Rose's husband of forty years, Frank Galigani, the best dressed man in Revere, who once helped relatives of the deceased prop up Great-grandpa's corpse so he could be part of a final family portrait. I remembered a favorite story of Robert Galigani, heir to the family business. He loved to describe the time he'd accepted help with his makeup chores from a lady of the night—she wanted her deceased friend to look the way she did as she practiced her trade in Boston's Combat Zone.

Bayside was a more modern chapel than Galigani's, with whitewashed walls, bright lights, blond paneling, and a pale blue carpet. The paisley seat covers were a soft blue-and-mauve fabric. I'd arrived in the middle of an upbeat hymn, sung by a group of teenagers wearing identical white robes with red collars. Is this Catholic? I wondered, as if it mattered.

I took one of the few empty seats, in the back of the parlor, my insides still in upheaval over Rita Johnson's incident, as the police probably labeled it. Not the first time I'd had to deal with the unfortunate consequences of my meddling, good intentions aside. At least Rita was still alive, I told myself.

It occurred to me that when she regained consciousness she might be more willing to help solve Manuel's murder—as if getting knocked off a bicycle made a person more cooperative and freed her from suspicion herself. In my mind, Rita's agreeing to meet me in the first place told me I was right about her having a confrontation with Manuel. If she lost the use of her arm in the struggle, maybe Manuel had lost his life.

Memories of other wakes floated in front of me. I'd witnessed an arrest at one not long ago, and had been threatened by a man pointing a gun at me at another. As the young voices filled the Bayside Chapel with lyrics of hope and redemption, I reexamined my life. A smart person would cut her losses, I reasoned. Send

Matt home to Revere and restrict my activities to comforting Elaine and José for a few more days before flying back to a normal retirement life.

But my purse was heavy with notes and lists about two murders, and my heart was filled with a sadness that would only be relieved if I could do something constructive with my time and my skills as a puzzle solver. I remembered a quote I used often in classes, by Marie Curie—"One never notices what's been done, one can only see what remains to be done."

By the time the program of hymns ended, I'd strengthened my resolve to find the murderer. As a concession to good judgment, I'd also decided to confess to Matt about my trip to the remote parking lot. Surely he wouldn't be able to resist honesty and sincerity.

I'd located Elaine and Matt, sitting together in the second row, behind José and Liz and other adults I took to be Manuel's aunts and uncles. Sidney and Jennifer Kellerman, the only other people I could identify, were almost directly in front of me, five or six rows away. I felt the Kellermans were central to the two murders, though I had nothing to go on except that Jennifer was Gary's housekeeper and Manuel's girlfriend. I wished I could talk to them again, and tried to think how I could approach them.

When I noticed Inspector Russell leaning against the wall on the other side of the parlor from me, I abandoned my plan for interviews and shrank as far as I could into my straight-backed chair. I wondered how his meeting with Matt had gone and whether he knew about Rita Johnson's alleged accident. If Berkeley were a foreign country, I thought, Russell would probably have me deported.

I stood up, prepared to join Elaine and Matt, but before I could move forward, I felt a heavy hand on my shoulder, pushing me back down to my seat. The law, I thought, come to arrest me.

I turned in my seat and came face-to-face with Lincoln Carver, his countenance grim, his breath reeking of alcohol and mouthwash.

TWENTY-TWO

"WE NEED TO TALK," Lincoln told me. He kept his voice low, though Bayside Chapel's guests had begun to mill around and speak in nearly normal tones. Apparently I'd missed most of the formal part, which ended with hymns by the glee club from Manuel's high school. The white-robed youngsters filed past us, not a gleeful smile among them.

Although I was in close proximity to police officers from each coast, I felt a twinge of anxiety as Carver's acid breath hit my neck. "Is that why you came to the service?" I asked him. "To talk to me?" I made an effort to sound annoyed rather than afraid.

"Can you step outside for a minute?"

"Certainly." As long as it's not in a remote parking lot, I added to myself.

As we stood up, I caught Matt's eye by accident. A tiny shiver went through my body as I gave him a weak smile. I turned and left the parlor with tall, handsome, slightly intoxicated Lincoln Carver.

"Okay," Carver said when we were a few yards from Bayside's entrance. I marveled at the steadiness of his gait and wondered if it meant he'd had a lot of practice drinking and walking. He leaned against a hydrant and expelled a deep breath. I turned my head from the odor. "I want to clear the air here," he said, apparently unaware of the irony in his remark. "I know you're working with the police."

I nodded, tipping my head from side to side instead of straight up and down, not quite as much of a lie, I told myself.

"I know you suspect me, but I did not kill that boy." Carver spoke slowly with a sincerity that I found myself trusting, in spite of the slight slur. I need to get training for this, I thought, I'm too easily fooled. "Manuel and I had a few chats on the Net about his beryllium paper. Then I guess he hacked into my system and found some things.''

I stood facing the entrance to the chapel, checking the groups gathering on the sidewalk. So far neither Matt nor Elaine had come out. I saw Inspector Russell talking to people I didn't know, and it occurred to me that he probably wouldn't have come to the wake if he'd already caught Manuel's killer, or thought he had. What did that mean about Marlene and Ted? I wondered. Had he questioned them and released them? Or had he not bothered at all with my theory of pornography-for-hire? And what did it mean about the man standing in front of me?

"What *things* did Manuel find?" I asked Lincoln Carver.

"Personal things. Like my stock market information, flyers for my singles' group activities. The schedule for the soccer team I coach. Nothing big, but somehow the kid knew we're not supposed to use lab computers for anything personal." Carver seemed to sober up as he talked. I had the thought that he wasn't a murderous alcoholic, but simply needed a drink before he could make this confession to me.

"Did he ask you for money?"

"Yeah. Fifty dollars. No big deal, I thought. I know it was stupid, but I sent a money order to this post office box he gave me." Carver frowned and crossed his arms over his chest. "You know, I spend all day and night at my job. I go in on weekends. And I'm exempt from overtime. And they won't give me a computer to take home. Of course I do some personal stuff while I'm there. Lots of people do. What do they expect?"

I wasn't anxious to get into a discussion of the lab's rules on appropriating government property for personal use, especially with someone not in top thinking form. I moved back on track.

"Did he ever ask for more?"

"No. Strange, huh? Makes me think he was basically not a bad kid, at least not yet. Though I don't know why I think that. He certainly wasn't good to me." Carver shook his head, rubbing his hand over his bald scalp, as if entertaining doubts about the deceased teenager.

"When did all this happen?"

"A few months ago. Maybe March. I could find out exactly if it's important."

"Didn't it occur to you that maybe this same kid was the one who hacked into Gary's computer and uploaded the pornography?"

"It crossed my mind, but why would I open that can of worms?"

Why indeed, I thought. "You know you should tell all this to the police."

"And have it get back to my boss? No way. Anyway, I'm too embarrassed. And I didn't kill the boy. I thought maybe you could put in a good word—don't bring it up, of course, but if it comes out while they're investigating..."

"It doesn't work that way, Lincoln. It's not as if I can vouch for you and that's all it takes. I can't force you to go the police, but I'd like you to reconsider."

"Yeah. Well, thanks for listening."

Carver gave me a thin smile and took off toward the parking lot. I wondered briefly if I should alert Russell of a possible DUI in the making. I found myself instead looking at Carver's shoes, checking whether they matched the ones I'd become familiar with at my rest room stop. Carver was wearing brown tassel loafers.

I HAD ABOUT two minutes between the time Carver left and Matt and Elaine's exit from the chapel. Behind them were Manuel's mother and a portly man I took to be her new husband, since he'd sat next to her in the chapel, with his arm around her shoulders. At least in outward appearance, Liz had chosen an extremely different type the second time around. Husband number two seemed older, the solid businessman type with a pocket watch and no landscaped facial hair. The man was carrying a box of tissues, holding it ready for Liz—leaving me with an odd, out-of-place recollection of allergy-ridden Gary Larkin.

"Busy day?" Matt asked, greeting me with a kiss on the cheek.

I felt a blush creep to the same spot, whether from the kiss or from the question about my day, I couldn't decide.

"I can't wait to hear about yours," I said, satisfied with the diversion I'd come up with.

"Where have you been?" Elaine asked. Her direct question gave me less room to waffle.

"I'll tell you all about it," I said. "How are things going here?"

"We're all going back to José's. But don't feel you have to come back again."

Before I could make a decision, Matt voiced his preference.

"I talked to Russell today, and Gloria and I have some things to work out about the cases. Maybe we'll come by later?"

"Fine," Elaine said, touching my shoulder. My friend seemed to have aged greatly since my arrival, and I wished I could ease her burden.

NOTHING ABOUT THIS TRIP has gone as I expected, I thought. A surprise dinner party organized by a woman I hardly knew, three frightening incidents, two murders instead of one. And Matt making coffee in Elaine's kitchen. I could hardly wait for our debriefing session, delayed by snack preparation and some welcome-back snuggling on the couch.

A phone call from Rita got the down-to-business ball rolling. I moved back to the rocker to take her call.

"I'm still at Alta Bates," she said. "But I'm expecting my roommate to come and get me any minute. I'm calling from a wheelchair. Hospital rules."

"I'm amazed you sound so good," I told her. "That was a nasty bruise." Maybe I can tell Matt about my day this way, I thought. The easy way out—let him eavesdrop.

"I can't believe I wasn't wearing my helmet."

"Didn't I see it next to you in the lot?"

"Yeah, but I had it hanging on my handlebars. Cool, huh?"

"Did you hit something in the road and fall?" I asked this for the benefit of Matt—a casual question from a routine day. I was glad he couldn't hear Rita's sarcastic laugh.

"Hardly," she said. "Somebody hit me with two tons of metal."

I mouthed a thank-you to Matt as he put a mug of coffee in

front of me, wondering how much longer I could play out two scenes at the same time. "Oh?" I said to Rita, as if she'd told me her latest beryllium calculations came out wrong.

"It was very scary. I took one of the lab bikes out to the lot the way I always do. I was a couple of aisles from my car and this SUV comes barreling down on me. It took me a while to react—I couldn't believe it was happening."

"Were you able to give the police a description?" I asked, the dark SUV that had run me off the road coming immediately to my mind.

"Not much. Dark green or black was all I could tell them. As far as they know, it was some nut pumped up on his new all-terrain vehicle."

I wanted to ask Rita whether she believed what she'd told the police—that it was a random act. I was even tempted to tell her my windy road experience, to see if we could come up with more details by brainstorming. Did she notice if the license plate contained 767 for example? Frustrated at not being able to speak more directly, I fidgeted in my chair, keeping my eyes on Matt sitting across from me on the couch.

He reached over and patted my wiggling ankle.

"Why don't you just have that interview as if I weren't here," he said, clearly pleased at his powers of observation.

I smiled and mouthed "okay," part of me relieved to have it in the open.

"Rita, I'm wondering why you parked in that remote lot," I said as if I'd forgotten the reason she'd given me earlier in the day.

"I usually come in late, and it's only place you can find a spot after nine."

"But I thought I remembered you were at the lab early the day Gary Larkin's body was found? Around seven-thirty."

"I don't like where this is going, but I'll tell you anyway. I had to leave early that day, so I made up the time in the morning."

"I'm sorry to annoy you. I'm trying to tie up loose ends." The old half-truth again. Maybe it was time I went to current movies and picked up some new lines, I thought.

"Anything else?" she asked me, annoyance still in her voice.

"Yes. Have you considered this incident today might have something to do with your meeting me?"

"Of course I've considered that. But I can't think of why. It's not that I have anything on anyone. Except myself."

"Who was in your office when we set up the time and place?"

"Let's see. Kellerman, Carver. I can't remember if Pursiano was still there by then. But so what? They wouldn't hurt me. And anyway, I know all their vehicles and that wasn't one of them."

I considered ruling out all the Larkin team on that basis, wondering what kinds of cars Marlene and Ted drove. Certainly Ted fit the stereotype of a muscle car owner. Also, it always did my heart good when I could eliminate a scientist from my list of suspects. As Matt once reminded me, I'd rather the cold-blooded murderer be a little old lady in tennis shoes than someone from the lofty profession I'd spent my career in.

"Are you still willing to talk to me? I could come there."

"I'll be leaving here in a few minutes I'm sure. And I can just tell you over the phone. It's not that much. I met Manuel and we had a fight."

That sounds like a lot to me, I thought, considering he's now dead. I refrained from making the judgment out loud.

Rita continued. "It was on Wednesday evening. He'd been shaking me down for money."

"He hacked into your computer?"

"Right." Rita didn't sound at all surprised that I'd know. Like Carver, she probably thought I had an inside track on information from the police. "We'd chatted a few times about his school paper on chronic beryllium disease. I actually gave him some data that he wouldn't have been able to get for months by any normal routes."

I imagined Rita slamming her fist on the arm of her wheelchair at the scam that had been worked on her by a teenage boy, especially one she'd helped with a term paper.

"What did he find on your computer?"

"I've been doing business for our gender lawsuit on my lab system. I don't have one at home. And I'm here all hours of the day and night, watching the data runs, setting up for experiments. You name it.''

I wondered if Rita and Lincoln Carver had gotten together on their excuses. Occult compensation seemed the defense du jour.

"So you arranged to meet Manuel?"

"Yeah, he said he wanted to show me some printouts he downloaded from my files. The kid was smart enough to know it wouldn't help our case in court. He thought it would be cool to meet at the pit. I wasn't about to pay him, but I figured it wouldn't hurt to meet him."

"And this was Wednesday evening, about what time?"

"Around five o'clock. Before dinner, I'm sure. It was still plenty light. We talked for about ten minutes. He told me what he had on me."

"Had he brought printouts or any proof?"

"No, but I could tell he knew what was on my system. He was such a wise guy, I hit him—just slapped him, really. The way you'd hit your kid. Well, maybe you wouldn't hit your kid. But I am old enough to be his mother. He pushed me away and we got into this ridiculous fight. I fell back into the freaking pit. It took me a while to climb out. I was in screaming pain."

"Did he help you out?" I asked.

"Actually, he did. He seemed almost apologetic when he realized I was really hurt. But not enough to suit me."

Rita's words sounded tough and unemotional, but her voice cracked several times during her clinical explanation. Whether from guilt or innocent grief, I couldn't tell.

By the time she got to the punch line, I could barely understand her, but it sounded like "I drove off and left him there."

TWENTY-THREE

I GAVE MATT a big smile as I hung up the phone. "Okay, it's your turn to share," I said.

Matt's laugh included the charming "whoa" sound that I loved, and was loud enough to reach the Galiganis in Revere, I told him.

I finally agreed to his terms, giving him a more full description of my trip to B-4 than he'd have gotten from my half of the conversation with Rita. To my surprise, he was interested in the technical details.

"Tell me again how you happened to hear that interview with Rita?" he asked me. "Where you catch her in the high-dusting lie."

"Call it fortuitous browsing. I came upon it while I was cruising BUL's pages on the Internet. The WOSE interview had been recorded on videotape and broadcast over the lab's closed-circuit television system and its website. Elaine has the right software on her computer to access it—it's called real audio client software. It converts the file to something you can hear and see. It's called 'streaming audio,' because the audio streams out..."

"I'm glad I asked," Matt said, holding up his palm in a "that will do" gesture.

I waited for his usual dressing-down about going to a remote location to meet a murder suspect, but it didn't come. Still Josephine's daughter, I found myself reverting to childhood, needing a reprimand to complete my day. I thought up reasons why Matt wouldn't admonish me—he didn't care for my safety anymore, came to my mind, but our last couple of weeks together helped me move quickly past that notion.

It could only be that some of my alleged meddling had paid off with Russell, I decided.

"My theory about Marlene and Ted's hiring Manuel was correct, wasn't it?"

Matt smiled and nodded.

"So?" I said, instigating him as I had many times when one of my theories passed a critical test.

"Nice work, Gloria," he said, and we enjoyed a congratulatory kiss.

MATT SHARED the information he had from his meeting with Russell. The disappointing news was that my partial license plate for the SUV—767—had turned up nothing. Better news was that after lengthy questioning in separate rooms, Marlene Korner and Ted Gernich, the khaki twins, as I thought of them, had confessed to hiring Manuel to hack into Gary's computer.

"I guess they realized it would show up in their bank records anyway."

"Have they been arrested?"

"No. Of course, they insist they didn't kill either Gary or Manuel. Their main goal seemed to be to give Gary the hardest time they could, and maybe have a chance at more money out of the divorce settlement."

"I guess they figured their lawyer could work his way around the no-fault policy."

"Right. But at the moment there's no evidence to connect them to either murder. Especially Gary Larkin's; neither one had anyway of getting into the lab."

"How did you convince Russell to question them in the first place?" I asked. "I'll bet you didn't tell him it was my idea."

Matt gave me an embarrassed nod. "He didn't ask, I didn't tell."

I remembered Russell's rudeness to me, interrupting the flow of polite, mild-mannered law enforcement personnel I'd dealt with since I'd begun consultant work with the Revere Police Department. I thought of the police-sponsored safety programs in the schools, and the dozens of RPD officers who volunteered to read to elementary school children as part of a national campaign to improve reading skills. None of them would have been rude to me, I decided.

Only Matt's partner, George Berger, had been resistant to my participation at first, and I'd won him over easily with a few flattering comments about his infant daughter. Russell was the exception that gave me more appreciation for the others.

"Is he going to check out the rest of the people on the beryllium team?" I asked, as if Russell's poor attitude meant he needed coaching in investigative procedures from a civilian. "We know Manuel hacked into both Lincoln Carver's and Rita Johnson's files. Shouldn't he question them?"

"I mentioned that possibility. I didn't know about Johnson's connection at the time, however. I'll give him a call. See if that tips the scales."

"Maybe we can add some weight in our direction." I moved my hands up and down as if they were the pans of an analytic balance.

Matt looked at me sideways. "What did you have in mind?"

"Kellerman and Pursiano, the other two team members. We could call them and ask..."

My voice trailed off as I considered the complicated phone calls my plan would entail.

"Ask if they've been blackmailed by a teenager lately?"

"Why not? What's there to lose?" I realized I was showing how unfettered I was by the usual rules and procedures that governed official investigations. "Let me call them. I've already established contact with them. If we see a pattern, it could be very useful."

Matt shook his head in a way that told me I'd almost won. I sweetened the deal. "You can sit right here and make sure I don't make any dates in dark alleys."

"It's bright alleys that seem to be your problem."

"Good point. No meetings in well-lighted places, then."

I flipped open my notebook to the page with key phone numbers in the cases and pushed the sequence for Pursiano at work. It was nearly nine o'clock, almost exactly the time I'd called him three days ago, and I was counting on his still being on swing shift. The line was about to switch to an answering service when he picked up.

"Beryllium Facility. Pursiano." Pursiano's voice was nearly

drowned out by equipment sounds. I pictured him in his coveralls, standing at a wall phone next to a vacuum pump or a lathe, and had a sudden longing to be in a lab coat, the kind I'd worn when my life was simpler.

"This is Gloria Lamerino. I talked to you last Saturday about..."

"I remember. What can I do for you?"

"You've probably heard the news that the teenager I asked you about, Manuel Martinez, was found dead over the weekend."

"No, can't say I did."

"I'd like to ask a question..."

"Can't hear you too well."

I removed the phone from my ear and looked at it, as if there were some way to increase the volume on my end. Get to the point, I told myself.

"Has anyone ever hacked into your computer?" I nearly shouted, speaking slowly. No wonder the police don't interview this way, I thought.

"Don't have a computer."

"No computer?"

"No computer. I've been asking for one, but Kellerman's cheap. Anything else? I've got to get back."

"Kellerman has to approve a computer purchase?"

"Yeah, he's the one with the purse strings for the team. Buys all the supplies for our group. And he's cheap. Has to have things in triplicate, if you know what I mean. Anything else?"

I thought about asking him how he liked his last performance review from the late Gary Larkin, but the noisy line and Pursiano's impatient tone dissuaded me.

"No, thank you," I said finally, and hung up the phone. I thought back to resource managers I'd known—purse string holders, as Pursiano put it—all of them as frugal as if the money were their own and not the government's. I supposed we should be grateful for their parsimony, but it was hard to deal with when supplies seemed necessary.

"No computer?" Matt sounded as surprised as I was.

"Can't get one out of Kellerman."

"Didn't you say he's the modeler for the group?"

I nodded. "Apparently, he's also the purchaser."

I punched the numbers for the Kellerman residence. After their traumatic appearance at José's on Saturday night, I was reasonably sure they wouldn't have gone back to the house after tonight's wake.

Kellerman answered on the first ring.

True to what I remembered of his general disposition, he sounded in no mood for pleasantries. I got right to the point of my call. "We've learned that Manuel might have taken advantage of his access to the beryllium team to hack into lab computers. I'm wondering if you had any such problem?"

Kellerman cleared his throat and uttered a laugh that sounded embarrassed, as if a calculational error of his had been discovered by someone right out of grad school.

"I guess there's no point in hiding it now." He said. "I didn't want to bother José about it, and now that Manuel's gone...But, yeah, he did approach me. He found out I do my personal banking on the lab computer."

"That's it?"

Kellerman coughed, as if considering whether to say more to another potential blackmailer. "And, uh, my stocks. Not that I have a lot of investments. But I have some, and I like to check everyday."

"Did he ask for money?"

"No. It never got that far. He, well, he died." Kellerman had lowered his voice, and I wondered if Jennifer might be in the room. "Did he get money from some people? Do the police think that's how he got killed?"

"They're looking at that," I said, grateful that Kellerman hadn't challenged my connection to the police. I didn't relish telling him my call was semi-authorized by a cop whose jurisdiction was three thousand miles to the east. I smiled at Matt to illustrate how completely safe I was keeping myself.

"I hope they get to the bottom of this," Kellerman said.

"So do I. One other thing. Would you be willing to let me talk to Jennifer?"

"You don't think she had anything to do with this?" Kellerman spoke like a concerned father, and I imagined he'd be merciless with anyone who tried to harm his daughter or accuse her of wrongdoing.

I rushed to reassure him. "Of course not. But it occurred to me that she's lost two people in the last couple of weeks—a neighbor she knew and worked for, and a young man who meant a lot to her," I said, relieved that I caught myself before calling Manuel her boyfriend. "I can tell how well you care for her, but she might need a woman to talk to." I half expected Kellerman to inform me Jennifer had three aunts, four female cousins, and two grandmothers, but instead he bolstered my case.

"Jennifer's mother died of cancer last year."

I drew in my breath. "I'm sorry. I'd forgotten it was that short a time ago. All the more reason for me to talk to her."

"I suppose it couldn't hurt."

"I could stop by now."

"No. She's already in bed. She's been sick all day." That's why you answered so quickly and are speaking so softly, I told him, but not out loud. "I'm not even sure I'm going to let her go to the funeral. I might take her out of school and go to our place in Tahoe. Just to get away from all this for a while."

"I understand why you'd make that decision, but remember, she's going to need closure somehow. Keeping her from the funeral might delay that."

"We'll see."

"I'll be going to the service. It's not till eleven o'clock. What if I stop by your house beforehand, whether Jennifer's going to the funeral or not?"

"I guess that could work."

Kellerman gave me his address, two doors from Gary's place, on Ashby.

"Thanks. And thanks for your time, Dr. Kellerman. I'll see you tomorrow."

I hung up the phone and frowned at Matt. I took a long breath and folded my hands on my lap as if it were recess at school.

"You may have a future on the force," Matt said. "That was pretty good."

"Then how come I feel so awful? I made it sound like I'm

God's chosen therapist for troubled teens, when I really just want to interrogate her.''

"It's part of the job."

I looked at Matt, moved that he seemed to be including me among his colleagues in law enforcement. He took my hands in his, and I became aware that he wanted to share this sometimes painful aspect of his life's career. Working with passionless lasers, steel chassis, and cold, inanimate DC power supplies for thirty years seemed the easy way out.

"You have to do this all the time, don't you? Push your real feelings down so you can get to the truth."

Matt nodded. "You tell yourself the end justifies the means. Maybe you can help this person through a difficult time, but that would be just a lucky spin-off. What you have to do is find out who broke the law, and how you can prove it."

He drew me off the rocker, next to him on the couch. "You're doing a great job," he said.

I wanted to tell him how grateful I was to be close to him, to learn more about him everyday. I had to rely on body language to communicate the message. All I could say was a soft "Thanks."

TWENTY-FOUR

BY THE TIME our phone interview session was over, it was after nine-thirty. I convinced Matt there was still time to drop in at José's. My motives were less than pure, a circumstance more and more frequent these days. For one thing, I hadn't seen José since Manuel's hacking had been confirmed, and I wondered if he blamed me for the discovery. Another reason not to envy the life of a cop, I thought. Even if turning up criminal activity helped find his son's murderer, José probably wouldn't thank me for it.

I also hoped to meet Russell in a less intimidating situation. Catching me snooping in Manuel's room put him at a considerable advantage the first time.

We gave brief consideration to walking the mile or so from Elaine's in Walnut Square to José's in the Elmwood district.

"Too late," Matt said.

"Everyone would be gone by the time we got there," I said.

"We can start our exercise program when we get back to Revere."

"Good idea."

We called a cab.

José's house was less crowded than the night before, his neighbors undoubtedly busy cooking for the reception after the funeral. Russell was present, as well as Manuel's mother and her husband, who was introduced to me as Steven Steelman. Even his name is solid, I thought.

I watched out of the corner of my eye as Russell worked the room. I wondered how much of his questioning was done this way, instead of at the station. I remembered Matt's showing me what he called the "soft interview room" at the Revere police station—a comfortable setting, with a window onto the street and pleasant landscapes hanging on the walls—for talking to most of the victims' family and friends.

For more likely suspects he used the "hard interview room." Innocent as I was, I'd shivered when I entered the tiny dark space with a single metal table and two chairs. The seemingly innocuous panels on the walls hid a tangle of wires that led to cameras and microphones.

"Confession by intimidation?" I'd asked, prompting a slightly embarrassed nod from Matt.

Looking at Russell in José's living room, I figured him for an excellent intimidator.

While José was busy on the phone, I took the opportunity to draw Elaine aside.

"How do you think he's doing?" I asked her, tilting my head in José's direction.

Elaine shrugged. "Who'd be happy to find out his son had a shady scheme to pick up extra cash?" she asked in a tone with a hard edge.

"Does he know how the police discovered it?"

"Do you mean, does he know you dug it up? And is he blaming the messenger? The answer is yes, and sort of." Elaine twisted her wrist from side to side to indicate a position halfway between yes and no on the question of my status with José. Her navy sweater, limp and wrinkled, hung crooked on her shoulders. The bags under her eyes and her lack of perfect grooming worried me as much as her coldness to me.

"Are you blaming me, Elaine?"

We'd been standing by the kitchen counter, piled high with the sour-smelling remains of a buffet. I'd skipped dinner, but the dry, crusty cheeses and droopy vegetables didn't tempt me. Elaine fell back onto the same stool where I'd brought Jennifer Kellerman to tears two nights before. I'm becoming a nasty person, I thought.

Elaine threw up her hands. "I'm sorry, Gloria. How can I think this is your fault? You did exactly what we asked you to do." I hugged my friend, a process made more difficult by her sitting on a high stool when there was already a four-inch difference in our heights. "It's hard enough to lose a son, but under these circumstances..."

"Maybe it would be better if I left, to give José sometime to adjust."

Elaine pointed behind me to where José was leaning against the door frame. He seemed comfortable enough to have been standing there through our whole conversation.

"I've already adjusted," he said, walking toward us. "At least a little. Now all I want is to find who killed my son. Whatever he did wrong, he didn't deserve to be murdered."

I breathed a long sigh. "You're absolutely right, José. And that's what we're working on."

"Who's working on it?" Russell swaggered toward us, his hands in the pockets of his suede jacket, like a tall, thin lawman of the Old West. Though José's kitchen was already very crowded, I wondered where Matt was. Maybe Russell ran him out of town, I thought, in keeping with the western motif. "Don't tell me you're still investigating, Dr. Lamerino?"

A host of sarcastic remarks came to my lips, but I chose a more or less polite response.

"Of course, I meant the Berkeley Police Department is investigating. But every now and then information critical to a case comes from ordinary citizens."

"Anything you'd like to share?" Russell had closed in on me. He'd insinuated himself between me and Elaine, bringing his breast-pocket badge on a level with my eyes. I'd dealt with men taller than me all my life, however, and knew exactly how far back I needed to step—three feet, and I'd significantly decreased the angle it took for me to look into his eyes.

"I'd be happy to share what I've learned," I told him.

"You can use the den down the hall," José said, apparently happy for any action in his son's case. "Second door on the right."

Russell nodded and led the way to the tiny room José used as a home office. I looked around for Matt but couldn't see him. He's either in the bathroom or Manuel's room, I figured, hoping for the latter.

We sat in the den, across from each other on two computer chairs. Entering first, Russell had taken the one with arms, undoubtedly a power move, as if to make it clear: No matter whose office we were in, he was in charge.

I wasn't surprised to learn that "sharing" for Russell meant I'd tell him everything I knew, and he'd listen. I gave him all the information I had on Manuel's attempts to profit from what he'd learned by hacking into the beryllium team's computers—Rita had been using the lab system for her lawsuit, Carver for personal activities, and Kellerman for his personal banking and stock market information.

"I'm convinced Manuel's hacking has to do with both deaths," I told Russell.

Russell frowned and shook his head. "Except for one sixteen-year-old girl, there's nothing to connect the two victims. The first guy died in the lab, and we don't even know where or when the second one was killed. By the way, I'd like you to account for your whereabouts since Wednesday evening."

My eyes widened at the implication, the first of my life, that I needed an alibi in a murder case. As much as I tried to present the posture of one deeply offended, I swallowed audibly and felt a flush come to my face. Russell's thin smile irritated me more than his pseudo-accusation, however, and I recovered enough to throw back my shoulders in righteous indignation.

"I was in Revere, Massachusetts, where I live, on Wednesday. I didn't arrive in California until Thursday afternoon. And Manuel was most likely killed at the pit on Wednesday evening, between five-thirty and six," I said.

Russell uncrossed his long legs and leaned forward, quick on the draw, so to speak. "And what makes you more certain of the time of death than the Alameda County coroner?"

For a few seconds, I considered retracting my remark or waving it off as a wild guess. I wondered if Fifth Amendment rights applied only to statements made under oath. I decided to tell the truth, at least most of it.

"I talked to Rita Johnson. She told me she met Manuel at the pit on Wednesday evening, around five o'clock. They discussed what he'd learned from hacking, then they had a fight. From the timing she gave me, I figure it was about five-thirty when she left him there alive. If she's telling the truth, of course."

"And if you're telling the truth."

I frowned at him, thinking of Russell as a wisecracking old sheriff instead of the Berkeley PD inspector he was. I pictured half doors swinging behind him, and continued as if he hadn't interrupted me.

"Manuel's bike was at the pit. It's too much of a stretch to think he rode down the hill, then back up before he was killed. My guess is the killer knew he was going to meet Rita and went up there himself. He waited until Rita left, then killed Manuel."

Just the way he knew Rita was going to meet me this afternoon, I thought—a bit of information I'd decided not to share with Russell. I concocted a half plan to ask Rita if she could remember how she set up the meeting with Manuel.

Russell took notes as I told him how I'd stumbled onto Rita's WOSE interview on the Internet, and then got her to confess about the pit meeting. He asked a few questions without looking at me. When we were finished, he flipped his notebook closed and stood up. It was clear he wasn't about to do his part in the sharing exercise. I imagined his grade school report card: "does not work well with others."

"And you knew Manuel's bike was at the pit, how?" Russell asked, moving my hopes of protecting Terry Spender to thin ice.

In my debriefing, I'd tried not to inadvertently reveal anything I could have gotten only from the police report Terry had smuggled to me. Implicating a suspect like Rita Johnson was one thing, but I saw no reason to reveal Terry's role. She'd have to work with Russell long after I'd gone home.

I swallowed hard. "Lucky guess."

Russell glared at me. "When did you say you and your boyfriend are going back East?"

"I didn't." I stood up and walked by him out the door.

At about ten-thirty, José's house emptied out, and he and Elaine replaced Russell and me in the den, for what turned out to be an hour-long private conversation. At the same time, Matt and I had our own chat in the living room. Like a medical/professional building dedicated to couples' counseling, I thought.

I could tell from Matt's demeanor he had something to tell

me, and I predicted the topic correctly: The case he'd been following in Revere had come to a critical point.

"I slipped out to that convenience store on the corner a while ago, and called in," he said in a voice that presaged bad news.

"The Chapman case?"

He nodded. "I promised to head right back when they needed me."

"And they need you?"

Matt took my hand. "I have to testify first thing Wednesday morning."

I swallowed my disappointment. Although I knew about his pending case I'd assumed Matt would be able to stay for the rest of the week, and return to Boston with me on Saturday. Why am I upset? I asked myself, since he wasn't supposed to be here in the first place.

I managed a thin smile. "So you'll have to fly out Tuesday. Tomorrow," I said, sticking to cold facts.

"I booked a flight at nine in the morning. I know the funeral service is at eleven, so if you don't have time to drive me, I'll take a cab."

I nodded. Under other circumstances I probably would have argued about driving him myself, but I didn't trust my voice not to crack.

"I'll see you Saturday, at home," he said with what sounded like a forced cheeriness. "I'm sorry I didn't get to show you around the Bay Area."

We moved closer together on the couch and rested against each other, waiting in silence for Elaine and José. I was sure an observer would have guessed we were about to part for longer than four days. How do these things happen? I wondered. A year ago I hardly knew Sergeant Matt Gennaro, and now I can hardly get through a week without him. Something else to ask Elaine about.

ELAINE, MATT, AND I left the house together close to midnight, leaving José by himself.

"I need my own bed and shower," Elaine said once we'd unlocked her front door.

"Matt will be back at his own bed and shower tomorrow night," I said, hoping I didn't sound as pouty as I felt.

"Oh no. You have to testify, huh? I feel terrible we haven't taken you anywhere. We didn't even get to San Francisco."

"It's not your usual vacation schedule. Don't worry about it," Matt said. "There'll be other times." I hoped he was right.

Elaine's answering machine had two messages, both for me. The first was from Rose Galigani, hoping we were all fine.

"It's almost one o'clock here," she said. "Thought I'd call since I'm awake. Frank got a late-night summons. He had to handle a client on short notice."

"Handling a client" was one of Rose's many euphemisms for embalming and preparing a corpse for burial.

The second call was from Lincoln Carver.

"Call me when you get in. No matter what time it is." I checked my watch, wondering if twelve-thirty was beyond Carver's threshold. I decided to take him at his word, and punched in his number.

"Are you trying to be funny?" he asked me as soon as he heard my voice. There was no hint of inebriation, or sleepiness in his tone, in spite of the hour.

"What are you talking about, Lincoln?"

"Someone's been hacking into my files again. I figure you're as good a candidate as any."

TWENTY-FIVE

IT TOOK A FEW MINUTES for Lincoln Carver to calm down enough to tell me the story. When he'd accessed his E-mail from his home computer, he'd come face-to-face with copies of earlier E-mails he'd sent to friends and business associates.

"Someone is sending your own E-mails back to you?" I tried to pull the facts out of his emotional outpouring.

"Yeah. There's nothing bad in them. Most of it's legitimate business. It's just to prove it can be done, I guess. To get to me." I heard a long, deep sigh, as if Carver had been doing push-ups while he talked.

A flag went up in my brain. "I thought you didn't have a computer," I said, happy I'd caught a suspect in an inconsistency.

"I just bought one. After all this trouble, I figured I'd better be clean."

How handy, I thought.

"So, it wasn't you?" he asked.

"No. Why would you think that, Lincoln?"

"I don't know. I thought maybe you were trying to intimidate me into going to the police."

"I wouldn't do that, even if I could. And the police are probably on their way to you anyway." At least I hoped Russell would follow up on what I'd told him during our so-called sharing session.

"Thanks a lot." Carver hung up with a loud noise.

I breathed out and rubbed the sore spot between my eyes.

"What do you think?" Matt asked when I relayed the latest conversation to him and Elaine.

"I haven't a clue, but it's late and I'm sure it will be clearer in the morning."

We sat in Elaine's living room, in our wrinkled clothing, almost asleep, as if we were all too tired to climb the stairs. We made plans for the morning—I'd drop Matt at Oakland airport at eight for his nine o'clock flight, have plenty of time to meet Jennifer, and then pick up Elaine for the funeral.

"We should all get to bed," Elaine said, echoing my thoughts. "Not that I'll sleep. I'll probably have dreams of Liz and her tissues."

I snapped to attention in my rocking chair. "Tissues?"

"Liz must have gone through a whole box just tonight. I felt so sorry for her."

"Tissues. That's what's missing," I said, suddenly alert.

"What do tissues have to do with anything?" Elaine asked. Without the advantage of my adrenaline rush, she sounded too weary to care about the answer.

"Gary Larkin had bad allergies. He had all the normal ones, like grass and pollen, and possibly even special sensitivity to beryllium. Everyone I talked to mentioned how he carried tissues with him, had them handy all the time."

"So?"

"So, why aren't there any tissues in his house or work space?"

While I talked, I shuffled through the envelopes and notebooks I'd scattered over Elaine's coffee table since I'd arrived. I found the envelope of photographs Terry Spender had given me, with shots from the lab the day Gary Larkin's body had been found, and from Gary's house. I spread the pictures on the table, one end of the array in front of Matt, the other in front of Elaine. I sat across from them, in the rocker, with an upside-down view of the evidence.

"There. Do you see tissues anywhere?" I asked, realizing my tone sounded like a dare.

Matt and Elaine studied the photographs, turning them sideways, clockwise and counterclockwise, as if they were pieces of abstract art with dubious orientation in the space-time continuum. The three of us took turns pointing to places where there logically would have been a box of tissues in Gary's home—on the table next to his bed, on the counter in the bathroom, by the computer in his office, next to the recliner that faced his television set. In the lab photos, only generic Labwipes were present: the large, rough tissue more suited to toxic spills than human skin.

Matt scratched his head and focused on the photographs. "No tissues," he said.

"Right. No tissues," Elaine said. "But I'm still not sure I know what it means."

"I'm going to check one more source," I said. I picked up the phone and punched in Pursiano's number, which I now knew by heart. I wondered if the night shift always got so many phone calls. While I waited for someone to answer, I heard Matt and Elaine's conversation.

"She thinks whoever killed Gary Larkin removed all his tissues," he said to Elaine.

"Because?"

Matt threw up his hands and shook his head. "The tissues are the murder weapon. I can hardly wait for the explanation."

"Who are you calling at this hour?" Elaine asked me.

I covered the mouthpiece and whispered. "Night shift." I tapped my fingers on my knees, from impatience, and also because I'd read somewhere that fidgeting helps burn calories.

"I'd better make some coffee," Elaine said.

"Is there anymore of that pizza?" Matt asked, alerting me to the fact that we hadn't had dinner, fine hostess that I was.

After a few rings, the night shift answered.

"Beryllium Facility. Daddario."

Another Italian, I thought. Not a statistically likely sample, since I'd only met one or two during my three decades in California. "Is Larry Pursiano there?" I asked, envisioning the group of technicians forming their own little Sons of Italy club. The smell of pizza being bombarded by microwaves while I was on hold reinforced my scenario.

When Pursiano heard my voice again, he sounded fed up.

"I have work to do," he told me. "And don't you ever sleep? This is beginning to seem like harassment, Dr....?"

"It's Lamerino," I said, hoping my name would appeal to his sense of Italian-American pride. "I'm really sorry to bother you. I know you're busy. I have just one important question."

"Okay, shoot."

"Do you remember seeing a box of tissues in the lab the morning you found Gary Larkin's body?"

In spite of the loud equipment hum in the background, I heard Pursiano's long breath, almost a whistle. "How would I remember something like that? The guy was on the floor, dead. I called for help. I didn't look around for something to blow my nose on."

"Just think for a minute. He always had tissues near him, didn't he?"

"Correct." Pursiano sounded exasperated.

I wanted to give him a mental exercise, or maybe hypnosis— close your eyes, Larry, I'd say, try to visualize the scene, look around for tissues, perhaps a small travel-size box—but I didn't think Pursiano was the meditative type.

After a few seconds of silence, during which I thought he'd stormed back to his bench, leaving the phone dangling from the wall, I heard his voice again.

"You know, I don't remember seeing tissues on the cart or the bench. There was always at least one box of some good stuff Gary brought from home. He didn't like the Labwipes you could get free from the supply closet. And lately his allergies had gotten worse, like he was having trouble breathing, so he had them with him all the time." Pursiano seemed lost in his own re-creation of Wednesday, May 17. "What does all this mean anyway?"

"We're not sure right now, but it could be very important. Thank you very much."

"That's it," I said to the now-awake and snacking Matt and Elaine. "Someone spiked Gary's tissues."

ELAINE HAD CUT the leftover pizza into bite-size pieces and arranged them with sliced pears on a lovely ceramic plate she'd bought at the classy annual Stanford crafts fair. I was sure the artist had envisioned more elegant hors d'oeuvres on the platter, but I greeted the gesture with a silent "welcome back" to Elaine's old, gracious self. Between gulps of coffee and nibbles of hot, stringy cheese, we talked through a plausible murder scenario.

"First, beryllium is not a controlled substance," I said. "You can buy it from a catalog."

"I've never seen it in any of mine—Neiman Marcus, Bloomingdale's, Nordstrom," Elaine said, showing she'd also recovered her sense of humor, and at one in the morning, at that.

"All the killer had to do was sprinkle Gary's tissues with beryllium powder. He—or she—would have had to start a few months ago. It would take a while for the damage to his lungs to build up and eventually kill him."

I spoke slowly, trying to remember what I'd read about the dosage it would take to accomplish a murder by such means. I'd heard that inhaling beryllium powder would be like breathing in finely ground china. I shuddered and took a sip of coffee as if to wash down bits of glass in my esophagus.

"Did Gary's allergies have anything to do with this?" Elaine asked.

"Maybe. For all anyone knew, he was allergic to beryllium as well as all the usual irritants, making it easier to kill him with it. Remember, he'd never take the new tests for beryllium sensitivity."

"Because he figured he knew how to handle it properly?" Elaine asked.

"Partly. Also, I think he didn't want to call attention to anything negative about beryllium."

"Didn't you say only about two percent of the population has beryllium sensitivity?" Matt asked.

"That's the current thinking. Scientists like Gary, intent on using beryllium more widely, stress how small that number is, but the Department of Energy is actually tightening regulations. The point is, however, that just about anyone would die from the kind of exposure I think Gary Larkin had—he'd have been breathing it in on a daily basis, every time he picked up a tissue. And a couple of people have mentioned his allergies had gotten worse lately, which could have meant that his lungs were deteriorating from the beryllium exposure."

Matt finished the last piece of pizza and leaned over the coffee table, summarizing out loud. "So, the murderer douses all Gary's tissues with the powder for several months, then gets rid of the evidence as soon as Gary's dead."

I nodded.

"So, we've got the evil tissues as the means for the Larkin murder. And hacking as the motive for the Martinez murder. We're still missing a few pieces here."

I couldn't argue with that.

"Someone had to have access to Gary's house and lab to keep spiking the tissues, then remove them at the end." Elaine said. "That could eliminate Marlene Korner and her boyfriend. They wouldn't have been able to get into the lab."

"No, but it's not clear that all Gary's tissue boxes had to be tampered with. Maybe just the ones at home. The more I think about it, it could be a coincidence that his personal tissues are missing from the lab. He went into the lab late that night, after a business trip. He might not have been organized enough to carry his tissues in to the work area."

"And you said Pursiano didn't mention the box of lab brand tissues that's here in the photograph," Matt said. "So how valid is his recollection of what was outside camera range?"

And how accurate is his observation that technicians don't compete for good raises? I wondered.

"Let's say the killer worked only with the tissues in Gary's house." Elaine spoke thoughtfully, then nearly jumped from her seat on her floral couch. "Kellerman," she said as if she'd cracked a code. "Jennifer worked in Gary's house. Her father would have access to a key. Or even Jennifer herself."

I had a hard time picturing the delicate young Jennifer Kellerman murdering someone by a process of deliberate, drawn-out suffocation. But murder isn't logical to begin with, I reminded myself. Before we had time to condemn the Kellermans by virtue of their having a key to Gary's house, Matt put a realistic spin on our deliberations.

"Do you know how easy it is to get into someone's house? With or without a key. A lot easier than getting into the lab. Most people leave keys to their doors in very obvious spots—above the frame, under the mat, in a plant."

Elaine's eyes roamed toward her front door, to where I knew

she kept her extra key. I pictured its shallow grave in the planter at the edge of the porch.

"So, the field is wide open? Badge or no badge?" Elaine said, discouragement creeping into her voice.

"Looks that way," said the only official investigator in our midst. "But if we're looking at an outsider to the lab, that means Gary just happened to die at his workbench because that's when this accumulation of powder caught up with him. And the lack of tissues at the scene means nothing."

"Which is possible," I said. "But it could have happened another way—say the traces of powder the medical examiner found in his lungs were the last big dose. The killer probably knew Gary's habit of going directly to the lab after a trip and he could have been waiting for him, making sure there was a large amount on the last box of tissues."

"Then whisk the box away," Matt said.

"Death by tissues," Elaine said. She removed the half-used box from an end table and threw it into the wastebasket. "I'm switching to handkerchiefs."

It still bothered me when I found humor in any aspect of a murder case, but it was hard not to join in the mild laughter at her action.

WE DECIDED TO SET a time limit of thirty minutes to explore connections between the two murders, then retire for a few hours' sleep. I took out the time line I'd drawn up during my scenic interlude on Grizzly Peak Boulevard.

We agreed that Manuel's hacking, which started in January, was the key, not ruling out the possibility that he hacked into Ted Gernich's computer, in a kind of ironic twist, and blackmailed him and Marlene.

"The timing is perfect for the start of the beryllium poisoning, too," I said. "Three or four months is about right, given the condition of Gary's lungs."

"Manuel gets a new computer, hacks around, uploads pornography to Gary's computer, finds something on everyone else, gets money when he can..."

I was impressed by Elaine's dispassionate summary, but not enough to miss an important point.

"But," I said in a voice loud enough to interrupt her flow. "One of the things Manuel found was too big to ignore, so he goes to the boss, to Gary, and tells him. Gary confronts the person, and gets killed."

"Then why wouldn't he kill him right away? If Gary was going to expose him, he wouldn't stretch it out over four months."

I sat back, defeated for the moment.

"Time's up," Matt said, and we all headed upstairs for bed, obedient to our own guidelines.

Although I fell asleep with my back against Matt's chest, I dreamed he left for the airport in the middle of the night, not waiting for me to drive him. I woke up at four-thirty in the morning as I was searching for him among the toxic waste at the pit. When I have time, I thought, I should look into my fears of abandonment.

TWENTY-SIX

NOT WANTING TO wake Matt, I slipped out of the room and went back to one of my favorite thinking stations: Elaine's green padded rocker. I was ready for the next phase of my own personal set of investigative procedures—considering each suspect separately as the murderer, to see how it felt to me. A departure from sound reasoning, and sometimes tedious, but often it generated an insight I wouldn't gain otherwise.

I started with Gary's ex-wife and her boyfriend. My usual practice was to bend over backward to spare the scientists and engineers on my list. I found it hard to imagine a person who dedicated her or his life to understanding the universe taking a pencil home from the lab for personal use, let alone turning violent. If you care passionately about the ultimate laws of the natural world, I reasoned, you'd never be callous about a single human life.

In this case, however, I was at a loss to determine how anyone but a technical person would know how to use beryllium to accomplish Gary's murder. I admitted the chance was slim that Marlene had learned enough about the element just by being married to Gary for more than twenty years. Quite the opposite, I thought. I remembered our café interview and imagined her doing everything she could to avoid becoming familiar with Gary's consuming interest. Her choice of Ted Gernich as a replacement for Gary confirmed my hypothesis.

I moved on to the technician, leaving the engineers as a last resort. I tried to envision Larry Pursiano in a rage over a poor performance appraisal, enough to come up with a scheme for murdering him. It was hard to imagine. Moreover, if I was sticking to my theory that Manuel's hacking uncovered the same thing Gary had suspected, the murderer would have to have a computer, and Pursiano had none. I decided for the time being to rule out Pursiano, hoping I wasn't being generous simply because of his ethnic origins.

I turned to the big three beryllium engineers, each with apparently the same motive to kill Gary—with or without Manuel's help, Gary had caught one of them in some form of criminal behavior. I created the only scenario that would work, given the time line.

1. Gary suspects illegal activity of person X in his group.
2. He confronts person X but has no proof.
3. Person X keeps Gary from finding out the truth, while
4. Killing him in a way that appears accidental.
5. Gary dies soon after, and
6. Person X removes the evidence (tissues), but
7. Manuel uncovers the illegal activity while hacking.
8. Manuel has proof that Gary didn't have, so
9. Person X has to kill Manuel immediately.

I looked at my yellow-lined pad, with its neatly sketched solution to a double murder. The only missing links were (a) what was the illegal activity? and (b) who is Person X?

Nice work, I told myself, you have all but the most important elements.

I put aside my pad, intending to show it to Matt and Elaine at a reasonable hour of the morning, and turned my thoughts to Jennifer Kellerman. Not because I suspected her, but to prepare myself for talking to her before Manuel's funeral service.

What did I know about the young woman? One, she'd been sick a lot lately, and two, she'd spent an inordinate amount of time with Manuel.

My sympathetic response to Jennifer's illness prompted a new idea, one I could check by a phone call to the East Coast. I looked at the clock on the mantel—nearly five, or eight at the Galigani residence in Revere. A decent time for a friendly conversation. I punched in Rose's number, imagining her picture-perfect in her pink chenille robe, every hair in place before breakfast.

"What a nice surprise," Rose said. "I've been trying to reach you. How's it going with Matt?'' Rose lowered her voice for the last part, as if Matt were listening in or a national secret of great scientific importance was under discussion.

"Things are fine. We had a little problem, but it's all worked out now.''

I heard a sigh of relief from Rose, who, I suspected, was setting up appointments for me in bridal salons from one end of Boston's Back Bay to the other. Evidently satisfied that her hopes of being my matron of honor were not dashed, she launched into her thumbnail sketch of the Galigani family, a routine we'd developed during my thirty-year-long stay in California.

"Robert and Frank, very busy this weekend. Multiple car accident on Route One. Three fatalities, all from Revere. Very sad.'' Rose paused for a moment, and I knew she was saying a silent prayer for the grieving families. I wished I could do better in that regard. Instead, I found myself focused on the mourners who'd be crowding my building, the Galigani Mortuary, hovering at the bottom of the stairs that lead to Rose's second-floor office and my third-floor apartment.

Rose picked up her telegramlike approach to an update of her family's activities. "John's going on a cruise to Bermuda as the official reporter. Hired by the rich, rich Dalandros. Taking his new girlfriend, Carolyn Verrico, Laura and Joe's daughter. And your godchild, Mary Catherine, who knows? Still finding herself in the desert.''

"I know MC is in Phoenix." Rose still hadn't recovered from her daughter's decision to take a job with a big oil company in Arizona. She'd often accused me of influencing Mary Catherine's choice of career as a chemical engineer, but I knew both she and Frank were proud of their daughter. "And I've met Carolyn Verrico. I've only been gone four days, Rose.''

"I guess I'm thinking you're going to stay for thirty years again.''

"Not likely.''

"We miss you both. Frank and I'll pick you and Matt up at the airport Saturday evening. No balloons, I promise.''

"Matt will be back there tonight.''

"Uh-oh. Business, I hope.''

"He has to testify on Wednesday in the Chapman case."

Another sigh of relief. After waiting more than three decades for me to have a steady boyfriend, Rose didn't want it to slip through our fingers, mine or hers.

"Gloria, what time it is there? The middle of the night? What's wrong?" Rose sounded as if an alarm clock had gone off in her head, alerting her to the unlikely hour for a casual conversation. "You're not calling just to ask how we are, are you?"

"Of course I want to know how everybody is. But I do have a question, too. It's about pregnancy, and you're as expert as anyone I can think of."

Rose's gasp sent a wave a laughter through me. "Gloria, I thought..."

"Ha. No, Rose, not me. No medical miracles. It's a young woman I met here. A teenager."

"Oh," she said, not revealing whether she was relieved or disappointed at the loss of a potential godchild.

"Here's my question. I know women get morning sickness when they're pregnant, but do they also get evening sickness? I mean do some women throw up anytime of day?"

"Absolutely. Especially at the sight of food. When I was carrying Robert, I couldn't look at pizza without getting sick. And with John, it was...What are you up to, Gloria?"

"Nothing you have to worry about."

"I'll bet."

ALTHOUGH I'D NEVER followed fashion trends for my own peer group, let alone Jennifer's, I knew I'd seen petite teens like her around Revere and Berkeley wearing tiny tank tops or cropped shirts. It seemed to me the oversize craze was over for high school girls, and I wondered if it meant anything Jennifer wore size XXL sweatshirts. I wrote my questions on the "Jennifer Kellerman" page of my pad. Was she trying to hide a pregnancy for as long as possible? Did her father know? Did any of this matter to our murder cases?

I considered the other fact I knew for sure about Jennifer—she'd spent her evenings and free time with Manuel. I also knew that hacking took a great deal of effort, a big investment in time.

A lot of it was trial and error and required as much patience as a police stakeout. With only so many hours in a day not committed to school, it stood to reason that Jennifer helped Manuel with his computer scams—or at least she was present when he worked on gaining access to files that weren't his.

It should have occurred to me as soon as I'd had the call from Lincoln Carver about the latest encroachment into his computer files: Jennifer was the new hacker. I imagined her doing it to cover for Manuel. Maybe he had more victims than we knew of, and maybe not all of them had met him in person—they might reason that if the scam is still going on, Manuel couldn't have been the original hacker.

I checked the clock—five-thirty—still too early to start the day on the West Coast. I briefly considered making enough noise to wake up the household, maybe turning on the television set or vacuuming the living room, but thought better of it. Nothing to do but plan how I'd approach Jennifer. Something more gentle than "Dear, are you pregnant—and have you been hacking into computers lately?"

I also needed to prepare myself for Matt's departure. I felt like a teenager getting worked up about a four-day absence. Maybe I was making up for skipping that phase in high school; Matt and I had discussed how we'd both had less than our share of the typical teenage emotional life. No cheerleader stage in my history, no jock status for him.

WHEN MATT CAME DOWN to the living room at six o'clock, I had the table set with plates of bagels and cream cheese, coffee brewing, and the newspaper brought in from the front walkway. Another nuclear family moment, I thought, as we kissed good morning.

"I'm going to miss you," he said, sending a shiver like an ultrasonic wave through my body. "I'm glad it's just till Saturday."

"Me, too."

Matt bit into a plain bagel, taking no advantage of the large selection Elaine had provided. I chose cinnamon raisin, equally predictable. We made plans for him to pick me up at Logan

Airport on Saturday evening and go straight to our favorite jazz club in Cambridge unless I was too tired. I was sure I wouldn't be.

"And in the meantime, there's nothing for you to do except take the tissue theory to Russell and let him work on it. He'll probably be at the funeral, so you don't even need to go to the station."

"Right. Good idea."

"Gloria?"

I gathered that something in my tone struck Matt as less than sincere. "I have some other avenues I'd like to pursue," I said, dragging out my latest list, the nine-point scenario, from Gary's suspicions to Manuel's murder.

"Not bad," he said. "You're only missing the killer and the motive—what the illegal activity was."

"I know that."

"You have no legitimate way to determine these missing pieces."

"What do you think Russell will do with this? I mean my tissue theory and this scenario?" I waved the yellow pad over his bagel, for emphasis.

It was Matt's turn for a tutorial. He put down his food and looked straight at me. I thought of a heat-seeking missile locking onto its target. "What can he do? He can go back and check alibis. He probably didn't do any kind of thorough job of it the first time, since the Larkin death seemed accidental. He can look into the backgrounds of these engineers and ten others if he wants to, see if anything turns up, something more serious than flyers for Little League games. He can send out uniforms, get warrants, court orders, look into bank records, bring in people for questioning. You can't do any of that."

"You're right."

"So you'll do some sightseeing with Elaine and be back home safe and sound on Saturday?"

Elaine had come into the kitchen in the middle of Matt's persuasive recitation of the resources available to the police. While I poured her coffee, she appeared to take his side.

"Wouldn't that be nice?" she said.

"Charming. Let's go for a cable car ride." I smeared a layer of apricot marmalade over the cream cheese on my bagel as if to mask my true feelings.

TWENTY-SEVEN

FIVE DAYS AFTER Matt had seen me off at Boston's Logan Airport, I sat waiting to kiss him good-bye at the Oakland airport. Blue plastic chairs in Massachusetts, orange in California. I had a hard time keeping my coasts straight. Which one did I now live on? Which one had Matt been visiting? He was wearing his traveling clothes, brown corduroys and tweed sports jacket, and no gun. Following procedures, he'd checked his weapon with airport security. I was glad he hadn't had to use it in California.

It was nearly eight in the morning, and we hadn't argued since breakfast. Our disagreement about my further participation in the murder cases hung between us, like a hovering, wide-bodied airplane with copilots who couldn't agree on the day's flight plan.

Instead of resolving the issue, we spoke of other important matters.

"I think the weather has turned hot in Revere already," Matt said.

"Yes. Rose told me to be prepared for higher temperatures than we've had here this week."

"I might not be able to give them this candy before the weekend," he said, holding up a box wrapped in plain white paper, a gold seal at the end.

"No problem."

We looked at the black-and-white See's Candies cart across the room from us, as if it cared about the disposition of the two-pound box of nuts and chews I'd bought for the Galiganis.

I checked my watch, torn between impatience to get back to work and not wanting Matt to leave, in spite of his utter lack of understanding of my need to finish the investigation I'd started.

"Are you ready with your testimony for tomorrow?" I asked, wondering if we could come up with enough neutral topics to fill the time till boarding.

He patted his black canvas carry-on. "I have a lot of hours to work on it."

"That's true. Maybe you'll have an empty middle seat."

"Are you at all glad I came?" Matt's sudden directness threw me off balance, and I retasted the extra dollop of breakfast marmalade. "I know we got off on the wrong foot, but I loved being with you anyway."

He'd taken my hand and turned his soft brown eyes to me, and for a minute I thought he was going to get down on his knees on the ugly, stained carpet. I swallowed the unsteady feeling that always surfaced when Matt said anything bordering on romantic. I wished he'd stick to numbers, like "it was twice as nice to be in Berkeley as Revere this week."

I gave him my best smile. "I'm very glad you came. I'm sorry you're leaving." I knew I sounded as if I were on the witness stand, and hoped my leaning on his shoulder, in spite of the public venue, conveyed more than my dull words. I heard his deep, comfortable sigh and felt confident he understood my feelings. I guessed he also grasped that I wouldn't be buying T-shirts on Fisherman's Wharf after he left.

AS SOON AS I saw the last of Matt's jacket on the boarding ramp, I left the airport and drove to Berkeley, making two stops on the way—one to Galvan's, my favorite deli and market, to replenish Elaine's food supply, and another to a drugstore for basic cosmetics I'd run out of. The errands gave me a sense of normalcy in an otherwise aberrant week.

I'd worn my jeans and Elaine's San Francisco Ballet sweatshirt to see Matt off, and needed to change my clothes. I was facing an interview with a teenage girl who might be pregnant with the child of her dead boyfriend, a funeral, and further investigation of my theory that a beryllium engineer might have been murdered by a box of tissues.

Just a normal day.

I walked into an empty house, greeted only by a note from Elaine and a blinking light on her answering machine.

"Gone with José." I read from Elaine's cryptic lines. "Keep car with you. See you there."

Easy enough to understand. The message on the answering machine was a little more complicated, and I had to play it twice to get it.

"It's Courtney from the library," the voice said. "I hope you're still in town, because I finally got that other report you wanted. The sixth one on your list. It took me a while because one of the authors mistakenly marked it DELTA, which means only certain people can look at it. I don't know why. It's nothing classified or proprietary. Anyway, it's here, and I put it in an envelope with your name on it in case I'm on my break or something."

While I listened to the message the second time, I remembered I'd asked Courtney for the six latest reports with Gary Larkin's name on them. I'd merely wanted representative beryllium articles written by his team, and the five she'd retrieved immediately were sufficient. I hadn't meant for her to bother with the last call number, and was unaware that she'd still been searching for it.

I sat on the rocker and stared at one of Elaine's Hummel figurines—a little girl carrying an apple, a pile of books tied with a strap slung over her shoulder. I thought of Courtney, with her perky, high-pitched voice and schoolgirl ponytail, a misleading image for the conscientious document handler she'd turned out to be.

I tried to contain my excitement, telling myself there was no reason to expect the sixth report to be any more valuable than the first five had been. Except for interesting reading and breaking the ice with the engineers, the beryllium articles had proved useless for my investigation. I wished I had the list, but I'd left the only copy with Courtney, and I hadn't had titles to begin with anyway, just call letters.

What was the combination of authors? I wondered, not that I could think how it would matter. Garkin Larkin and Person X in my murder scenario, perhaps?

Elaine had a lab phone book handy in the living room, and I used it to find the library number.

"You have reached the library and information services desk at Berkeley University Laboratory. No one is available to take your call, but if you leave your name and number, someone will get back to you as soon as possible. Your call is important to us…''

I hung up without leaving a message. Probably a staff conference, I decided, and it would be just as easy to stop by the library after my meeting with Jennifer Kellerman.

For interviewing and funeral participation, I chose one of my many black suits, this one in a soft knit fabric, with a long skirt and waist-length jacket. I passed up my conversation-piece jewelry in favor of a simple silver pin in the shape of a leaf. A sign of life, I thought, in the midst of death.

I arrived at the Kellermans, two doors from the late Gary Larkin's flat on Ashby, at about nine-thirty. Unlike Gary, who lived in one quarter of a fourplex, the Kellermans had a one-story, single-family dwelling in cream-colored stucco, with its own narrow driveway.

Jennifer opened the door, wearing a hooded Cal sweatshirt big enough to hide a pile of laboratory equipment. "Hi," she said, her small voice barely reaching to where I stood on the porch.

"Good morning, Jennifer. I'm glad to see you." I should have looked up some teenage jargon, I thought, or this will never work.

Jennifer led the way into a small living room, with seventies-style earth-tone furniture. Landscape prints on the walls matched the decor, featuring artificially dense forests and autumnal hillsides in the sunset. "Dad says we have until ten o'clock."

We took seats opposite each other in orange-and-brown-plaid easy chairs. "Is your dad home?"

"He's in the back at his computer. He has a pretty elaborate system here, so he works at home a lot." Jennifer flung her head back to where I pictured Sidney Kellerman in his maroon outfit, bent over beryllium calculations. "We're getting ready to leave."

"You're going to Tahoe, right?" It was almost every Bay Area resident's fantasy to have a second home on the magnificent Lake Tahoe, half of it in California, half in Nevada. I was impressed that Kellerman had managed to achieve the dream.

"Yeah, we have a place there. It's quiet. We used to go there with Mom, especially when she was really sick at the end."

"I'm sure that was very hard for you."

She nodded. I tried not to look at her deep blue eyes. I knew if I saw tears welling up, I'd pat her on the shoulders and leave without an interview. I focused on her hair, a soft red, falling in front of her face.

"I'm sorry you've lost Manuel, too. Do you want to tell me about him?"

Jennifer bowed her head as if she were praying for his soul. Or simply remembering beautiful moments with someone she loved. "We hung out a lot."

"Did you have some special place you went to be together?" I asked, choosing a question at random. It wasn't as if I'd planned to revisit their lovers' lane and look for clues. Not for the first time, I resolved to learn more about interviewing techniques if I decided to stay in the crime-solving profession.

Jennifer gave me a smile, the first since I'd met her. "The pit. We used to go to the old pit."

"The battery and capacitor pit?" For a moment, I wondered if Jennifer knew that's where Manuel had been murdered, but apparently she'd already processed the facts.

"Yeah, we'd go there sometimes to fool around. Manuel liked it. I guess if he had to die somewhere..."

I cleared my throat, coming to grips with the idea of the waste pit as a death site of choice for a young man. "Any particular reason he liked it there?"

"We'd talk about how pretty it was all around it—the trees and the hills, and sometimes you could see the whole bay—but on the other side of the fence was this gross stuff. It was ironic, or poetic or something. I didn't really like being there as much as he did, but it was just the idea of having some place that was our own."

Whatever happened to watching the submarine races by the water? I wondered. Even the backseat of a Chevy seemed preferable to the pit. I pictured the chain-link fence topped with nasty spirals of barbed wire, separating the old waste site outside the fence from the new one, with thousands of cubic feet of material not fit to be buried in the earth. Times have changed, I thought. Whatever the drawbacks of hazardous waste, however, talking about the pit seemed to enliven sixteen-year-old Jennifer Kellerman.

"Dad caught us there once," she told me, a tiny smile lingering on her lips. "We were all pretty surprised. He came up there to dump a bag of trash. I couldn't imagine why he'd go all the way up there when we have our own recycling bins. He said it was flammable or something. And there we were, sitting on some empty barrels."

Jennifer stopped talking. The flow of her memories seemed to have caught up with her, and she started to cry, softly, into the sleeves of her sweatshirt. I moved my chair closer and took her hands, wishing an adolescent psychologist were sitting in front of her instead of me. Someone who could really help her, not a pretend cop who should have been sightseeing.

"I wish I could help you feel better," I told her, when her breathing had slowed down. "But it's going to take a long time before that happens."

She shrugged her shoulders. "I know. I'm okay, I guess." Jennifer had pulled at the cord of the hood on her sweatshirt, wrapping and unwrapping the ends around her fingers.

Hard as it was, I had at least two more important questions to ask. I folded my hands on my lap, although the same priestly gesture hadn't worked at all when I'd tried to pump Marlene Korner and Ted Gernich for information on Gary's finances. I remembered another trick that had done well by me this week, however, and decided to risk it: pretend you know more than you do and see what results. I started with the easier of the two topics.

"Jennifer, your hacking into computers doesn't really help the way people think of Manuel."

She nodded. I wasn't surprised that my interviewee offered no resistance to my accusation. She seemed to have been beaten down by life, and nothing I'd say could match the tragedy that she was living through. "I'm not doing it anymore."

I decided that was enough on topic number one. One more question, then I'd leave this child alone.

"Jennifer, does your dad know you're pregnant?"

Jennifer dropped the ends of her sweatshirt cord and turned her eyes on me, her eyebrows raised, her neck stretched to its limit. She opened her mouth to speak, then closed it. She folded her hands over her stomach, in a gesture that looked like protection for her unborn child, and nodded her head. "That's sort of why we're going away."

I sat back in my chair. "When is your baby due?"

"Early September. If it's the third, it will be Manuel's birthday. We were going to name it Manuel Jr. if it was a boy. We were going to get married, in the summer, before..." Jennifer looked beyond me and stopped in midsentence, as if an alarm had gone off, signaling our time was up.

I turned to see her father in the doorway leading to the dining room, out of his maroon outfit and into olive green pants and shirt that blended with the living room palette. I wanted to tell him we still had fifteen minutes before our time was up, but thought better of it.

"Good morning," I said, hoping I'd struck a note between cheery and morose.

"Good morning." Kellerman's tone was cordial. "Jennifer, are you finished packing?"

Jennifer left the room quickly, without a nod or a good-bye to me, as if she'd been caught at the pit with her boyfriend again.

I stood up and gathered my purse and jacket. "I hope you have a good trip," I told Kellerman.

"I'm looking forward to it. It's very peaceful up there, and that's what we need right now. As you can tell, we won't be going to the funeral."

"I'm sure you know best," I said, wondering if he could tell I didn't mean it. In my opinion, his daughter needed a funeral service to say a proper good-bye to the father of her child. Or, I conceded, maybe I was influenced by my more than forty-year friendship with the Galiganis and my year-long residence in their mortuary.

"I'd offer you a cup of coffee, but I want to get on the road soon," Kellerman said.

I checked my watch. "Thanks. I don't have time anyway. I need to stop at the library before the funeral to pick up a report I ordered."

Kellerman walked to the door with me. He lowered his voice,

although I couldn't imagine Jennifer eavesdropping. "Thanks for trying to help my daughter. Jennifer's the world to me now," he said. I looked at his sad, drawn face and had no trouble believing him.

As I left, I cast a glance at the car in the Kellerman driveway, some part of my subconscious still trying to find the owner of the vehicle that bullied me and possibly Rita. A white Lincoln Town Car, certainly not the kind that could be mistaken for an SUV, and no garage.

TWENTY-EIGHT

I DROVE NORTH toward the lab library, my brain busy with the puzzle pieces I'd accumulated during my conversation with Jennifer. One or two things twitched in my mind as significant, demanding attention, but navigating the Saab through Berkeley streets took most of my concentration. I had thoughts of Elaine and José also, hoping the day would pass quickly for them, and wondered where Matt was with respect to the Rockies.

When I had mental leisure, at traffic signals and stop signs, I considered again how different this case was from the others I'd worked on. This time, instead of thinking everyone guilty, I found it easier to dismiss each suspect as an innocent victim of my meddling. Maybe all I'd done was uncover the scheme that gave Marlene satisfactory revenge on her ex-husband and a bigger share of the *Larkin v. Larkin* divorce pie.

If my tissue theory of Gary's death was correct, the killer most likely needed access to the lab to administer the last large dose. That cleared the badgeless Marlene Korner and Ted Gernich. The team of Kellerman, Carver, and Johnson had been unearthed merely from my library browsing. Not the most exhaustive search for suspects.

Going through the events of the week, I had to admit Kellerman seemed too sad a figure to have the energy for murder. And would he really kill the father of his future grandchild? The others seemed just as easily let off the hook. Rita Johnson probably didn't knock herself off her bike to look innocent. Carver was noticeably anxious, calling too much attention to himself to be guilty, and he hadn't lied when he claimed to be the victim of further hacking activity. Pursiano had no motive worth killing for, since raises in salary at BUL never exceeded a few percent, even for the most stunning performance evaluations.

I wondered if Inspector Dennis Russell and the Berkeley Police Department were correct after all—Gary Larkin had simply had an accident while handling beryllium. All I'd done was to determine it was on the same day he ran out of tissues. If so, I'd upset many lives for nothing. Or, worse, I'd done it to satisfy my need to solve problems, whether they exist or not; maybe I'd retired from physics too soon, I thought. Not only Kellerman, Carver, and Johnson had been perturbed, but also the delicate relationship between Lamerino and Gennaro.

As for Manuel, he could have been the victim of a random killing. If he and Jennifer found the pit an intriguing site for hanging out, probably many others did, too. I pictured it a cozy retreat for drug dealers and gangs, as well as young lovers.

Another possibility was that Manuel inadvertently came upon midnight dumpers—people who brought their hazardous waste to the site after dark, breaking the rules anonymously. I thought about dumpers I had known—scientists who had just enough money for research but not enough for the cleanup they'd committed to, engineers who had a mixed toxic waste stream and neither the time nor the funds to determine the constituents. Not knowing what their waste was made up of meant they couldn't dispose of it properly, so they'd dump it after hours, leaving it for someone else to figure out.

Poor and rude as this practice was, the penalties were small for such offenses, and it was difficult to imagine a scientist, even an environmentally unaware chemist, murdering a teenager to avoid paying a fine. I brushed away the idea that Manuel had taken his entrepreneurial skills to the limit of trying to blackmail midnight dumpers.

All the way to the library, I worked hard at convincing myself I'd headed down the wrong mental path from the beginning. Couldn't all these events—two deaths, computer hacking, a stalking in a ladies' room, a harrowing tailgating incident on Grizzly Peak Boulevard, and a hit and run in the parking lot—be unrelated?

But I loved things to be neat, like all scientists, and I balked at the idea that so much disaster could randomly pile up around the BUL beryllium team in two weeks.

In science, when too many little theories were necessary to

account for events, physicists looked for the one big theory, the overall pattern, like the current superstring theory. I thought about the bizarre hypothesis—that everything in the universe can be explained as the manifestation of vanishingly tiny, vibrating strings, detectable only with sophisticated equipment. But as long as it accounted for seemingly unconnected behaviors in the physical world, it would not be rejected.

I must be on some other plane, I told myself, comparing my theory with the elegant superstrings of physics, but beryllium-doped tissues did account for everything in the Larkin and Martinez cases.

By the time I got to the library, I was in a dead heat with myself: 50 percent sure Gary Larkin had an accident and Manuel Martinez was a victim of random foul play, and 50 percent sure Person X, who was one of my suspects, had deliberately killed both men.

I needed something to break the tie.

I PICKED UP the envelope at the reference desk, still unstaffed, making a note to send a thank-you card to Courtney for her diligence. After I write to the person who supervises Randy, my personal bus driver to lot B-4, I thought, wondering when I'd get to normal chores like penning notes and reading *Science News*.

With about a half hour to spare before Manuel's funeral service, I decided to have a seat in the library's reading area and skim the report. I expected to find another briefing on the uses of beryllium in fusion reactors, but the sixth report had dollar signs where metric dimensions would have been, columns of financial data instead of measurements of energy output and power. I stared at my lap, where I'd placed my copy of *Beryllium Purchases—Fiscal Year Report* by Sidney Kellerman and Gary Larkin. It had a January date, representing the expenditures of the beryllium team for the preceding calendar year.

I flipped through the pages of the report. They may as well have been sheet music or written in a foreign script—Cyrillic, perhaps, or Mandarin. This is hopeless, I thought. I didn't understand my own simple money market accounts and left anything more complicated than interest checking to a financial advisor. As long as I had enough money in my purse for a cappuccino, I didn't pay much attention to the finer details of fiscal management.

Focus, I told myself. If I could grasp how mixing copper with beryllium improves the strength of the material while not interfering with its electrical conductivity, I should be able to understand a simple financial accounting of beryllium purchases.

The first few pages at least were in English—two sections described the kinds of purchases required to carry out the experiments for the current contract. The list included one-of-a-kind optical components such as an oversized mirror, and finely ground lens, plus specialty parts that couldn't be bought from a catalog: pumps, filters, feedback systems, temperature controllers, cutting tools with unparalleled precision.

The next page gave details of the sole source agreement with the supplier, a company outside Cleveland, where Gary had gone on his last business travel. I'd done my share of sole-sourcing as a researcher; it was a semi-legitimate way of circumventing the need for government purchasing offices to ask for bids for supplies, a process that could take longer than the duration of the contract.

What we'd do is determine for ourselves where we could get our components, then give the lab buyers a request for parts so narrowly specified that only that one company could provide them. To accomplish this, we stopped just short of saying "it must have company X's logo in the corner," telling ourselves we made up in efficiency for a certain lack of fairness to other suppliers that might want our business.

Kellerman had done the same for the beryllium team supplies. Nothing startling in that, certainly nothing to incriminate him in two murders.

The final section contained the expenditures for the previous fiscal year, long lists of unit prices, deposits, credits, returns, and other quantities headed by dollar signs. I almost wished I had traded in a few units of calculus for a bookkeeping class. Not knowing the going rate for precision-ground optics, I could hardly tell if the prices were reasonable, and couldn't think of a reason it would matter. I felt I'd come to another dead end, like

Rita Johnson's interview and Lincoln Carver's initial denial that he knew Manuel, all with perfectly reasonable explanations in the end.

I stood up, prepared to put the cases aside while I attended Manuel's funeral service. Courtney's ponytail, back from its break, poked at the corner of my vision, however, and I couldn't resist another quick question. Holy Angels Cemetery was not far from BUL, just down the hill, and I could go straight there, I decided, saving the trip to the chapel on San Pablo.

"Thanks so much for retrieving this document," I said, resting my arms on the counter in front of Courtney's neat cubicle.

"Oh, hi, Dr. Lamerino. I'm glad you're still around. Is that report helpful to you?"

I nodded, unwilling to explain that it didn't have the impact I'd hoped on a double murder investigation. "I'm wondering why it was marked DELTA," I said. "As you pointed out, there doesn't seem to be anything in it that's classified or proprietary."

"Funny, isn't it? Dr. Kellerman changed it to DELTA soon after it was released, sometime in January. Then the strange thing was even Dr. Larkin couldn't take it away or make copies of it. He had to read it right here and he's the second author."

"He wanted to copy it?"

Courtney nodded, giving her hair a life of its own. "He had some problem with it, and wanted it released in the normal way so he could have complete access, but it took all this time to clear it. And then..."

He died, I thought, mentally finishing her sentence. Courtney bit her lip, and I thought I saw her eyes stray to a group photograph pinned to her felt wall. A picnic? A retirement party? The last time she saw Gary Larkin alive? Courtney seemed another victim of sudden death—of the sort where you wish you'd been kinder to someone who died.

"I'm sure he appreciated all your efforts," I said as if I had an inside track on Gary Larkin's dealings with information services.

"Well, I hope the rest of your trip is good," Courtney said, recovering her poise. "At least I could help you a little."

"You've helped a great deal," I told her. I'd added the enthusiastic last phrase mostly to assuage Courtney's guilt at not doing more for Gary Larkin, but at the back of my mind was the nagging feeling that late-arriving report number six held a clue that might provide a breakthrough in my investigation.

I gave Courtney a smile meant to come from both me and Gary Larkin, and left the building.

TWENTY-NINE

SOMEWHERE BETWEEN Courtney's desk and Holy Angels Cemetery, the collection of words and phrases from my interview with Jennifer Kellerman sorted themselves out as if they'd been puzzle pieces, tossing and turning on their own in my mind, until they found their proper orientation and dropped into place.

The first fragment that came to my mind in a new way was Jennifer's comment about her father's working habits: "He has a pretty elaborate system here, so he works at home a lot."

As far as I could determine, Kellerman was the only one of the beryllium team who had a home computer besides Gary Larkin. It made sense that he would have computer power at his residence, since he was the computations engineer, the modeler for the group.

But when Kellerman admitted to being approached by Manuel, his confession was "He found out I do my personal banking on the lab computer." Now I questioned why Kellerman would use government property to take care of his mortgage payments if he had his own system at home. And if he didn't, why would he lie to me about it? Why make up a crime? Unless you're trying to cover a bigger one.

I thought of the inscrutable fiscal report I'd just tried to read. It has to be there, I decided, possibly illegal transactions were really what Manuel uncovered through his hacking. I'd thought all along that Manuel had something bigger than I'd uncovered so far on one of the beryllium engineers. It was one thing to run off your Little League flyers and party invitations on the company copy machine, it was another to make thousands of dollars profit from your role as a lab employee.

The scenario that was taking shape in my head was so all-consuming, I pulled off the street into the parking lot of a supermarket and took out the nine-point list I'd drawn up in the early hours of the morning. I'd torn it from the yellow pad and stuck it in my purse for just such an enlightened moment.

I made a guess that the generic illegal activity I'd listed as item one had something to do with Kellerman's responsibilities as purchaser of supplies for the beryllium team. Thinking of Kellerman's unimposing presence, I suspected something uncreative, like kickbacks. Suppose Gary Larkin suspected Kellerman of charging BUL more for supplies than he was paying the vendor, and pocketing the difference. Gary would try to get proof, but, following step three in the scenario, Kellerman would stall, creating an obstacle to anyone's determining the facts.

Say *Beryllium Purchases—Fiscal Year Report* had the incriminating data—Kellerman as the first author could submit a classification request and have the report labeled DELTA. Even though Gary was second author, his hands would be tied as far as making the report public. Scientists often have their names on reports as formalities, without knowing the contents in any detail, so it's possible that Gary didn't know what the report contained until after it was printed.

Kellerman would want Gary's death to look like an accident— my theory of dousing Gary's tissues with beryllium powder fit the bill. In the end, perhaps because Gary was closing in on proving his suspicions, Kellerman had to up the ante and give him a large dose, which would be fatal. It was easy for me to picture Kellerman sneaking into Gary's house and lab and removing all remaining tainted tissues.

The rest of my list flowed smoothly.

7. Manuel uncovers the illegal activity while hacking
8. Manuel has proof that Gary didn't have, so
9. Person X has to kill Manuel immediately.

I clicked my pen, crossed out "illegal activity" on my list and wrote "kickbacks." I took a deep breath and looked around me at the Tuesday morning shoppers, mostly women and children. I studied their faces, as if I were searching for a murderer among them, then crossed out "Person X," and wrote in "Sidney Kellerman."

I STILL HAD some questions. What tipped Gary off in the first place? Reading the printed report for the first time and comparing it with other invoices? I couldn't figure a way to trace back the audit trail. And what could Manuel have seen that he would understand? If it was Kellerman's home computer that he hacked into and not the lab computer, he could have seen the real data—perhaps some private notes Kellerman made, keeping track of his illegal earnings.

I let those details go unaccounted for; I had to leave something for Inspector Russell and the proper authorities to figure out, I reasoned. Meanwhile, I tried to figure out what else pointed to Kellerman.

A strange place for crime solving, I thought, as I sat in a prime spot of the supermarket lot. Ignoring the noisy cart traffic, I built the case against Sidney Kellerman, coming up against pros and cons. Although I believed Matt's assessment of how easy it was to get into someone's house, I knew it was even easier for Sidney Kellerman, whose daughter had a key. One pro-Kellerman vote in my mind.

When I tried to picture Kellerman outside my stall in the ladies' room at Walnut Square, however, I couldn't in all conscience say I recognized his shoes. I tried to make my mind see maroon pant legs, but the image wasn't there. One con-Kellerman vote.

I had a tie-breaker in my recollection of the SUV. Besides recalling the 767 combination, I'd been having fleeting images about another unique feature of the license plate, but couldn't zero in on it. Now, sitting in the parking lot amid vanity plates, motorcycle plates, and cars from out of state, it became clear.

The dark-colored SUV that did its best to push me off Grizzly Peak Boulevard into the depths below had an out-of-state plate, not any of the California styles I knew. During my thirty years' worth of cars in the Bay Area, I'd gone through many designs—black with yellow letters, dark blue with yellow letters, ending with blue letters on white for my last Jeep. The SUV's plate was pale green on the bottom and white on the top, like the mountains of Nevada. I wished I'd asked Jennifer which side of Lake Tahoe the Kellerman's home was on. It was worth a try to see if he had a SUV licensed there.

I needed a phone, but both pay phones at the corner of the parking lot were in use, both by scroungy men I was sure were drug dealers. I wished I were in Revere in my own well-equipped Cadillac, with its captive cell phone. Elaine had a modular phone that she kept with her, which did me no good at the moment.

By the time a phone was free, another pro-Kellerman vote emerged. I rushed to the booth and punched in the numbers for the Kellerman residence, hoping they hadn't left and that Jennifer would answer.

Shivers of excitement and relief ran through me when I heard her voice.

"I'm sorry to bother you again, Jennifer," I said. "I have one more thing to ask you. Do you remember what night your dad caught you and Manuel at the pit?"

"Not exactly." Jennifer's small voice sounded worried, as if she'd never be rid of me.

"Try to think, Jennifer. It could be really important." I neglected to clarify that her answer could clinch my suspicion that her father was a double murderer.

"Well, I know it was a Tuesday, because both our dads go out on Tuesday nights. My dad plays the violin with this group, and Manuel's dad has some kind of class he goes to, so we're sort of free. My dad was supposed to be practicing."

"But instead he showed up at the pit?"

"Yeah, with this special trash, like I told you." Special trash indeed, I thought. Tissues doused with enough beryllium powder to kill a man.

I shook my head, as if I didn't want to be correct. When I thought about all Jennifer had been through, I couldn't imagine taking her father away from her also. And did I really think this horrible double murder was perpetrated by an overweight computations engineer who dressed in matching polyester and played the violin? I wanted to believe otherwise, but the evidence was mounting. The medical examiner had determined that Gary had died during the evening on the Tuesday he'd come back from Cleveland.

"Jennifer, could it have been almost three weeks ago that it happened, two weeks before Manuel disappeared?"

"I guess. I don't know. I have to go."

Jennifer ended the conversation before I could ask which state her new home was in. Her hang-up was as weak as her voice. Since I didn't peg her for a rude young woman, I figured either her father had summoned her or she'd started to put the pieces together herself.

I had another call to make, to the Berkeley Police Department. My second telephone wish of the morning was granted when Terry Spender answered her extension.

"Terry, I have a request. I don't know if this is your province or if you can do it even if you wanted to."

"It might help you to know that technically we're all on this Martinez case. So if you have a lead, ask away." Terry laughed, as if she'd already gotten used to my meddling after only a few days' acquaintance. I thought of enlisting her to call and explain me to a few people in Revere.

"Thanks. I do feel better knowing that I'm just being a good citizen. I'd like you to run a license plate for Nevada."

"Nevada? Can do."

"All I have is, it's a dark sport utility vehicle, with 767 as part of the ID."

"It'll take a few minutes. That system is always busy and I have to wait my turn. Shall I call you back?"

"No. I'm at a pay phone. Here's what I'd like," I said, feeling as though I were her commanding officer. No wonder Pursiano gave me a salute in the cafeteria, I thought. "If the vehicle is licensed to Sidney Kellerman, meet me at the pit."

"The pit? The old waste dump outside the lab fence?"

"The same. I'm going there now. If I'm right, I'll have something to show you."

"Why don't you wait for me and we'll go together?" Terry sounded nonchalant, as if she were suggesting lunch and a movie, but I suspected she was worried, the way Matt would have been under the same circumstances.

"No, I'm ready to go. And I'll be fine alone. It's broad daylight."

THIRTY

As I CHECKED MY WATCH—after eleven o'clock—I could have sworn I heard church bells in the distance. It was Tuesday, however, not Sunday, and I chalked the imaginary sound up to my feelings of guilt at choosing a visit to a waste dump over Manuel's funeral service.

Did I really expect to find a few boxes of tissues that had been dumped three weeks ago? I asked myself. Or was it my morbid curiosity that brought me here? One thing I knew: I felt a strong urge to inspect the site that turned out to be the nexus between the two cases that had nagged me since I had been in California.

I wondered how the police had handled the pit as a crime scene when Manuel's body was discovered on Saturday. I knew from conversations with Matt that cops were authorized to remove whatever could be important from a crime scene. They'd been known to take whole segments of a wall from a victim's house, entire sections of plumbing, or a three-tiered entertainment center, if there was blood spatter, or a chance of finding other forensic evidence.

The area known as the pit was at the top of the hill, outside lab property, and technically contained only nonhazardous material. It was separated from the new waste handling area by a chain-link fence and a security booth. I tried to picture the Berkeley police van driving away with a standard fifty-five-gallon drum of paint thinners like xylene, toluene, and methyl ethyl ketone. I figured that, instead, they immediately ruled out toxic waste exposure as cause of death and didn't enter the secured area.

I drove as close as I could to the pit and parked in front of a pyramid of rusty drums I assumed were empty. I brushed away a temptation to guess what substances had leached out of them into the soil. I thought of Elaine several hundred feet below me, expecting her Saab to pull up any minute with her houseguest, and hoped she'd understand my choice.

I realized with dismay that I was dressed in funeral clothes and would have a hard time walking on the gravel. I knew Elaine kept tennis shoes in her trunk, but I didn't think she'd appreciate radioactive mud on her soles, even if the amount easily met the "ALARA"—as low as reasonably achievable—criterion for exposure. Another pair of black pumps for the cause of justice, I thought, remembering a similar incident when I was inappropriately dressed for a visit to a trailer site in Revere.

I walked to the spot where Manuel's body had been discovered, at the edge of the large crater that gave the pit its name. In my early days at BUL, before the strict regulatory environment that began with problems at Love Canal, the pit had been the only waste dump for laboratory operations. I remembered inventories I'd seen, listing the programs and services that generated hazardous waste. Acids, electrolytic solutions, and rinse water from the group that made printed circuits. Solvents and reagents from analytical chemistry experiments. Cyanide from the metal-plating shop. Solids contaminated with heavy elements from radiochemical research projects. All put to rest, or unrest as it turned out, in the pit.

I had confidence in the tight regulations that currently governed hazardous waste, and I was used to being around toxic materials, but I still had a hard time envisioning the pit as a popular spot for necking.

A small scrap of yellow-and-black tape stood out against the dull blacks and browns of the pit. The crime scene markings had come and gone before Manuel's body was buried. I'd learned so much about him since he'd disappeared; I wished I'd known him while he was still stealing time with his girlfriend.

I stood for a moment and looked across the hole in the ground at the clearing sky over the bay—my own private service for Manuel Martinez. I thought of an invocation from my childhood at St. Anthony's Church in Revere. *Dear St. Anthony, look around. Something's lost and can't be found.* I prayed for Manuel's parents, hoping they'd find a way to move on in spite of their great loss.

I brought my mind around to the job at hand. Maybe Saint Anthony, restorer of lost things, would extend his talent to help me find the tissues.

Beyond the pit was the new handling-and-treatment facility, a small building with several detached trailers. I wished I'd thought of asking Jennifer whether her father had gone inside or dumped his bag of special trash outside the fence in the pit area. Fortunately for my career, my physics research life had been considerably more well organized than my interview techniques were.

I pulled my retiree badge from my purse and debated whether to try to use it for entry through the security booth. Retirees were issued special badges that would admit us only to unclassified areas of the lab, and I had no idea how the waste dump was categorized. Not only that, I'd never used my badge since it was issued on my last day of regular work and I took off for Massachusetts soon after. For all I knew, the badge didn't work at all.

I inspected the workings of the security system as well as I could from outside it, and concluded it was the old style, a glassed-in booth with two sets of doors, the kind that would set off an alarm and trap me inside if my PIN number wasn't accepted. At that point, I would be stuck in the booth until a PSO—a personnel security officer—came to investigate the intrusion. What would I tell the PSO? I wondered. I got lost on the way to Holy Angels? Although I'm relatively well dressed, I'm really a bag lady looking for recyclables? The truth, that I was looking for boxes of tissues laced with beryllium, probably would not set me free.

My hunch was that Kellerman would have taken the deadly trash inside, to mix with the other deadly trash, and I decided to take the risk with my badge. I hoped a better cover story would come to me should the need arise.

I looked over my shoulder, as if hoping someone would dissuade me, but I was alone on a hilltop, Berkeley's biggest and most interesting collection of trash on the other side of the fence. I wiped my sweaty hand on my skirt and reached for the large metal handle.

The first door opened easily and closed behind me with a loud thud that seemed to echo throughout the Berkeley hills. No going back. The system would not let me out in either direction without a valid badge/PIN combination.

The floor of the booth was covered with a special mat that weighed me, ready to check the result against the code in my badge. Besides me and my doctor, the lab's security system was the only other entity, human or otherwise, that knew my weight. I remembered there was about a forty-pound margin in the system, and felt pretty sure I'd neither gained nor lost that much since I'd weighed in to activate the badge a year ago.

I took a deep breath and slid my badge along the groove of the reader. I raised my eyes to the camera mounted on the upper left corner of the booth and gave it a smile, as if to say "please." I didn't know if anyone was watching in real time, but I wanted to cover all bases. My fingers were sticky with perspiration from the sun-baked booth and my own nervousness. I entered my PIN number, 11767, based on Marie Curie's birthday, November 7, 1867. If she were a saint, I thought, I could pray to her. Canonized or not, I decided she qualified, and I invoked her help.

The loud buzz startled me, and for a minute I couldn't tell if the sound heralded good news or bad. A click from the second door and a flashing green light told me I was in. I let out a long sigh, pushed the door open, and walked out of the booth, happy to join the company of containers filled with radioactive, hazardous, and toxic waste.

THE TREATMENT BUILDING was a one-story structure, one step up from a trailer, but I knew it housed sophisticated equipment that rendered some forms of waste harmless by elaborate separation and filtering processes. The plant appeared empty, and there were no hours of operation posted. I suspected the site was staffed on an as-needed basis, probably to minimize occupational exposure. I walked among the barrels and tanks, reading labels, as if I were in a laboratory supply room looking for a new ammeter or power supply. I saw a few labels with names I recognized, the "generators" of the waste. The description on one of the waste drums—an aqueous solution from sample analysis—

identified it as corrosive, but not ignitable. There's a break, I thought.

Where would Kellerman dump the tissues? I asked myself. In a container no one would be likely to open, came the answer. I looked around for the oldest drums, sometimes referred to as "legacy waste." They were identified by the old-style label, one that didn't comply with new regulations. I'd always thought it ironic that the new rules were a handicap to disposing of old waste. Current federal codes prohibited the disposal of unidentified waste or certain combinations of mixed waste, which meant that drums filled under old rules had to sit on the lot, waiting for some future technology that could characterize their contents in a noninvasive way.

If Kellerman chose these drums for the evidence, I thought, he could be sure no one would be breaking the seal to look in. No one was that foolish.

Moments before I became a foolish person, a drum labeled Gloves, Glassware, and Labwipes caught my eye. Usually this would be the least harmful drum on the lot. But not if Kellerman had chosen it to dispose of his evidence, I mused. The drum appeared to be sealed by a band around the top, but I knew this kind of seal was easily removed and replaced. I walked up to it, and rubbed my hands, with more excitement than I'd felt in front of the pile of presents waiting for me at Siad's on Saturday evening.

"No need to do that, Dr. Lamerino."

The voice came as such a surprise, my hands stopped in midair. In my focused state, I hadn't heard a sound other than the noisy birds that inhabited the hillside and the faint rush of traffic far below me. I turned to see Sidney Kellerman. He stood with his arms over his head, holding on to the chain-link fence between the pit and the treatment area where I was. He looked like a prisoner wanting to get out. Or in.

Squinting in the sunlight, I saw the dark SUV of my nightmares pulled up close to the Saab. Elaine's car was hemmed in between the SUV's bumper and the pile of waste drums, beyond which was a drop of at least a thousand feet. No sense leaping over the eight-foot, barbed wire-topped fence to jump in the car and drive off, I mused.

I opened my mouth to speak, but nothing came out, and I had no idea what I'd intended to say anyway—hello, where did you dump the tissues? Or, why aren't you in Tahoe? Kellerman, having no such problem with his larynx, had talked right through my musings. When I tuned in again, he seemed to be inviting me to join him outside the booth.

"Why don't you come out and we can talk about this."

"I don't think so," I said. "I'm waiting for Officer Spender." That is, if she was able to get a turn on the computer. And if she was able to trace the license plate to you.

Kellerman laughed, as if he sensed a bluff. Although he was several meters away, I could see that his eyes were wide open and unblinking, his hair wilder than usual, as if he'd been caught in an unexpected storm of static electricity. His olive green shirt was open at the neck, revealing a dirty undershirt.

In his hand was what I knew to be a deadly weapon: a large white handkerchief. I could neither see it nor smell it from where I stood, but I guessed it was doused with ether. Sidney Kellerman, the chemical killer, I thought.

Is this going to be easier than dodging a bullet? I wondered. Unlike Manuel, who'd had no idea Kellerman had followed him to the pit to kill him, I had forewarning.

I just had to keep away from his right hand.

THIRTY-ONE

"I HAVE SOME information you might find useful," Kellerman told me in a singsong voice that sounded insane, and worried me more than any amount of shouting. Had he lost his mind entirely? I decided my only recourse was to stay behind the fence and engage him in as normal a conversation as possible, while straining my ears for the sound of Terry Spender's patrol car.

"What is it you want to tell me?" I asked him.

"You'll have to come out, and then I'll show you." I couldn't believe he didn't realize how transparent his intentions were—his right hand holding a handkerchief, his left fist closed over a small, shiny container. I knew he'd have to have a supply of ether with him since it evaporated so quickly once exposed to the atmosphere.

Kellerman stood leaning against the fence, making no attempt to enter the area through the security booth. I knew he could come in easily, not having to wrestle with doubts about his regular employee badge as I had had to about my retiree version. Then why was he trying to lure me outside the fence? Did he not have his badge with him? Most lab employees kept their badges in their vehicles whenever they weren't wearing them, although it was technically a violation of security procedures.

The more obvious answer brought a measure of relief for me. If he used the booth to join me in the waste area, the camera would record his entry. If he then killed me—here I paused in my reasoning for a labored, dry swallow—he wouldn't be able to get me out. The booth allowed only one person at a time to exit. If my body were found in the area, whoever reviewed the videotape would know Kellerman had followed me in, and that much alone could incriminate him.

So, he wasn't that out of his mind, I thought. I nearly threw up my arms and cried "I'm safe—as long as I stay behind this fence." As if this exercise had itself saved my life, I walked toward Kellerman with a boldness inappropriate to the situation.

My lack of panic was probably due also to Kellerman's persona. Not that of a typical killer, I thought, as if I were an expert FBI profiler. I had a fleeting image of him at the control panel of an old Bendix computer, like the kind I'd used in graduate school in the basement of the physics building. Only the evidence and logic of the cases forced me to change the picture to one of a middle-aged man in brightly colored polyester outfits, wielding a cloth full of $C_4H_{10}O$, ready to anesthetize and strangle his victims—when he didn't have time for slow beryllium poisoning.

In the back of my mind, I thought it important to keep Kellerman talking, but couldn't remember whether that applied only to hostage situations. I wondered if this would qualify since I was as captive to the waste area as if I were chained to one of its tanks of hydrochloric acid.

"I know how you killed Gary Larkin," I said in as calm a voice as I could manage. "And Manuel Martinez. And so do the police. But why would you do such a thing?"

Kellerman threw his head back, then shook it, as if he were about to explain murder to the mentally challenged. "Larkin was closing in on my little kickback scheme. I knew it was a matter of time before he'd figure it out. Especially once he was promoted and had access to anything he wanted."

"Two murders, Sidney?" I asked him, as if identifying him as the killer put us on a first-name basis. "Could the money have been worth it?"

He shook his head again, his hair falling in front of his eyes. "I only charged the lab five percent more than I was paying the supplier."

"And put the difference in your pocket."

Kellerman shrugged. "It was a drop in their billion-dollar bucket. It didn't even come close to the raises I've lost over the years. The promotions."

"You think you should have gotten the promotion Gary did?"

"Absolutely," he said. He glared at me, causing me to take a step back, in spite of the fence and security booth that separated us. I remembered reading in a general science magazine that it was possible to die of fright. Medical researchers had recorded above-average numbers of heart attacks during natural disasters such as earthquakes and hurricanes. Doctors claimed the only connection to the physical events was through their frightening affect on the victims.

Unwilling to be in the next table of statistics on the topic, I stared back at Kellerman, who had continued to rave about his ill treatment. I almost suggested he start his own discrimination lawsuit.

"The lab always gives people a promotion when they get close to retirement age. It's a token of goodwill, you know. Makes the pension a little better. It's a sign of respect." The liquid from Kellerman's S's nearly reached me through the fence. "Do you know why I was passed over?"

Quizzes always made me nervous, and this one topped the list. I managed a weak "no."

"Because I was out too many days taking care of my wife and daughter. My wife, who was dying." Kellerman's voice cracked.

I let out a long sigh. "That's terrible, Sidney," I said. And I believed it was. "That's illegal." Not to mention immoral, I said to myself.

"Ha. Try to prove that. I'd have to be a woman or a minority."

I decided to let that go and moved on. I wanted desperately to check my watch, as if knowing the time would help me determine if Terry were on the way, but I was afraid Kellerman would react to the gesture.

"What about Manuel?" I asked him, stretching out the time until sirens I hoped to hear eventually approached. "The father of your grandchild." I knew I sounded like someone auditioning for a part in a daytime soap, but Kellerman's highly agitated state seemed to evoke an equally irrational response in me.

Kellerman slapped his thighs in another comic gesture that lead me to believe his lethal chemistry projects had affected his brain. "That Martinez kid? He was so naïve, telling me he'd found my financial files, trying to bargain with me."

"What did he find?"

"My memos. The ones I wrote to the supplier. He compared them with the ones to the lab purchasing office. The same thing

Gary noticed when he saw the figures in that report I tried to bury." Kellerman tapped his forehead. "Stupid. I copied the wrong set of numbers into the report I released. Stupid me." Kellerman pressed his finger into his head, as if to drill some sense into it. "And stupid Manuel Martinez."

"It wasn't money Manuel asked you for, was it?"

"No. Worse," Kellerman said, confirming my guess. "He wanted Jennifer. He wanted to marry her." He spit out the last words, and looked at me as if he knew that fact alone should win me over to his side. "That was the last straw."

Kellerman had started to pace, covering a few feet in each direction, along the fence. He swung his arms, releasing the sweet odor of ether, the same aroma I'd detected in the ladies' room the day I was rescued by my fake phone call to a nonexistent Mike.

The small camera in the security booth and the fifty-fifty chance that an armed Terry Spender would appear were all that stood between me and a double murderer. I tried to breathe normally, reminding myself that I was still in a secure area.

How is this going to end? I wondered. I'm surrounded by toxic waste on three sides, and a wild-eyed, anesthesia-wielding killer on the fourth. Maybe the climax will be another Love Canal. I remembered the seventies again and the famous incident that instigated regulatory reform in the United States—abandoned waste drums exploding in New Jersey, sending the toxic fumes drifting off into the atmosphere. I looked over my shoulder at the two-story-high treatment vat next to a large trailer, as if it might ignite at any minute, providing a spectacular final scene for Sidney Kellerman and me.

New sounds woke me from my special effects daydream— rustling, clinking, the clearing of a throat—the noises of a man moving into action. Kellerman had transferred his handkerchief to his left hand and with his right hand reached for his badge.

Evidently he no longer cared who knew about his felonious choices.

A second or two before true panic set in, I noted that his badge had been in the typical location chosen by male employees, his left breast pocket, even though he was supposedly headed to

Tahoe for a long retreat with his daughter. I wondered at what point I'd rated a premeditated detour on his itinerary. When I mentioned picking up the report at the library? Or had he been listening in on my call to Jennifer when I asked about his appearance at the waste site?

I realized I'd probably given him cause to worry the minute I started questioning his colleagues and entertaining police officers with Sunday coffee in Elaine's living room. He'd been ready to give me an anesthetic in the ladies' room even before I met him, right after my interview with Rita Johnson.

With dismay, I acknowledged it didn't matter what particular incident brought him to me this morning. Kellerman was about to enter the security booth.

I weighed my options, a life-threatening exercise too frequent these days, I thought. Running as far as I could past forklifts and transuranic waste would bring me only to the back fence, which offered no way out of the area. I knew the treatment building would be locked, and even if it were open, it was bereft of hiding places that weren't at least as lethal as Sidney Kellerman.

I looked around at the odd-shaped containers in the lot. Drums, vats, tall cylinders, and long metal boxes that reminded me of the caskets in the showroom at Galigani's Mortuary. I thought of Matt and the possibility that I'd never see him again. I wished for a more peaceful ending to my life than death under a thousand-gallon tank enveloped in—I paused—scaffolding.

I could climb the wooden structure the waste handlers used for looking down into the contents of the twenty-foot-high tank. Then what? Jump into a vat of unknown chemical constituents? I might be better off taking my chances with ether.

Kellerman had made it through the security screening. Evidently the camera didn't freak out at his wild look, if it was monitored at all and not just a videotape system. I figured he looked more normal than the women and men who passed under its lens wearing bright yellow plastic suits and booties.

As he walked quickly toward me, Kellerman opened the bottle of ether and doused the white cloth. My breath came in short spurts, and my feet already burned from taking only a few steps on the gravel after abandoning my pumps so I could move faster.

I backed into the metal scaffolding, debating whether to climb it. One or two rungs would at least give me a height advantage, I thought, and took a step up. A slotted landing halfway up was connected to the ground by another set of stairs, giving me an alternate route down. I pictured Kellerman and me running up and down the scaffolding, like overgrown children in a laboratory playground, until the Wednesday shift of waste busters arrived.

By the time I reached the first step, Kellerman had arrived at the bottom and pulled my leg with both hands, one of them holding the deadly cloth. I hoped my panty hose would protect the pores of my calves from the ether. I struggled to make it up to the landing, trying to kick Kellerman at the same time.

At one point my slippery legs got away from him and I made it up another step. Two more to go, but high ones, made for people taller than my five foot three. Kellerman had a good three inches on me, and probably fifty pounds. I had no idea whether that was good or bad.

I was almost at the landing when Kellerman made another grab and overcame the friction of my panty hose. He pulled me back down toward him, but I struggled free when he maneuvered to get the ethered cloth into position to cover my face. I wondered how long we could seesaw this way. We were both breathing hard, and our grunts were louder than the wildlife noises from the dense patch of trees. I wished I had a weapon, like Terry's pepper spray, to subdue him.

Maybe I do, I thought. Although I'd kicked off my pumps, my purse was still hanging at my hip, its strap tight across my breast. What is it about a woman and her handbag? I wondered. It's the last thing we want to give up. Except maybe the fanny pack generation. I pictured myself evacuating a burning home, passing by precious photos of my grandparents and scooping up my pocketbook.

My stop to pick up groceries and cosmetics flashed through my mind. I realized I had a chemical weapon of my own in my purse, where I'd stuffed my drugstore purchase. Spurred by this new awareness and the energy of adrenaline, I hoisted myself to the next step, away from Kellerman, grateful that he'd spent no more time in a gym than I had.

I opened the zipper of my purse, reached down, and pulled out a can of deodorant spray. I remembered scooping it into my handbag as soon as the clerk rang it up.

While Kellerman reapplied his ether, I prepared my own weapon: a pink-and-white can. Excited and frightened as I was, breathing hard and clenching my jaw, it didn't escape my notice that we made a pathetic sight. Two overweight, middle-aged people wrestling with a pitiful arsenal of weapons. No Uzis. No switchblades. Not even a small pistol. Not the stuff of action movies.

Kellerman, with increased adrenaline of his own, I guessed, took a giant leap to my level, surprising me by covering two steps in one move. He hadn't said a word since accessing the area through the security booth, and I abandoned my strategy of keeping him talking. I knew all I needed to know about his motives and his deeds.

I closed my lips tight and held my breath as the white cloth came toward me, at the same time spraying my deodorant in the direction of his face. I hoped I'd come closer than eight inches of his eyes, enough to qualify for the misuse of the product that could be harmful or fatal according to the label.

Kellerman and I both scored, I realized, as I heard him scream the B word, as Elaine would call it in my presence. At the same time, my tongue responded to the burning taste of ether he'd forced into my mouth. I felt dizzy immediately, but the sound of his cursing gave me hope, as well as the sight of the cloth in my hand. I'd managed to confiscate part of his weapon.

I crawled onto the landing and dragged myself across to the other set of stairs. I knew he'd need a minute to clear his eyes, locate the bottle of ether and find something else to apply it to. Or, he could pour it on me, I realized, moving as fast as I could in my groggy state.

My nose itched, my eyes watered, and I felt ready for surgery. I nearly slid down the stairs on the opposite side from Kellerman's perch, and hobbled to the security booth, half on my feet, half on my knees. I'd snagged my bare feet more than once on the jagged metal steps and hoped I'd live to bathe them in warm water.

I reached the door of the booth on my hands and knees, almost out of energy, ready to give in to a comatose state. I heard Kellerman behind me.

"It's no use," he was barking. He sounded completely recovered from the deodorant that was supposed to leave him with a permanent disability. "Your car is hemmed in. You'll never make it down the hill."

Kellerman's taunt, almost a laugh, seemed to propel me. I stretched my arm up to the long metal handle of the door and used it to lift myself to almost standing position. In one movement, I pulled at the handle in a direction that opened the door and fell onto the floor of the booth. I heard the loud thunk of the lock as the heavy glass closed behind me. I uttered a silent thank-you to the absent designers of the security system. As long as my weight registered on the mat, no one else would be allowed to enter the booth, and if I didn't leave within four minutes, a PSO would be dispatched to the post to investigate. I knew I could wait that long, since I felt more than ready for a nap.

Although he must have known the system as well as I did, Kellerman, still screaming, used his free hand alternately to try to force the door open and to bang on the glass. I sat quietly and looked through bleary eyes at the bright metal can of ether glinting in the broad daylight.

Through the thick glass pane on the other side, I saw a black-and-white police car driving up the hill, followed close behind by a pale blue car from the lab's security fleet. They passed Kellerman's SUV, Elaine's Saab, and the pit area, heading straight for the chain-link fence.

Just before I passed out, I worried that they would crash through the booth and kill me.

THIRTY-TWO

I WOKE UP IN A small peach-colored room in St. Leander's Hospital, both my feet bound in white bandages, thanks to my running around on gravel and broken glass.

A young attendant, looking fuzzy through my half-closed eyes, entered with a clipboard.

"You were really lucky," she told me, patting my toes on her way to the head of the bed.

Lucky would have been a nice vacation with Elaine, no brushes with death, and no bruises, I thought, but I didn't have the energy to voice my opinion. Instead I smiled at—I strained my eyes to read her badge—Stacianne the nurse.

"How long have I been here?"

Stacianne shook her head and laughed, as if amused by the meandering mind of a senior citizen. "Only a few hours. Your friends just left to grab some coffee from the cafeteria. They'll be right back." In her throat, the *I* in "right" became an elongated sound, a high-pitched humming, and "back" grew into a two-syllable word.

My head hurt too much to tolerate perkiness, and I wished I were in the cafeteria with whoever my friends were. They probably left to get away from Stacianne, I decided.

I shook my head, as if to reorient my brain, to rattle it into the thinking position.

"When will I be able to leave?" I asked Stacianne. "I have a flight to Boston on Saturday."

"You're going to Bah-ston?" she asked. I groaned and figured she'd think it was from pain. "I have some friends there."

"How nice. So will I be able to fly on Saturday?"

"Oh sure. You'll be out of here in a few minutes. You won't be running any Bah-ston marathons, though. The soles of your feet are pretty raw. Next time wear your safety shoes," she said with a grin as if she'd come up with brilliant repartee.

My friends, who turned out to be Elaine and Terry, came back from coffee, just in time to see Stacianne wiggling my toes again.

"Take me home," I whispered to them as the young nurse left the room. "I feel like I've been left in day care too long."

Elaine and Terry laughed and gave me understanding nods.

"Terry's here to give you an escort home," Elaine said.

"Yeah, how would you like to ride with a blaring siren?"

I looked at the Terry in her full regalia and decided she might not be kidding. Clutching my bottle of pain pills, I gave my head a vigorous shake.

"I think I'll take the Saab."

IN THE NEXT FEW DAYS at Elaine's, I was treated in turns like a patient, a heroine, and a foolish old woman who didn't know enough to keep out of trouble.

I was happy Elaine's car insurance settlement was generous, in spite of the added damage when Kellerman had not very gently boxed me in, in front of the waste drums.

"I'm surprised at what they offered. Maybe they're rewarding its use in solving two murders," Elaine said.

Terry was a welcome visitor on several occasions, and I enjoyed talking about the cases with her and Elaine. I'd gotten used to the fact that even though a case might be "solved," there were always a few unanswered questions.

"My problem is—didn't Jennifer know Manuel found something criminal in her father's computer?" Elaine asked. She'd gotten over apologizing for putting me in a danger. It helped that I'd place my life in jeopardy before, without prompting from her. "Wouldn't that make her suspicious of her father when Manuel disappeared?"

"When I talked to her at José's house, she said something had been bothering him, and he wouldn't tell her what it was. Given the way he felt about her, it's likely Manuel would have tried to keep it from her."

"I suppose. True love and all," Elaine said in a sarcastic tone that led Terry to ask how she and José were getting along.

She shook her head. "We have a lot to work out. I don't know what Manuel's horrible death means to our relationship in the long run. But I know it's going to be a while before José will be able to focus on anything else. He describes it as having a permanent lump in his throat."

I nodded and remembered the lump I'd felt for months after my fiancé, Al Gravese, died in a car crash, three months before we were to be married. For a while I was afraid to drive myself, and left the house only when it was necessary. When I finally decided to continue my life, I took off for California. Smart reasoning, I thought in hindsight—it's too scary to travel Route 1 in Revere where Al died, so avoid it by moving across the country.

José had come by once and offered a perfunctory thank-you to me for finding his son's killer. But I couldn't shake the feeling he thought I should have been able to prevent the murder also, even though I was in Boston at the time.

"Then there's that thing with the tissues," Elaine said, bringing us back to the cases. "Why wouldn't Kellerman just dump them in his own trash? Who would have found them?"

It had never occurred to me that Kellerman would treat the tainted tissues like ordinary trash, and Elaine's question forced me to determine why. "Maybe it's because of television and movies," I said. "He couldn't be sure the police wouldn't search his personal trash. You always see cops and FBI agents going through the suspects' rubbish."

"That's right," Terry said. "And we do. If we'd had any reason to suspect Gary Larkin was murdered that way, we'd have looked at the property of everyone Gary was close to."

I smiled at the idea that, once again, I'd thought like a cop.

FROM A DISTANCE, Rose Galigani had her own comments on my latest cases, calling often to be sure I was doing well and planning to return home as scheduled.

"Ether. Imagine that," she'd said when I told her one of Kellerman's murder weapons. "I remember they used to put us under with ether when we had our tonsils and adenoids removed as children, in the old days. Did you start to count backward from one hundred?''

"No, but I did remember all the ice cream I had to eat when I lost my tonsils."

Rose laughed. "You would."

From a mother's perspective, Rose was also concerned about Jennifer and the baby she was carrying, and I was happy to be able to reassure her.

"She's going to stay with her mother's younger sister in Brookline, just a subway ride away from us," I told her. "She seems to be holding up better than I would under the circumstances."

"She may want to come visit you when you're back home." Rose stressed the word "home" in a way that told me she still had some residual fear that I'd stay in California for the next thirty years.

"That's not a bad idea," I said. "In fact, that's a wonderful idea. Let's make sure that it happens."

ON FRIDAY, my last day in California for a while, Elaine and I decided to take a day trip.

"We have to do something to make this a vacation. How about Santa Cruz?" she asked with a smile that told me she knew she'd selected my favorite spot on the Pacific Ocean. About two hours from Berkeley, Santa Cruz offered a long, sandy beach and a boardwalk full of amusements and refreshment stands, reminding me of the Revere Beach of the fifties. Elaine looked at her watch. "We can be there by lunchtime."

"I'm ready. But you'll have to drive," I said. I pointed to my feet, encased in soft, blue slippers, the backs of which Elaine had slit down the middle to accommodate the thick bandages.

OUR DAY IN Santa Cruz provided many moments for "remember when" for me and Elaine.

I paddled along the boulevard in another new pair of slippers, hard-soled and backless, until we came to our favorite seaside deli for lunch. Elaine had always teased me about my reaction to a sign the owners put on the door when they closed for a short break between two and five o'clock. Back Momentarily, the sign read. "Momentarily is not a meaningful unit of time," I'd responded the first time I saw the notice. Now, part of me wanted to be able to travel across the country quickly enough to be on either coast momentarily, for the rest of my life.

"We have to finish that talk about *it*," Elaine said over eggplant sandwiches, equally good as the one prepared by Rose Galigani for my flight to California.

"It?"

She laughed. "The S word."

I put down my sandwich and covered my mouth with the thin paper napkin, inadequate to the occasion. I felt my face flush and a tingle run through my body as if I were back on the scaffolding with Kellerman. "I think the time has passed," I said.

"You're blushing even at the letter S," Elaine said, shaking her head. "I'm tempted to draw you some pictures."

Under different circumstances, I might have been annoyed at her persistence, but I was relishing the return of our easy friendship. I took both our napkins and crumpled them beyond use as a sketchpad. "Not today," I said.

Elaine laughed, apparently willing to drop the subject, and I sighed with relief. I figured the rest of what I needed to know about the birds and bees would take care of itself.

A LITTLE BEFORE six o'clock, we felt a light drizzle and headed for the parking lot. It was about time for our trip home anyway. But there was one more bit of sightseeing waiting for us, in the direction of the Santa Cruz mountains. A glorious rainbow.

I'd been in California only a month or so when I saw my first rainbow. I'd been working at a sister lab in Livermore, about fifty miles away from BUL. I'd stood by my car in the parking lot, much as I was now in Santa Cruz, and stared at the perfect arc of vivid colors, from red to violet, the result of double refraction through water droplets in the air. I'd half expected to see a "color by Technicolor" credit along the horizon.

"If there's one thing the open desert does better than the East Coast," I told Elaine, "it's rainbows."

I took this one as my personal farewell from the western skies. I wished I could share the sight with Matt, but I was happy enough to be flying home to him the next day. There was always the sunrise on the Atlantic Ocean.

ON FRIDAY EVENING, Terry stopped in to say good-bye.

"I have something for you. Since you cleared up that four-fifteen with your friend from the East Coast."

"Excuse me?"

Terry put her hand to her mouth, like a little girl caught saying a naughty word. "Sorry. It's dispatcher talk for 'a fight.' We use these codes all the time. Like, we'll say, 'Are you ten-six?' meaning 'Are you busy?' Or 'It's code seven,' which is mealtime. I'm so used to thinking of you as a detective, I lapse right into copspeak."

"I'm flattered."

Terry looked at me sideways as if she didn't know whether I was serious. I didn't know either, but I tried to put her at ease. "I appreciate all your help this week," I told her.

"I'm the one should be saying that to you. Don't expect anything from the top brass, however."

"You mean Inspector Russell isn't going to submit my name for a special commendation? Maybe the key to the city?"

Terry smiled and shook her head, reaching into the pocket of her khaki pants. I couldn't imagine a handkerchief or a wallet fitting in the tight space and wondered briefly where she kept essentials like a comb and deodorant spray.

"This is as official as it gets." She handed me a small, thick piece of blue-and-gold fabric—a Berkeley Police Department patch. "I thought your policeman friend might like this. Some guys collect them." I laughed and took the souvenir, fingering the gold stitches around the edge of the shield. I envisioned Matt's face when I showed it to him. "This is perfect, Terry. Thanks so much."

MATT CALLED late Friday night. As we chatted, I sat on Elaine's floral couch, one of my bags already packed, waiting at the door.

"I have a patch from Berkeley PD," I told him.

"I don't collect those things."

"I do."

"Fine. I'll give you the one from my old uniform."

"A relic."

Matt laughed. It doesn't get much better than this, I thought. Going home to Scrgeant Matt Gennaro.

"How do you feel about the bad guy being a scientist?" Matt asked me.

"He wasn't a scientist. He was a computations engineer."

"And that makes a difference?"

"You bet. Also, I verified the lab is still a safe place to hang out. I was saved by the workings of a security booth."

"I give up," he said in a playful tone. "I can't wait to see you tomorrow."

"My feet are still pretty sore. I might want to skip the club and go straight home."

"That sounds better to me, too."

Elaine came downstairs and stood in front of me. She pointed to my bandaged feet.

"Tell him if he has any new cases for you to work on, it will have to be at a desk for a while."

I grimaced at her remark, but thought it was a good topic anyway.

"What's new at work?" I asked Matt.

He sighed, as if he'd rather not talk shop, but he went ahead. "You're not going to believe this, but the library director found the body of a woman in the basement of the building this morning."

I gasped, thinking of the beautiful old brick edifice on Beach Street in Revere. I'd shelved books there as an after-school job when I was a teenager. Revere High School was next door until it was moved a few blocks away, giving me quite a surprise the first time I tried to visit my alma mater in the old location.

"That's awful," I said. I pictured a dead woman sprawled at the bottom of the narrow staircase, although Matt hadn't told me exactly where she'd been found and I had no idea what she looked like. "Who was it?"

"We don't know. Unidentified so far. I suppose you're hoping she was reading a book on boron at the time."

"Very funny." I feigned annoyance, but I was impressed Matt knew which element followed which in the periodic table. "As a matter of fact, there is something controversial about boron," I said. "A new study on the nutritional value of boron in the human diet—it's being disputed..."

Matt's laughter thrilled me. I could hardly wait to get back to him. Boron murder or no boron murder.

AGATHA AWARD WINNER

JEANNE M. DAMS

KILLING CASSIDY

A DOROTHY MARTIN MYSTERY

Though Dorothy Martin is quite content with her new life in a cozy English village, she looks forward to an unexpected trip back to her Indiana hometown. Sadly, it is the sudden death of a longtime friend and a small inheritance that offer Dorothy this brief holiday in the States.

Along with her inheritance, Dorothy gets a cryptic note from her deceased friend claiming he was murdered. Now, back among the friends and acquaintances of her past, she must find out if one among them is a killer—and why.

"Altogether, this is a warm and worthy read…"
—*Publishers Weekly*

Available November 2001 at your favorite retail outlet.

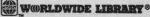

W⬤RLDWIDE LIBRARY®   WJD402

E. L. LARKIN

DIE AND DIE

A DEMARY JONES MYSTERY

Though genealogical research is her specialty, Demary Jones takes on a murder case with a most interesting twist: the woman found with her throat slashed died three years earlier in a tragic plane crash.

Rumors of Carolyn Zimmer's previous death were highly exaggerated. Or rather, manipulated by the victim herself. Alive and well, she not only remarried, but lived a mere four blocks away from her twice-bereaved husband.

Yet few mourn Caro's second—and this time, true—death. Caro specialized in alienating women, seducing men and skillfully hiding her past. To get to the truth, Demary realizes that she must confront a killer—with every reason to kill again.

Available November 2001 at your favorite retail outlet.

WORLDWIDE LIBRARY®

WELL403